D1737288

GET A FREE BOOK!

I'm a pretty nice guy once you look past the grisly images in my head. Most of all, I love connecting with awesome readers like you.

Join my VIP Reader Group and get a FREE serial killer thriller for your Kindle.

Get My Free Book

www.danpadavona.com/thriller-readers-vip-group/

THE SHADOW CELL

A WOLF LAKE THRILLER

DAN PADAVONA

A CHILLING PSYCHOLOGICAL THRILLER

1

Hushed whispers echoed off the steepled interior of St. Mary's church, lending an air of secrecy to the place of worship. Father Josiah Fowler roamed the basement corridors, ambling from his office to the stairs, before he turned left and strode past the shadowed pews toward the confessional booth. The church was gloomy and cool and blanketed by the reserved hush common to all places of worship. A handful of guests mingled in the vestibule, though it was too dark to make out faces as Fowler slipped inside the ornate structure.

He fiddled with his hands. After two decades of listening to confessions, he'd never acclimated to the suffocating confines or the heavy gloom of the booth. The inside smelled of cheap cologne, aged leather, and the sweat of old men. The cushioned chair was murder on his back. He always felt off balance when he sat here. Curtains cloaked a latticed opening on both sides. A kneeler lay against the dividing wall with a matching hassock in the opposite compartment.

Fowler sat in silence, sensing eyes on him. Judging. He'd made his share of mistakes, some he never learned from. The whiskey on his breath an hour before lunch spoke to his longest running vice. Several years ago, he'd blacked out driving on a rural road outside Wolf Lake. He awoke on the gravel shoulder with the engine still purring and no idea how he'd gotten there. He'd heard the distant sirens drawing closer. Fowler drove home before the authorities wandered past and ticketed him for driving while intoxicated.

The morning after the drunken ride home, a knock on the rectory door tugged him out of sleep. Lana Gray, Sheriff Stewart Gray's wife, had crashed on the same road Fowler had driven. They'd found her dead behind the wheel, the front end of her car crumpled and wrapped around a tree. A witness claimed a vehicle resembling Fowler's had weaved across the centerline moments before Lana Gray came around the bend.

Fowler peeled back the curtain and assessed the empty compartment opposite his. Had he murdered the former sheriff's wife? He prayed it wasn't so, that he'd pulled over before he blacked out. The investigators discovered skid marks from one car—Lana Gray's. No proof someone forced her off the road.

As Fowler shook away the memory, footsteps trailed between the pews and angled in his direction. Each step reverberated like faraway thunder, unsettling the priest for reasons he didn't understand. The door opened on the other side. A black silhouette filled the opening before the figure sat across from him. No greeting, just the man's steady breathing beyond the lattice.

Fowler waited. Sometimes, a man needed time to gather his thoughts. The priest lifted his wrist and glared at his watch.

"Bless me, Father, for I have sinned."

The sanctimonious voice made Fowler wonder if another priest sat across from him.

"How many days since your last confession, my son?"

A pause.

"I don't remember. Not since I was a young adult, I suspect. And I'm not your son."

The words sliced like tiny razors. Why did the stranger unsettle him? In that moment, he imagined not another priest beyond the lattice, but the devil himself. Father Fowler's instincts told him to walk away, hurry down the staircase to his office, tucked at the rear of the basement, and lock the door. Fowler cleared his throat and wiped the sweat off his forehead.

"What is your sin?"

Fowler was careful not to address the stranger as his son this time. Whoever sat in the neighboring compartment, it wasn't a parishioner. Or at least, the man hadn't visited St. Mary's in many moons.

The priest checked the time again and tapped his foot. He was scheduled to speak at a fundraiser for the local food bank in an hour.

"While we're young," Fowler said, hoping to draw a laugh out of the man. The curtained lattice made it impossible to identify faces, only the shape of the man. Agile, strong, a few hairs taller than Fowler. "Your sin?"

"What is the ultimate sin, Father?"

Fowler peered through the holes. The man hadn't moved since sitting down. It was like chatting with a bronze idol.

"The three unforgivable sins involve the murder, torture, and abuse of others, especially children and animals."

"I see. Interesting, the church equates children with animals."

The quiet stretched out like a tether tightened to the point of snapping.

"And how many of these sins have you committed?" the stranger asked, continuing.

"I'm unsure I understand the question."

"It's simple, Father. How many unforgivable sins do you beg forgiveness for?"

"I thought you came to me to confess. That's how the process works."

A laugh followed. Like parchment paper crackling inside a fire.

"A woman murdered the sick and weak under your nose. Right here, in God's house."

The stranger spat *God* with derision. Fowler thought of Thea Barlow, his former assistant. Barlow believed herself an angel of mercy. Over several nightmarish days last year, she murdered the sick and dying before the sheriff stopped her. A shiver rolled down Fowler's spine.

"You watch the news and read the papers, I see. I assure you God will pass His judgment on Ms. Barlow. But that's not why you're here, is it? You didn't come all this way to question me about Barlow. Unless you're a reporter. You aren't, are you?"

Another snicker.

"I'm no reporter, Father. But I know more than any newsman would about what goes on in your church."

Father Fowler groaned.

"If you came for an apology, I couldn't feel worse over what happened. The victims Ms. Barlow attacked were my friends, loyal parishioners who filled my Sundays with joy. Every time I stand behind the lectern, I look out at the crowd and expect to see their faces. Then I don't, and the memory of what happened rushes back to me. Satisfied?"

"No. You have a rather short memory, Father Fowler. It's as if nothing significant occurred within these hallowed walls before last year's tragedies."

Fowler shifted. Soaked with sweat, his back stuck to the chair.

"But we all assume risk when entering a new situation," the stranger said.

"As an example?"

"Take flying on an airplane. The moment you strap yourself into your seat, the attendant explains how to breathe or float should the airliner crash into a body of water. Not reassuring."

"The odds of a crash are low."

"So are rare cancers and heart attacks among the healthy. Yet the newspapers are full of tragedies of people who drew the joker card from the deck."

"This is all very interesting. But I have a pressing meeting, sir. If you've nothing to confess, you'll understand my need for haste."

"Oh, don't rush off, old friend. I brought you a gift."

"A gift?"

"Something for you to remember me by, since your memory fails you."

"This is highly unusual. Perhaps if you visited outside confession hours, we might sit and talk. I'm certain if I saw your face, I'd remember you."

"I'm sure you would. But I won't keep you, Father. Run along to your little meeting. My gift lies beside my feet. You may retrieve it once I exit."

Silence.

"Is that it, then?"

"For now. We'll meet again, Father."

The shadowed figure rose. With a creak, the door opened and banged shut.

Father Fowler sat breathing in his private compartment, the old leather and sweat smell returning now that the man's overbearing presence didn't dominate his thoughts. He didn't want to peer inside the neighboring compartment. As he procrastinated, footsteps warned him as another person approached the confession booth. Elderly Mrs. Carr covered her mouth with her hand when Fowler burst into the aisle, waving his arms.

"If you'll give me a moment, Mrs. Carr. I must attend to the booth before you . . . never mind."

She turned and clicked her heels toward the vestibule, shooting him a confused glance before she pushed through the doors.

Fowler stood outside the confession booth. His heart jackhammered. As if viewing his actions through a camera lens, he felt displaced while his hand reached for the handle. He pulled the door open and ducked his head inside. The booth appeared empty until his eyes settled on a wooden box tucked beneath the chair. With trembling arms, he removed the box and glanced around the church. No one watched.

He set the box on a pew and lifted the lid. Fowler gagged and glared up at Jesus, hanging on the cross.

A bloody, severed hand lay inside the box.

2

Chelsey Byrd glanced up from her desk when the front door to Wolf Lake Consulting opened. Her noon appointment was here, and LeVar Hopkins's voice carried down the hallway as he directed the client inside.

She stood when Lawrence Santos entered. Though Santos was thirty-five and physically fit, the lines in his face and the charcoal gray dotting his hair spoke to the hardships he'd endured.

"Thank you for seeing me," Santos said, offering his hand.

She shook it and gestured at the open seat across from her desk.

"You came a long way. Poplar Corners, that's near Kane Grove. There's a fine private investigation firm in Kane Grove near the university. I'd be happy to—"

Santos waved her offer away.

"I read about your team. You're the best in upstate New York."

Two desks away, LeVar rolled his chair in front of his computer and clicked his mouse. LeVar ran with the notorious Harmon Kings gang before Sheriff Thomas Shepherd offered him a way out of gang life. Now LeVar lived in a guest house behind Thomas's A-frame overlooking Wolf Lake. The teenager swore off his old life, earned his GED, and enrolled as a freshman at the community college where he took criminal justice classes.

"That's kind of you to say. How can Wolf Lake Consulting help you?"

Santos slumped his shoulders forward. From a manila folder, he removed a photograph of a smiling woman with flowing auburn hair. Her Irish green eyes commanded Chelsey's attention.

"My wife, Harmony, disappeared four years ago, less than a year after our wedding day. The police never found her. Nobody gave me answers. I realize four years is a long time, but I never gave up hope."

Chelsey picked up the photo and tilted it toward the window light.

"I'll ask the uncomfortable question first, Mr. Santos. Is it possible your wife left on her own and doesn't wish for anyone to find her?"

"We had a healthy marriage," Santos said, pushing his fingers through his hair. A few strands fell to the floor. "No problems between us. Someone took her, and I can't sleep another night until I learn the truth."

"You understand the statistics. The odds of finding Harmony alive aren't in our favor."

"I understand. Goodness knows my family never stops reminding me. They're not in favor of me hiring you." An ironic grin formed on the man's face. "Last week, they held an intervention." Santos made air quotes around *intervention*. "They told me I needed to move on and live life before it passed me by, that Harmony would have wanted it that way."

As Santos spoke, his eyes darted around the room. His gaze

settled on LeVar, who focused on his computer. Chelsey nodded at the folder.

"What else did you bring?"

"Photographs from our wedding day," Santos said, fanning the pictures out across the desk.

He'd labeled each person and noted who they were. A great aunt from Lawrence's side of the family, Harmony's college roommate, the parents of the bride and groom, Harmony's sister, Adele. Santos reminded Chelsey of herself—obsessive and meticulous. He made quick glances over his shoulder as though he didn't trust humanity. Chelsey had survived major depression during her teenage years and still suffered from anxiety issues. She'd almost died when a bullet fired by fugitive Mark Benson grazed her head.

"I can work with these, and the labels will save me time. Is there anyone you suspect?"

"Gerald Burke," Santos said without hesitation. His mouth twisted. "Burke was Harmony's boyfriend during college. After the breakup, they remained best friends. If you ask me, he never got over Harmony."

"What makes you say that?"

"He didn't bring a date to the wedding. As far as I know, he never married. Creep was hung up on Harmony."

"Why did you invite him to the wedding?"

"Harmony insisted. How could we marry without her best friend in attendance?" Santos scoffed. "Every time I spotted him across the room, he was staring at Harmony."

"Can you point him out in a picture?"

Santos shuffled the images and tapped his finger on a photograph of Harmony dancing with another man.

"That's him."

Gerald Burke stood a foot taller than Harmony. Shadows pouring off his forehead hid the man's eyes, giving him a mysterious look that Chelsey didn't trust. She scribbled his name on a memo pad.

"Who else?"

"There was a guy named Kit at the reception." Santos rested his chin on his fist. "Sorry, but I don't have a picture of him."

"Was he Harmony's friend?"

Santos shook his head.

"He claimed he was with the band. But I spoke with the band members after Harmony's disappearance, and they never heard of anyone named Kit."

"What do you remember about Kit?"

"He was short and average looking, a little dumpy. The guy talked everyone's ears off and hung around the buffet table. I never saw him without a plate of food in his hand."

"Did the authorities look into Gerald Burke and Kit?"

"Nothing came of the investigation. They declared Burke clean, and the team never located Kit. Not that they put in much effort. The investigators were more interested in me."

Chelsey wasn't surprised. Statistics proved husbands abducted their wives more often than strangers. Chelsey rearranged the photos and pointed at Harmony's sister.

"What's Adele's last name?"

"Sowl. She's four years older than Harmony."

"Do you have a better picture of Adele? A closeup?"

"No, why?"

"Sometimes a kidnapper changes the appearance of his captive so she's not easily recognized. Harmony disappeared four years ago, so it's possible she looks more like her sister did on your wedding day."

"I never thought of that. I'll search through our pictures and see what I have."

Chelsey crossed a leg over her knee.

"Now the matter of compensation."

"I have the money."

"This investigation could take weeks, and there's no guarantee I'll find Harmony."

"You'll find her, Ms. Byrd. Your firm is the best in the state."

Chelsey tapped her nails against the desk. Santos was determined to pay any price for information on Harmony's abduction, though Chelsey doubted she'd find the woman alive. Too much time had passed to believe in fairytale endings. But she'd try.

"Let me start with the names you gave me." Chelsey pointed at the pictures. "May I hang on to these?"

"For as long as you need."

"I'll make copies and hand the originals back to you at our next meeting."

"How long before the investigation begins?"

"Right away. I'll call you with a progress report in forty-eight hours."

Santos thanked Chelsey and shook her hand again. LeVar watched him leave and waited until the front door closed. A car motor fired in the parking lot.

"What's your opinion of Santos?" he asked.

Chelsey knew LeVar had listened in while he worked on a different case.

"The numbers say the husband is usually responsible. Sounds like the investigators wanted Santos for the abduction."

"But you don't believe he killed Harmony and disposed of the body."

Chelsey anchored her dark, wavy hair behind her ear.

"If he did, why would he open up an investigation?"

"For appearances?"

"Doubtful. The investigators gave up on Santos four years ago." Chelsey tapped a pen against the desk. "I'll make a few calls. Poplar Corners doesn't have a police department, right?"

"It's too small."

"That means the Nightshade County Sheriff's Department has jurisdiction." Chelsey chewed her lip. She dated Thomas Shepherd, the county sheriff. But Thomas had worked in Los Angeles as an LAPD detective four years ago. "I'll speak to Thomas. Maybe his deputies recall the case."

Through the window, Lawrence Santos's car turned out of the parking lot and raced past the village shops. Chelsey wanted to trust him. But she'd learned to never let her guard down. Was Santos a murderer hiding behind a sob story?

3

Thomas Shepherd stopped his silver Ford F-150 along the curb outside St. Mary's church. So much for his day off. Deputy Lambert's cruiser stood two spaces ahead of the sheriff's truck. Outside the doors, Lambert strung yellow police tape, the wind forcing the tape to dance and snap at its whim.

The church was a mammoth concrete structure with intricate carvings etched into the exterior. Eight stone steps led to the entry doors, where a greeter would welcome parishioners for service under normal circumstances. But there was no service today.

Thomas assessed the disheveled mop of sandy hair across his head. No comb could tame the beast. He fixed his hat over the hair and tugged it down, then he hopped out of the cab. As he climbed the steps, a truck backfired. He flinched, spun, and reached for his weapon. Loud noises always bothered and confused him. Since a gunshot nearly took his life in Los Angeles, he jumped at anything that sounded like gunfire. He counted each step as he swept his gaze across the entryway. It was a habit he hadn't kicked since the family doctor diagnosed him with Asperger's syndrome during his childhood.

Gloom hung heavy inside the church vestibule. He blinked and forced his eyes to adjust to the darkness. Voices carried from inside the church as Deputy Lambert questioned Father Josiah Fowler. Thomas didn't trust Fowler. Sheriff Gray felt convinced the priest ran his wife off the road and killed her, and Thomas held Gray's opinion in high regard. Last year, the Thea Barlow murders tore the village apart. Why hadn't Fowler suspected his assistant? Still, Wolf Lake villagers worshiped Fowler. Even Thomas's own mother had loved the man, until Thea Barlow broke into her house and attempted to murder her husband. The doctors had diagnosed Mason Shepherd, Thomas's father, with late-stage lung cancer. Since the Thea Barlow arrest, Thomas's father had passed.

Father Fowler appeared as if he'd gained twenty pounds since the last time Thomas saw him. Girded by black horseshoe shapes, the priest's eyes looked tired, defeated.

"Sheriff," Fowler said in acknowledgment, as Lambert stood off to the side.

"Tell me what happened here." Fowler repeated his story for Thomas. "And you've no idea who this man was?"

Fowler drew his lips tight.

"Even if I did, I wouldn't tell you. The sacramental seal binds me."

"A madman leaves a severed hand in your church, and you won't reveal his name?"

"Confession is between the confessor and God. I would never break that trust."

Thomas held Fowler's eyes. How would he figure out who left the box in the confession booth, if Fowler protected the man's identity?

"Is there anything you can tell me?"

"I must respect the man's privacy, depraved as he is." When Thomas blew out a breath, Fowler raised a hand. "There is one thing. The man seemed to know me. He assailed me with the horrible murders, and he spoke of St. Mary's church many years ago, though he remained vague and spoke in circles. He's a troubled man, I fear."

"Many years ago, you say? You were the priest when I was a child."

"Yes, and I recall you rarely attended mass."

"I came out okay. How long have you been at St. Mary's?"

"Twenty-four years this August," Fowler said, puffing out his chest.

Thomas glanced at the towering ceiling, then across the walls. Though the stranger's confession remained sacred, perhaps modern technology would provide Thomas with the answers he sought.

"Do you have a security system, Father?"

"We have alarms on the front and back doors. But the church is open to the public during confession hours."

"What about cameras?"

Fowler shook his head.

"None."

Of course.

"Did anyone see the man coming or going?"

"I queried my assistants, and nobody saw the man."

"Anyone else in the building for confession?"

"Mrs. Carr arrived two minutes after the man departed. She didn't see him, either." Something buzzed inside Fowler's robes. Though he held to the old ways and refused to break his sacramental bond, Fowler embraced technology. He removed a phone from his pocket and squinted at the screen. "My apologies, Sheriff. I must take this call."

"Don't go far, Father. I'm not finished questioning you."

Fowler's robes fanned out behind him as he strode through the entry doors and descended the steps toward his basement office. Thomas turned to Lambert.

"Please tell me you have something to go on."

Lambert motioned Thomas to follow. The sheriff slipped gloves over his hands when they stopped at the third pew from the back. Thomas gazed down at the severed hand inside the wooden box. The flesh was pallid, almost snow white, the blood dried and crusted where the madman had sawed the hand off at the wrist.

"Fowler claims the man placed the box beneath the seat inside the confessional booth. He carried it out and placed it on the pew so he could get a better look. After he opened the box, he called our department."

The slight fingers branching out of the hand told Thomas this was a woman's hand. Pink fingernail polish strengthened his opinion. He searched for an identifying mark—a wedding ring, tattoo, deformity. Nothing stood out.

"Any women go missing over the last few weeks?"

"None."

Thomas scratched his head.

"All right. We need to dust the box for prints. And fingerprint Fowler so we can rule him out."

"Gotcha. I started dusting the booth before you arrived. There must be three or four dozen sets of fingerprints on the walls, the chair, and the door. It's a cluster."

"Concentrate on the box. We know Fowler and our visitor touched the box. There should be prints. That is, if the guy didn't wear gloves. We need county forensics. I'll call them in."

Thomas peeked inside the booth. The compartment held a putrid, stuffy smell. He ran his eyes over the room. Nothing but a chair, a box of pamphlets, and a latticed opening on the wall. While Lambert worked, Thomas passed through the vestibule and stepped into the bright outdoors. He was perplexed and troubled. This couldn't be happening again in his county. There were still people in Wolf Lake who trusted their neighbors. Few locked their doors at night. How would they react if they discovered someone sliced off a hand, placed it in a box, and delivered it to Father Fowler?

Shielding his eyes from the sun, Thomas studied the road. The church owned an expansive plot of land. One hundred yards down the street, the neighborhood began. Someone must have seen the stranger's vehicle pull up to the church. A blue SUV and a white hatchback were parked along the road. He took a photograph with his phone, zooming in so he recorded the license plates. Chances were the vehicles belonged to residents. But he wanted to be sure, just in case the stranger was nearby, observing him.

The obvious question tugged at him. Why deliver the body part to Father Fowler?

Someone had emerged from the priest's past to haunt Nightshade County. And his work had just begun.

4

At the top of the stairs, he pulled the string and shed light on the basement. Then he descended the steps, passing the washing and drying machines. Spiderwebs hung like silk from the rafters, the gossamer alive with black, spindly legs as he ducked beneath. At the rear of the basement, he pushed aside a fifty-gallon plastic box and moved his hands along the concrete wall. Even with the light on, he had a hard time finding the entrance. His hand touched the subtle imperfection in the wall. With a shove of his shoulder, he muscled the hidden door open.

The atmosphere inside the secret room was humid, neither warm nor cold. A vast nothingness hung over this enclosed space. Water bled off the earthen walls and formed puddles in the corners. Along the far wall, a tree root snaked through the dirt and protruded into the prison.

He kept the light off inside the underground enclosure. A small rectangle of illumination extended from the basement into the prison. Thick iron bars divided the enclosure into three cells. He wrapped his hands around the bars and tugged, satisfied when they refused to budge.

One person occupied the cell on the left. The other two cells remained vacant. For now.

The man bent on one knee and observed his prey through the bars. On the dirt floor, a young man lay naked and curled into a ball with gooseflesh rippling along his body. The victim was Scott Rehbein, a nineteen-year-old college student. The man gleaned this information from Rehbein's driver's license. He snickered. Young people today were stupid animals. They were experts at posting videos and pictures to social media sites, and they craved attention from people who didn't care about them. These idiots measured their worth by the number of *likes* their posts received. But they had no useful skills.

Capturing the boy had been easy. After following him through the parking lot to the college library, he slipped behind the boy's car. Certain nobody was around, he stuffed an old rag into the tailpipe, grinding it in good and deep. Then he sat inside his Tesla in the neighboring lot and waited. Rehbein studied for almost two hours before he exited the double doors with a backpack slung over his shoulder. The man remained calm as he waited for his prey to take the bait.

Rehbein unlocked his car and tossed the backpack onto the passenger seat. A moment later, he slammed the door and turned the key in the ignition. The engine sputtered and failed. Three more frustrated turns of the key got Rehbein nowhere.

The man started the Tesla. It was dark then, the dim glow on the western horizon the only memory of the departing sun. Nobody came to help the boy. Rehbein leaned against the door. The boy punched the hood, blaming the car for his incompetence. Predictably, he pulled his phone from his pocket and fired off a text, no doubt a plea for help from a friend or roommate. Or an angry post to social media about the dealership that sold him the car.

With the parking lot vacant of students, the man pulled into the next space and waved a friendly hand. Rehbein glanced up for a moment, then back to his phone.

"What seems to be the trouble?"

Rehbein shoved the phone into his pocket and tugged at his mahogany hair.

"Goddamn car won't start. I just changed the oil. This shouldn't be happening."

The man struggled to contain his laughter. Rehbein knew nothing about cars.

"Hmm. It's probably something simple. Let's see if we can get you started."

"Thanks, bro. I was about to call my roommate for a ride."

"No sense troubling your roommate." The man nodded at Rehbein's car. "Pop the hood and I'll have a look."

Rehbein gave the man an uncertain glance and slid into the car. With the door open, the dome light cast dim illumination over the interior. Rehbein's hand moved to the gas cap release as the man bit his tongue.

"It's under the headlight. Reach down, my boy."

With an embarrassed grimace, Rehbein searched for the hood release. A loud pop announced the boy had passed his first test toward becoming a functional adult. The man lifted the hood and gave a cursory glance at the engine.

"Ah."

Rehbein poked his head through the door.

"You figured it out already? Can you fix it?"

"There's a toolbox in the backseat of my Tesla. Bring it to me, and I'll have you on the road in seconds."

A relieved grin spread across the boy's face.

"Right away. And thanks."

The man waited until Rehbein crawled inside, searching for the nonexistent toolbox. The boy balanced one knee on the seat as he swept his hand through the dark.

"Hey, man. I don't think there's a—"

The Taser shot Rehbein from behind. The boy lurched forward and twitched on the seat like a dying fish. After he confirmed nobody had wandered past, the man zapped Rehbein a second time, shoved his legs into the Tesla, and slammed the door.

Now in the secret room beside the basement, he snapped a finger to bring the naked boy awake. Nothing. A second snap, and the boy groaned and rolled onto his stomach.

"That's it. Up and at 'em, as the old saying goes."

Something wriggled across the boy's leg. He yelped and slapped at the insect. The centipede scurried into a dark corner.

Instinctively, the boy covered himself with his hands, even as he drifted half-in and half-out of sleep. He didn't know where he was yet. Rehbein had slept for eighteen hours after the man injected him with a sedative. The boy's eyes tracked to the dirt ceiling, the walls, the bars holding him in place. Rehbein jolted and crab-walked backward when he spied the man beyond the cage.

"I know you," Rehbein said, pointing. "You're that guy who . . ."

"Yes, yes. The guy who helped you start your car."

"What did you do to me? Where the fuck are my clothes?"

"No need to cuss, young man. There is no need for clothes here. No one will see."

"Did you kidnap me? What are you, some kind of sicko? Let me the hell out."

The man didn't reply. This further unsettled Rehbein, who crawled to the bars dividing his cell from the vacant prisons. The boy yanked the bars, desperation sending him into a panic. On his hands and knees, he skittered to the front of his cell and pushed and pulled on the bars.

"No sense wasting your energy. Those bars are iron. You won't pull them out of the ground with your bare hands."

"This is bullshit! You can't do this to me."

The man produced a plastic container of food. A slat at the bottom of the cell allowed him to slide the container into the cage.

"I cooked the meal myself. Linguine. One of my best efforts, though it's several hours old now. You'll understand I didn't wish to wake you."

Rehbein glanced at the container and crawled backward.

"I'm not eating that. You poisoned the food."

"To what end? I'm in control, my boy. I see no reason to rid the world of you when we've only just met."

"Met? You attacked me from behind and locked me in a cage. You're a pervert or something. Bet you get off locking people up."

"Don't argue, my son. Eat your food before it gets cold. I'm not reheating it."

Rehbein peeled the lid off the container and hurled the food at the cage. It smashed against the enclosure. Linguine wormed down the bars.

"You'll attract bugs if you make a mess of your food."

"Screw you."

The man gathered a clump of linguine in his hand and tossed it to Rehbein. It landed on the boy's knee and trailed down to his shin.

"Eat, or incur my wrath."

"What?"

"Eat, or incur my wrath. Don't test me, boy."

"Or what? You're a coward. Open the cage and see what happens when I get hold of you."

The man chuckled.

"You're hardly convincing, covered with leftover dinner and

your private parts dangling like a dead eel." He stood and ran his eyes up and down the cage. The locked door stood in front of him. The key remained in the house, tucked beneath his mattress. "If you wish to survive, you'll respect my authority. Unlike you, I have useful skills. I control light and dark and hold mastery over your existence."

"You're insane."

The man's mouth twitched.

"Where I work, I have access to rattlesnakes and black widow spiders. If you wish to awaken to absolute darkness with snakes and spiders inside your cage, I can make it happen."

"You lie."

The boy rubbed his arms and edged toward the rear of the prison. As Rehbein took in his surroundings, his gaze fixed on a red splotch of moist earth in the neighboring cell. The blood still held a sharp, coppery scent.

Rehbein screamed.

5

L eVar bent at the knees and lifted Scout Mourning out of her wheelchair. He hadn't expected the teen to be this easy to carry. Scout seemed feather-light as he hauled her from the handicap accessible ramp fronting the Mourning's house to his black Chrysler Limited in the driveway. Scout had turned fifteen this year. While she'd lived in Ithaca, Scout lost the ability to walk after a truck slammed into the back of her parents' car, crumpling the rear compartment where Scout sat.

Yet the girl's troubles had just begun. Stricken by guilt over the accident, Scout's father blamed himself. He distanced himself from his family, forcing Scout's mother, Naomi, to start a new life with Scout in Wolf Lake. The teenager's classmates were uncomfortable approaching the new girl in the wheelchair. Scout found purpose in online sleuthing forums, where she solved crimes with fellow teenagers.

"Comfortable?" LeVar asked as he sat her in the front seat of his car.

"Perfecto."

"You sure?"

"I'm not a fragile piece of glass. Stop worrying."

But LeVar worried. He'd wanted to do this for a long time, and he couldn't bear the thought of injuring Scout. Today, he was researching a case for Wolf Lake Consulting. No big deal, just an infidelity case. But this was Scout's first time solving a case in person, instead of researching on her computer. The excitement on the girl's face suggested they were about to solve a national mystery or catch a murderer.

He reached for the seatbelt, but she'd already pulled it across her shoulder and clipped it below her waist. LeVar ran a hand through his hair. She appeared snug in the seatbelt. Her legs dangled off the seat with her feet resting on the floor.

"Really, LeVar. You did great. Snug as a bug, see?"

She tugged the shoulder strap. He checked the slack.

"You sure everything feels all right?"

"Well, there's one issue."

"What's that?"

"Ever since you sat me down, I can't feel my legs."

His brow creased in worry before he caught the joke. Leave it to Scout to laugh over her paralysis.

"You're a regular Rodney Dangerfield," he said.

"I'm surprised you know who Rodney Dangerfield is. I'm the one who schools you on seventies and eighties pop culture."

He rolled his eyes.

"I've seen *Caddyshack*, Scout. And *Back to School*, if you must know."

"Impressive."

He gave the seatbelt one last tug for posterity. Over the last week, he'd searched the internet for a swivel seat, a device that would make it easier for him to lift Scout out of the car. He didn't figure he'd need it, given how little she weighed. LeVar shook a finger at her.

"We need to load calories into you. Pizza, burgers, or a big ole steak. Are you dieting?"

"Are you saying I'm in good shape, LeVar?" She batted her eyes. "You know just what to say to a girl."

LeVar cleared his throat.

"Watch your legs. I'm closing the door now."

"I'm watching them. Is something supposed to happen?"

He sighed.

"Why did I agree to this?"

LeVar closed the door and slung the dreadlocks over his shoulder. He rounded the Chrysler and slid into the seat. Scout switched the Bluetooth to a hip-hop mix she'd created. He nodded in approval as he turned the ignition.

They took the lake road into the village of Wolf Lake, passing the shops and eateries. Ruth Sims swept the sidewalk outside the Broken Yolk Cafe. When LeVar honked the horn, Ruth raised her head and waved. LeVar still worked a few hours per week at the cafe between summer coursework and his job at Wolf Lake Consulting. Last year, Ruth's business almost collapsed before Scout's mother offered ideas for attracting a younger crowd. Now Ruth barely kept up with demand. Customers poured through the doors as the Chrysler drifted past.

Wolf Lake Consulting stood to the left. Chelsey's Honda Civic sat in the parking lot beside Raven Hopkins's Nissan Rogue. LeVar's sister worked as an investigator with Chelsey inside the converted home. An old Boogie Down Productions track played over the stereo. As LeVar drummed his fingers against the steering wheel to keep beat with the song, his gaze drifted to Scout in the passenger seat. She fixed her eyes on her phone, a giant smile curling the girl's lips.

"What's so interesting?"

"Remember when I told you I sent a message to that FBI

profiler?"

"Scarlett Bell?"

"Yeah, she wrote back."

"No kidding? What did she say?"

"She thinks it's cool I want to learn more about profiling serial killers, and she says she'll answer any questions I have. We might even do a Zoom call someday."

"That's awesome."

LeVar had completed a criminal profiling course at the community college during the spring semester. Scout hadn't stopped talking about profiling since. She'd spent the last two years solving crimes in internet forums. Though Scout's condition prevented her from chasing after criminals like an action movie hero, there was no reason she couldn't excel as a profiler. Given Scout's intelligence and work ethic, LeVar pictured the girl working for the FBI after college. But that was a long way into the future. Today, she'd start in the minor leagues and help LeVar catch a cheating spouse.

Across the seat, Scout beamed.

"Scarlett Bell caught something like fourteen serial killers over the last decade. She's the FBI's top agent."

"Well, maybe you'll meet her someday."

"Or work with her. That's my dream." Rich greens and a kaleidoscope of flowers flew past the car as they drove into the village suburbs. The smile faded from her lips as she stared out the window. "It's probably a dumb idea. How am I supposed to catch a killer with these?"

Scout gestured at her legs.

"You'll catch him with your noggin," he said, tapping his forehead. "Just like you caught Jeremy Hyde last year. Scout, you can accomplish anything you set your mind to."

She glanced at LeVar.

"So who are we going after today?"

"A woman named Halle Clem visited the office yesterday. She's convinced her husband, Andy, is cheating on her with his secretary."

"What does he do?"

"He's a loan manager at a bank in Wolf Lake."

"Hmm, he sounds guilty already. How will we catch him?"

"First, we'll drive to the bank and wait for Clem to leave for lunch." LeVar's eyes flicked to the dashboard clock. "Which should be ten minutes from now. Then we'll follow him."

"And if his voluptuous secretary shows up?"

"Who said she is voluptuous?" LeVar shook his head. "Never mind. If we catch them together, we'll use this."

LeVar patted the black camera bag on the seat between them. Canon was emblazoned across the top.

"You mean we'll take pictures."

"That's right. This is a high-end DSLR Canon with a 200-millimeter zoom. That allows us to maintain distance. We'll record him from across the street, and he'll be none the wiser. If Andy gets frisky with the secretary, we'll have proof in pictures."

"Then we'll sell them on the internet. Lots of money in porn these days."

LeVar snickered.

"Will you be serious for a second? I'm offering you the opportunity of a lifetime here."

"Say, you're not even twenty yet. I thought you couldn't get your private investigation license until you turned twenty-five."

LeVar winked.

"Hey, we're not breaking any laws. Just taking pictures on a beautiful spring day."

Scout laughed.

"That's our story, and we're sticking to it." She tilted her head. "But someday, I want to catch a real bad guy."

"Ease up, Jodie Foster. Your time will come."

Deputy Veronica Aguilar watched Thomas and Lambert through the tops of her eyes. While they worked on a potential murder case, she hunched over her desk with reams of paperwork spread in front of her. She wanted to join them in the field and catch the monster who'd left a woman's hand inside the church. Until the shrink cleared her, she was stuck on desk work with no high-speed chases in her future.

Standing a shade over five feet in her shoes, Aguilar rippled with muscle she'd carved from hard work in the gym. Full body squats, deadlifts, overhead presses. No sissy bicep curls with pink dumbbells. She ate right, favoring a protein shake loaded with spinach, matcha tea, and frozen fruit over a burger from the local grill. But what good did staying in shape do her when the county forced her to slave over boring desk work?

Last month, she'd shot a man in the line of duty. Worse yet, the man was a police officer. Officer Avery Neal with the Wells Ferry Police murdered attorney Megan Massey and her client after they built a corruption case against him. Aguilar, Lambert, and State Trooper Fitzgerald blocked Neal from escaping the county before the officer opened fire. Aguilar's bullet ended the fight. Neal died before the ambulance arrived.

Though she realized Neal was a criminal and had given her no choice, she harbored guilt. The firefight marked the first time she'd aimed her weapon at a person, let alone taken a life. Her hands clenched as she remembered the booming gunshots, the bullets whistling over her head while they sought refuge behind a cruiser. It seemed so easy in the movies. Shoot the bad guy. Be the hero. Dirty Harry never cried himself to sleep after he blew away the villain.

"Anything on the severed hand?" Thomas asked, setting another folder on her desk.

Great, more papers to file.

"County sent the hand to the lab for processing. We won't hear anything for days, possibly weeks."

The sheriff grunted and started away.

"Hey, Thomas . . . Sheriff."

"What's up, Aguilar?"

She swept the papers into a neat stack and raked her fingers through her hair.

"I was thinking. Things are going well with Dr. Mandal."

"Terrific. I knew you'd like her."

Thomas visited Mandal every week.

"There's really nothing for me to do here. I finished every case file you gave me. Maybe it's time I left the office for a bit. I could patrol the village and ensure no shenanigans are going on."

The sheriff's mouth quirked into a half-smile.

"You know the rules, Aguilar. It's not up to me. Until Dr. Mandal clears you to return to duty—"

"She's taking forever. I can't keep doing this," Aguilar said, gesturing at the folders. "I'm not helpful. Heck, I'm not even a public servant. No offense to Maggie," Aguilar said, lowering her voice and tilting her head at the administrative assistant's desk at the end of the hall. "But I'm not accomplishing anything she can't do. I'm losing my mind."

"This too shall pass. Please be patient."

When Thomas stuffed his keys into his pocket, Aguilar stood from her chair with panic fluttering through her chest.

"Where are you going now?"

"Lambert and I are canvassing the neighborhood near the church."

"Take me with you. What harm is there if I interview people? I won't have my weapon with me."

Thomas set his hands on her desk.

"That would break the county's rules. Except for emergencies, you're not allowed in the field until the county clears you."

"This sucks."

"Believe me, I don't like this anymore than you do. But therapy is for your own good. I'm living proof it works. When you're ready, Dr. Mandal will tell you."

Lambert strolled out of his office and adjusted the hat on his head. Aguilar scowled. To make matters worse, Lambert and Thomas bumped fists.

"Ready to roll?" Lambert asked.

"I'm ready." As they walked down the hall, Thomas glanced over his shoulder. "We won't be long."

Aguilar blew the hair off her forehead and pounded her fist against the desk. This was going to be a long day.

7

W ith Scout riding shotgun in the Chrysler, LeVar trailed Andy Clem from Wolf Lake Bank and Trust to a cheesy-looking hotel called the Pink Flamingo. They'd seen no sign of the secretary Halle Clem claimed her husband was having an affair with. But that didn't mean she wasn't already inside a room.

Clem sat inside his Volvo for five minutes before he glanced around the parking lot and strode toward the building. He kept his head down and his sunglasses on, and he stared over his shoulder, as though he sensed eyes on him. LeVar doubted Clem had spotted them. He parked his car near an outlet mall across the street where dozens of cars surrounded the Chrysler, and the sun glared across the windshield, making it impossible for anyone to see inside.

LeVar fired off two dozen pictures with the zoom lens fixed on Clem, who wandered back and forth on the walkway outside the garish hotel. A staircase rose to a second flight of rooms. In the grass, a pink flamingo sculpture welcomed guests. Beside the hotel, a gas station convenience store bustled with activity. Signage in the windows announced a lunch special on sausage sandwiches. LeVar would have preferred eating out of a garbage can to taking a chance on a gas station sausage.

"What's he doing?" Scout asked.

"No idea. Could be he's waiting for his date."

Just then, Clem glanced down at his phone, gave the parking lot another glance, and hurried to room nine.

"Someone sent him a text."

"It's action time."

LeVar zoomed in on the door, eager to capture whoever answered. He let out a frustrated groan when the door opened a crack, revealing only a thin line of shadow before Clem slipped inside.

"Was that the secretary who answered?"

"If it was, she stayed behind the door. Gotta hand it to them. They're careful."

"What do we do now?"

"We wait until they show their faces. They can't stay in there forever. Do me a solid and record the time Clem entered the room."

Scout scribbled the time and set the notepad on the dashboard. LeVar tapped a hand against his thigh. The curtain covering the window jostled as someone pulled the cord tight.

"So I guess there's a lot of sitting around and waiting," Scout said, brushing her hair back.

"Are you bored?"

"Not at all. I wonder how long they'll be."

LeVar was certain Scout's mother had given her daughter the birds and bees talk years ago. Still, he felt uncomfortable estimating how much time it would take for Andy and his date to finish their business. He took a bite of his sandwich and chewed. Scout sipped Pepsi through a straw.

"Do you want chips?"

"Please."

LeVar handed Scout the bag of kettle chips. Between them, they split a submarine sandwich. The inside of the car reeked of onion, vinegar, and oil.

"Now we wait," LeVar said, setting the camera inside the bag so he didn't spill sandwich fixings on the equipment. "I can't imagine they'll spend all afternoon in the room. They need to keep up appearances at the bank."

He crunched on a chip and squinted at the locked hotel room door. As he turned the music on again, Scout glared at an SUV parked two spaces away. A man in black sunglasses sat in the driver's seat.

"Who are you staring at?"

"That guy in the SUV. Is it just me, or has he been canvassing the gas station for the last ten minutes?"

LeVar shrugged.

"He's probably eating lunch like us."

"Where's his food?"

LeVar sat up in his seat and angled his head around Scout. The man hadn't budged. LeVar imagined the SUV's interior was steaming with the windows up and the noonday sun blasting down on the parking lot. He worried the man had passed out before he coughed into his hand and returned his gaze to the gas station.

"Don't bother the guy. And don't let him know you're watching."

Scout kept her head pointed straight ahead, angling her eyes toward the SUV.

"You know what would be funny?" LeVar asked. "What if he's another investigator, and the secretary's husband hired him to follow her to the hotel?"

"He's not canvassing the hotel. He's monitoring the gas station."

"Maybe he works there, and he's enjoying his break across the road."

Scout shifted her upper body toward LeVar.

"I'll tell you what I think. He's about to rob the place."

LeVar laughed.

"How can you tell?"

"He parked his vehicle in a crowded lot so nobody would notice, and he's across the road, out of view of the security cameras."

"Or," LeVar said, twisting around to face Scout. "He finished shopping at the mall, and he's wasting time before he returns to work. We should let him be."

Scout shook her head.

"What about the black sunglasses?"

LeVar gave Scout an exasperated glance and gestured at the sky.

"I could go for black sunglasses right about now. If he's a robber, shouldn't he use binoculars? Something like these."

LeVar reached below the seat and removed his binoculars. After focusing on the window outside room nine, he handed them to Scout. To his horror, she swung the binoculars toward the SUV.

"Don't do that!"

"Why?"

"It's rude. Let the poor guy enjoy his lunch hour."

The SUV backed out of its parking space. A moment later, the man navigated the vehicle down a crowded row and turned out of the parking lot. Scout bit her lip.

"I hope he didn't see me."

"He didn't," LeVar confirmed. The man never peeled his vision off the convenience store until he drove away. "But my point stands. It's bad manners to stare."

"Yeah, my mom taught me not to stare when I was like . . . two, I guess."

"Anyhow, when you're on a surveillance mission, you need to be subtle. Act like you aren't paying attention and monitor them out of the corner of your eye. Pointing binoculars out of the window is like screaming into a bullhorn."

Scout handed the binoculars back.

"Sorry I blew our cover."

LeVar laughed.

"Hardly. Andy Clem hasn't shown his face since the door closed. It appears he's enjoying himself."

"Hey, LeVar?"

"Yeah?"

"Did you mean what you said earlier? That I could catch criminals as a profiler without entering the field?" She glared at her legs. "Because I won't win too many footraces with these legs."

"Sure. I mean, I suppose so. Not that I've read job descriptions for criminal profiling positions, but I guess they have openings for people with your . . . unique circumstances."

"I wouldn't have to work for the FBI full-time. They might have consultant positions too."

LeVar snapped his fingers and pointed at Scout.

"There's a question you should ask Scarlett Bell the next time she messages you." He threw up his hands. "Now who are you staring at?"

Scout pushed herself up on her seat for a better view.

"Isn't that the guy from the SUV?"

LeVar followed Scout's eyes to the sidewalk. A man in a t-shirt, running shorts, and a baseball cap approached the convenience store from a busy intersection, jogging at a brisk pace.

"I'm not sure."

"It's him, LeVar. Check out the sunglasses, the leathery skin, the square chin. That's the guy from the SUV."

LeVar picked up the binoculars, one eye watching room nine in case Andy Clem and his secretary revealed themselves. Damn, Scout was right. Same guy from the parking lot. He appeared a little too inconspicuous in his running gear, though LeVar acknowledged the guy might just be out for a lunchtime jog. The man shot a quick glance into the store as he approached. LeVar's heart hammered until he ran past the convenience store and continued down the block.

"That's the same guy. But he's just out for a run."

Scout squirmed.

"He's up to something."

"Tell you what. If he circles the block and comes back, I'll call the sheriff's department. The office is only three blocks away."

"Promise you'll call?"

"I swear."

Scout chewed her nail, dividing her attention between the Pink Flamingo hotel and the empty sidewalk that led toward the convenience store. A minute later, the jogger returned. LeVar sat forward. No way the man had circled the block in that amount of time. He must have cut through an alley.

As LeVar reached for his phone, the jogger stopped on the sidewalk outside the convenience store, hands on his knees as he pretended to catch his breath. The distinct bulge in the jogger's pocket grabbed LeVar's attention.

LeVar dialed the sheriff's department before Scout shouted, "Gun!"

8

A little after noon, dispatch radioed Thomas and Lambert about a robbery in progress at the gas station convenience store beside the Pink Flamingo hotel. Thomas punched the accelerator and blared his siren, lights whirling as he raced across the village. With a pale face, Lambert held the door handle until the cruiser screeched to a halt outside the store.

Thomas and Lambert shared a confused glance. Deputy Aguilar held an unknown man face-down on the blacktop, the suspect's arm twisted halfway up his back in a painful hammerlock, Aguilar's free hand pressed against the guy's cheek to stop his squirming. A revolver lay beyond the suspect's reach. Aguilar let up on the man's face and retrieved the gun.

"She's not supposed to be here," Thomas said, shoving the door open.

Lambert hopped out on the passenger side with his gun drawn.

"Easy now, Sheriff. I'm sure there's a reasonable explanation."

Aguilar swung her head when they approached. Until now,

Thomas hadn't noticed LeVar Hopkins kneeling beside his lead deputy, keeping the suspect under control. The motor of his black Chrysler Limited purred beside the pumps. To the sheriff's astonishment, Scout Mourning sat in the passenger seat, pushing herself up for a better look. The girl gave Thomas a hesitant wave. He blinked at the teenage girl as he approached Aguilar.

"The creep's name is Oliver McCoy," Aguilar said.

"Let go of my arm," McCoy said, wincing.

"Not until you stop fighting."

Lambert took a knee beside Aguilar and wrenched the man's other arm behind his back. With Lambert's help, Aguilar slapped handcuffs on McCoy. Thomas moved his eyes between the prone suspect and his deputy, who was supposed to be on desk duty.

"What happened here?"

"LeVar Hopkins observed Mr. McCoy canvassing the convenience store. After McCoy pulled a gun, Hopkins phoned the department."

"And you responded?"

"Sheriff, you were on the other side of the village with Deputy Lambert. I was the closest deputy to the scene, so I responded."

Thomas worked his jaw back and forth.

"You took him down unarmed."

"No," said LeVar, rising to his feet. "I did."

"You?"

"I was across the street, working a case when I . . . when Scout caught McCoy removing a gun from his pocket. He'd canvassed the store for at least twenty minutes."

"You know better to confront an armed criminal. Leave it to the sheriff's department, LeVar."

"I wanted to. But the cruiser wouldn't have arrived in time, and I couldn't let him rob the place with the store packed with shoppers."

Thomas scratched his head and shared a glance with Lambert. The tall deputy shrugged.

Aguilar said, "When I reached the scene, Mr. Hopkins had Mr. McCoy on the ground and was fighting for control of the gun. I stepped in and took the gun from McCoy."

"That asshole knocked my tooth out," McCoy said, wrenching his head toward LeVar. "I'll sue him, and I'll sue your entire department."

"Good luck with that," Thomas said. "You read McCoy his rights?"

"I did," Aguilar said.

She gave Thomas a blow-by-blow description of the arrest. Thomas tilted his head at Lambert.

"Take him away." As Lambert yanked a protesting McCoy to his feet, Thomas rounded on Aguilar and LeVar. "What's gotten into you two? You're supposed to be on desk duty," Thomas said, glaring at Aguilar. He swung his eyes to LeVar. "And you're an unarmed citizen fighting a thug with a revolver."

"County law allows me to intervene in an emergency," said Aguilar, straightening her back. "Regardless of my status, I'm still an active deputy, sworn to protect Nightshade County and its citizens."

"And McCoy gave me no choice," LeVar said. "Either I tackled him from behind, or he barged into a crowded store with a gun. Who knows how many people he might have hurt or killed?"

The cruiser pulled away with Lambert driving and McCoy in the back. Thomas released a breath.

"I'll need a lift back to the station. We'll discuss what happened during the ride. Right now, I want a minute alone with LeVar."

"That's perfect. I should interview the store manager. Maybe this McCoy guy caused trouble in the past."

When Aguilar entered the store, Thomas threw his hands up.

"Before we get into what happened here, will you explain why Scout is in the passenger seat of your car?"

Scout appeared to be reading a magazine and sipping a soda, though Thomas caught her stealing glances at the two of them. LeVar pushed the hair off his forehead and swiveled his eyes toward the Chrysler.

"I wanted to bring Scout on a surveillance mission. You know she always wanted to help in the field."

"Is that wise? I'm all for including Scout, but not putting her in danger. LeVar, the guy could have turned the gun on you and shot Scout next."

LeVar studied the tops of his sneakers.

"I acted without thinking."

"Look, you'll get no argument from me as the sheriff of Nightshade County. You're a good Samaritan, and it's probable you saved multiple lives. But as a friend and someone who cares about you, I'm begging you to exercise better judgment. If McCoy shot you—"

"He's not a hardened criminal, Shep. I guarantee you'll find this is the first time he's ever done something like this. Getting the jump on him was easy. He never saw me coming."

"It was still an unnecessary risk. Does Naomi know Scout is accompanying you on cases?"

"She approves. And for the record, Scout caught the guy. I was too focused on the infidelity case to notice McCoy. Scout picked up on all the clues—McCoy studied the storefront from across the street, then jogged past the front door before returning."

"He was checking the place out, likely assessing the security."

"Right. By the time he returned and pulled the gun, I had no time to think things through. I just reacted."

Thomas removed his hat and wiped the sweat off his forehead.

"I'll need statements from both you and Scout."

"Understood."

Scout waved her arms over her head and pulled their attention. The girl twisted around in her seat and pointed at the Pink Flamingo hotel. LeVar's eyes widened before he sprinted to the Chrysler, snatched a camera off the front seat, and shot pictures of a man in a business suit leading an unknown woman out of room nine. After the man and woman piled into separate vehicles, LeVar reached across the seat and gave Scout a high five. Then he jogged back to Thomas and pumped a fist in the air.

"I take it you cracked your case."

"The infidelity case," LeVar said with a wide grin. "I can't wait to tell Chelsey I caught them on photo. And this time I remembered to remove the lens cap."

Aguilar finished her interview with the store manager and pushed through the doors. Thomas set a hand on LeVar's shoulder.

"Follow us back to the station. And, LeVar?"

"Yeah?"

"You did good."

9

Incense sharpened the air inside Dr. Ryka Mandal's office. The doctor kept the shades drawn. The atmosphere matched the color of the decor—caramel and mahogany. A glass coffee table divided the room. Deputy Aguilar slouched in a cushioned chair on one side. Mandal crossed her legs as she wrote on a notepad on the opposite side. Mandal's sable hair dangled past the middle of her back. She had a long, pointed nose and a thick accent Aguilar couldn't place. Something Middle Eastern. The doctor scribbled without looking up. Aguilar didn't trust what she was writing.

The doctor set the pen and pad aside and clasped her hands over her knee.

"Tell me again about the incident at the convenience store."

Aguilar cleared her throat. This was the second time Mandal had asked about the arrest. It was standard procedure for law enforcement officers to ask the interviewee the same question multiple times. It was an old trick to trip up the interviewee and catch him in a lie. Was Mandal following the same playbook?

"Dispatch received a call about an armed robbery in

progress. The sheriff and Deputy Lambert were on the other side of the village, interviewing neighbors about another case."

"The woman's hand inside the church."

"Yes. The convenience store is three blocks from the station. I responded."

"Did you carry your service weapon?"

"No. I don't have access to my gun. Haven't since the county told me to undergo therapy."

"So you responded to an armed robbery without sufficient means to defend yourself. How do you feel about that?"

Aguilar crossed her legs and scrunched her brow.

"I'm not sure. I didn't have time to question my actions. When I arrived, a friend of ours had the suspect on the ground. I took over and wrestled the revolver out of the suspect's hand."

"You could have been shot. That didn't worry you?"

"Not at all." Mandal gave Aguilar a telling glance that unsettled her. "Should it have?"

Aguilar hoped Mandal was ready to declare her healed and fit for field duty again. The doctor paused several seconds before continuing.

"Let's return to the Officer Neal shooting."

Aguilar's pulse raced. Just thinking about the shootout slicked her brow with sweat.

"Okay."

"Do you still dream about Officer Neal?"

Aguilar shook her head, biting her lip to cover the lie. Every night, she bolted upright with the image of Neal's bloody face burned into her vision. Which made little sense. She'd shot Neal in the chest and shoulder. Strange how the subconscious morphed her memory into a macabre scene from a horror movie.

"Never?" Mandal asked, cocking an eyebrow.

"Not since we last spoke."

"That's encouraging."

"Is it normal for the dreams to go away?"

"In due time, yes. Your recovery seems to be moving at an unusually fast pace. How are you around loud noises?"

Aguilar shifted in her seat.

"Sometimes they make me flinch."

"Also normal," Mandal said, softening her eyes. "Like the bad dreams, the fear of loud noises will go away in time." Mandal leaned forward. "Something else is bothering you, Deputy."

"Why do you say that?"

"Your body language. Now is the time to talk about what you're going through. You won't recover until you're honest about your feelings."

Aguilar chewed her thumbnail and stared at the window. A sliver of sunshine crept around the curtain and drew a sharp line across the carpet.

"Deputy?"

"It's just that Officer Neal must have had family, right?"

"You told me during our first appointment that Neal was unmarried, no children."

"But he must have a brother or sister. At his age, I assume his parents are still alive."

"That would be simple to confirm. But yes, I assume you're correct."

The deputy lowered her face into her hands and massaged the guilt away.

"I should be sad. No matter what Neal did, somebody loves and misses him. His coworkers pass his desk every morning, and Neal isn't there anymore. No more stupid jokes at the water cooler, no more rides in the cruiser."

"That's Officer Neal's fault. He murdered his own partner, correct?"

Aguilar nodded to herself. It seemed she was alone with her thoughts, Mandal's presence like a voice from another room.

"It's just that I should experience guilt for taking a loved one away. And I don't."

Mandal waited until Aguilar met her eyes.

"Isn't that what you're expressing now? You experience guilt every waking moment, Deputy Aguilar. It's plain in your facial expression, as well as your words. But your actions were justified. Would you experience the same guilt if Deputy Lambert or Trooper Fitzgerald shot Officer Neal?"

Aguilar sat back.

"I suppose not."

"Stop being hard on yourself." Mandal glanced at the clock. "It's time we wrap up our discussion. Thank you for opening up today. You're making excellent progress."

Mandal closed her notepad and clicked the pen. Hope thrummed through Aguilar's body.

"Does that mean I'm ready for field work?"

"Not yet. I'd like to see you again next week."

"Can't we move the appointment up?"

"I'm booked through next Tuesday. Besides, you can't rush the process. Like the body after experiencing a traumatic injury, the mind requires time to heal."

Aguilar sighed. Another week of desk work awaited her.

She blinked and sucked in a breath. A dead man lay between them, torrents of lifeblood pumping out of his chest, his punctured neck, and from the hole between his eyes.

Aguilar rubbed her eyes and looked again. Officer Neal vanished. The coffee table and carpet replaced the horrific image. Her eyes darted to Mandal, who adjusted her skirt. Aguilar leaped from the chair, afraid the doctor had noticed.

"Is something wrong, Deputy Aguilar?"

"No, it's nothing. I just remembered I had another appointment in fifteen minutes." Mandal narrowed her brow, unconvinced. Aguilar threw her bag over her shoulder. "I gotta run. See you next week."

Aguilar closed the door and leaned against the wall. Her head spun, black dots blanketing her vision like a swarm of bees. This was the first time the visions of Officer Neal attacked her in broad daylight. Who was she kidding? Things had gotten worse, not better.

But if Aguilar told anyone, Dr. Mandal would never allow her to return to field work.

10

Thomas ruffled his hair with a towel. Still damp from the shower, he tossed on shorts and a T-shirt and wandered out to the deck. Late afternoon sunshine painted the lawn in orange and yellow tones.

Outdoors, the lake breeze carried smoke from the shore where LeVar's mother, Serena Hopkins, grilled grouper. LeVar carried dishes to the picnic table as Naomi wheeled Scout down the concrete pathway. Jack, the enormous puppy Thomas rescued from the state park, wagged his tail beside the grill and accepted scraps. A warm contentment settled in Thomas's chest as he crossed the lawn to join the others. After a long day, it was nice to spend time with friends. Which upset him, because he needed to confront LeVar and Scout over the surveillance mission with Naomi present. He couldn't keep the robbery to himself. Naomi needed to know.

LeVar saw Thomas coming and busied himself with the grouper. With his mother's help, LeVar sliced the grouper onto buns and constructed sandwiches.

"Hey, Thomas," Naomi said, parking Scout's wheelchair beside the picnic table. "How was work?"

"Eventful. I'll tell you about it after we eat."

LeVar and Scout shared a glance.

The sandwiches featured a tangy mango dressing of LeVar's design. After they finished eating, Thomas set his hands on the table and turned to Naomi.

"There's something I wish to discuss with you."

"Is this about work?"

Thomas retold the story, emphasizing that the would-be thief pulled a gun before LeVar brought him down. Scout lowered her eyes as Naomi placed a hand against her chest.

"It's true I gave my approval. I'm all for Scout pursuing her interests, provided LeVar doesn't mind her tagging along. But I hadn't heard about the gun."

Naomi glared at her daughter. Scout sighed and opened her mouth to answer before LeVar cut in.

"If it wasn't for Scout, that guy would have held up the convenience store. He might have shot someone."

Naomi quirked an eyebrow.

"How did my daughter prevent a robbery?"

LeVar recounted Scout spotting Oliver McCoy as he studied the storefront from across the road.

"She's the real deal, Mrs. Mourning. I joke that she blabs about profiling all the time, but she profiled that guy to a T."

"Even so, I'm uncomfortable putting my daughter at risk. Has anything like this happened before?"

"There's risk during any case, but surveillance is usually pretty safe. Boring, even. The robbery wasn't related to our investigation. It was a matter of wrong place, wrong time."

Serena glared at her son. It was clear this was the first she'd heard about the incident.

"You could have been shot, LeVar. What got into your head, jumping out of the car and tackling a man with a gun like some half-ass superhero? And you left Scout alone."

LeVar shook his head and stared at his half-eaten dinner. "I messed up."

"LeVar was right about one thing," Thomas said, interjecting his opinion. "Oliver McCoy isn't a hardened criminal. He's an average Joe down on his luck, and he made a terrible decision. A little jail time will scare him straight. I doubt he's ever fired a gun. He was more apt to shoot his foot off than hurt anybody."

"That only means LeVar was lucky," Serena said, placing a comforting hand atop Naomi's. "Something terrible might happen next time."

"Mom, I'm entering law enforcement after I graduate. Sooner or later, I'll confront an armed suspect. You can't protect me forever."

"Fool." Serena rolled her eyes. "The academy will train you before they hand you a service weapon. You're still green. Think before you act, especially with Scout in the car."

"Yes, ma'am. I won't let it happen again."

Thomas glanced around the table and settled his attention on Naomi.

"Where do we stand? Do you still approve of Scout investigating with LeVar?"

Naomi set her chin on her fist and peered over the water. The sun reflected on the lake in an elongated blaze.

"I'm fine with Scout and LeVar working together." When Scout clapped, Naomi raised a hand to silence her daughter. "But only on one condition. LeVar needs to be her guardian and keep her safe. No more running after armed bad guys."

"I messed up," LeVar said. "Scout's my priority, I swear."

LeVar carried the dinner plates into the guest house with Naomi and Serena. Thomas slid along the bench so he sat across from Scout.

"I'm impressed. Where did you learn to profile so well?"

Scout straightened her shirt.

"Mostly through YouTube videos and articles. LeVar lets me borrow his textbooks too."

"Don't believe everything you read on the internet. But LeVar's books are excellent resources. What I said about Oliver McCoy was true. But anyone with a gun is dangerous. You saved lives today, Scout."

The teenage girl blushed. Looking out at the boats, she raised her water glass to her lips.

"I want to be a profiler after college. Obviously, I can't do things normal FBI agents do. But I can figure things out and help them find dangerous criminals."

"You're off to an amazing start. I've told you this before. When I was your age, Sheriff Gray hired me as a student intern. I never wanted to be a profiler, but I wanted to fight crime like you. Besides your mother and LeVar, have you discussed your interests with anyone?"

"I messaged an agent named Scarlett Bell at the Behavioral Analysis Unit. Working for the BAU is my dream."

"You're in luck. I know Agent Bell."

Scout's eyes widened to full moons.

"You know her?"

"Well, I met her once. I'm friends with her partner, Agent Gardy. We worked together on joint task forces when I was a detective with the LAPD."

"This is amazing. Can I meet them someday?"

"Maybe I can arrange a meet and greet. I talk to Agent Gardy every few weeks. The next time I do, I'll put in a good word and tell them how serious you are in your endeavors."

"Thank you. I can't believe this is happening."

Over Scout's shoulder, Thomas spotted LeVar exiting the guest house.

"Why don't you take Jack into the guest house and help your mom and Ms. Hopkins?"

"Sure. Thank you, Thomas. Come on, boy."

Jack woofed and followed Scout into the guest house. Now that they were alone, Thomas motioned for LeVar to join him at the table.

"I hope I wasn't too hard on you."

"Nah, you weren't. I had that coming."

"You saved everyone inside the store, LeVar. Your mother and I will always worry about you because we care. Please don't tackle another criminal with Scout in the car."

"I won't."

"To tell the truth, I haven't been myself, either." Thomas lowered his head and scratched behind his ear. "Between Deputy Aguilar fighting me to reenter the field and this new case, I'm having a difficult time keeping my head straight."

"The woman's hand?"

"That's the case." Thomas blew out a breath and searched the guest house windows. Two silhouettes worked at the sink. "I'm at a loss. This psycho walked into St. Mary's church during confession hours, claimed he remembered Father Fowler from years ago, placed the box, and left with no one identifying him. Fowler won't discuss the man's confession."

"Because of the sacramental seal."

"Are you Catholic?"

"We haven't set foot in church in so long, I don't remember what denomination we followed. But I read about the sacramental seal once."

"It's frustrating. Fowler is the only person who can help us catch the guy, and he's sticking to the rules. We don't know if the woman is dead or alive, or where she came from. No women have gone missing in Nightshade County in the last month."

LeVar snapped his fingers.

"Chelsey is working a missing persons case from four years ago. What's her name?" LeVar scrunched his brow in thought.

"Harmony Santos. You should put your heads together. Perhaps there's a common thread between the two cases."

"Four years is a long time." Thomas took a breath. "Thanks for the advice. I'll ask Chelsey about Harmony Santos after she returns from the office."

"We cool now, Shep Dawg?"

"Always, LeVar."

LeVar stuck his hand out, and Thomas bumped fists with the teenager.

The boy returned to the guest house to help Naomi and Serena. Thomas gazed along the shore. His eyes followed the trail to the state park where Ranger Darren Holt and Raven Hopkins lived. He thought about the woman's hand and the stranger's relationship with Father Fowler. The shadows lengthened, portending the coming dusk.

Was a murderer loose in Nightshade County? And why would Father Fowler protect him?

11

C helsey Byrd returned from her morning jog through the village. As the calendar moved deeper into spring, green leaves replaced the barren trees of winter, and rising humidity formed fog at sunrise. Sweat soaked her shirt as she fit the key into the lock at Wolf Lake Consulting. Musty stale air caught her nose upon entry. She wrenched the windows open inside the office and kitchen, allowing the house to breathe. Chelsey loved running the investigation firm inside the converted one-story house. She worked with all the comforts and amenities of home at her disposal, including a full kitchen and two bedrooms outfitted with blackout curtains. The bedrooms came in handy after Chelsey or Raven worked late into the night and needed a place to sleep. The bedrooms had also saved their hides more than once when snow bands rolled off the lake and stranded them at the office.

Chelsey showered at the end of the hall and changed into her work clothes. As she brushed her hair in front of the mirror, she thought about Thomas's offer. She loved the A-frame and loved Thomas even more. Accepting his offer made fiscal sense. With the housing market overheated, she'd sell her house in no time if she put it on the market. But there was Tigger, her rescue tabby, to think about. How would Tigger get along with a monstrous dog? Thomas claimed Jack was some form of Siberian Husky. She'd met her share of huskies over the years, and Jack appeared too wild to be one.

And there was the matter of commitment. It's not like Thomas had asked Chelsey to marry him. But moving in together was a huge step toward marriage, and she wasn't sure she was ready.

After she fried eggs and ate half a cantaloupe, she returned to her desk and studied the Harmony Santos file. During the early days of an investigation, she preferred to begin with a fresh perspective. Lawrence Santos suspected Gerald Burke and a mysterious guy named Kit. But the police followed both paths four years ago and reached dead ends.

She spread the wedding photographs across the desk and scanned each picture, searching for a frequent face, a common theme. Nobody stood out, yet her skin crawled with trepidation whenever she discovered a photograph of Harmony. Odd. Chelsey sensed eyes on the woman. Studying the pictures under a magnifying glass, she didn't find anyone sneaking glances at Harmony. Maybe Chelsey was overreacting.

Chelsey scanned the address book Lawrence Santos had copied for her. She located the entry for Harmony's Aunt Ella. The woman lived on the western edge of the county, a forty-five-minute drive from Wolf Lake. With the sun shining and the temperature reminiscent of early summer, Chelsey looked forward to getting out of the office. She called ahead and confirmed Ella would be home.

Chelsey followed the lake road and reached the highway fifteen minutes later. She lowered the windows and relished the cross breeze as it ruffled her hair. The trees rustled in the wind, the flowers in full bloom.

After inviting Chelsey inside, Harmony's Aunt Ella offered her coffee and croissants from the town bakery. Chelsey declined the croissant but accepted the rich homemade brew.

"I can't wrap my head around it," Ella said, drying her eye with a tissue. "It's been four years since Harmony disappeared."

"Thinking back, do you believe someone kidnapped Harmony?"

"Absolutely. When the sheriff's department suggested Harmony ran off, I bit my tongue. There's no way Harmony would have left her husband. She loved Lawrence."

Chelsey kept her relationship with the current sheriff to herself, not wanting to upset the applecart. She wasn't sure who the deputies were four years ago when Sheriff Gray ran the department. Chelsey couldn't imagine Lambert or Aguilar messing up the investigation.

"Lawrence mentioned a man named Kit. The police never found him. Do you remember who he was?"

Ella giggled.

"Oh, I remember Kit. That guy must have refilled his dinner plate three or four times. Every time I looked up, he was back in the buffet line."

"Did you speak to him?"

"Didn't we all? Friendly fellow, though bizarre. He kept taking pictures of himself with his phone like the kids do these days."

"You mean a selfie?"

"Is that what you call it? Then yes, a selfie."

"Do you recall Kit speaking to Harmony and Lawrence?"

"Just a quick congratulation. Kit said he was with the band, but I didn't see him on stage. As soon as they shut down the buffet, Kit vanished."

Chelsey bit her lip. She wasn't trailing a murdering kidnapper. Kit was a wedding crasher, no doubt snapping photographs of himself to show off for his friends. Ella offered Chelsey a refill on her coffee, but Chelsey declined. Together, they sifted through the wedding photos Chelsey brought along. Ella teared up multiple times. To Chelsey's chagrin, the aunt couldn't accept anyone in the pictures would hurt Harmony.

Back in the car, Chelsey searched for Gerald Burke's address. Harmony's ex-boyfriend lived in Dewitt, a wealthy village outside Syracuse. The drive would take an hour, depending on traffic. This time, Chelsey didn't call ahead. She wanted to catch Burke off guard. If the man wasn't home, she'd spend the day shopping and catch Burke after he returned from work.

It was a half hour before lunchtime when Chelsey stopped the Civic outside Burke's home. The cul-de-sac buzzed with lawn mowers and hedge trimmers, though none of Burke's neighbors worked in their yards. Instead, they contracted others to do the work for them. Trucks belonging to landscaping companies lined the street, and most of the houses featured privacy fences and security systems. Chelsey's heart thumped with anticipation when she spied the BMW parked in Burke's driveway. Someone had swept fresh grass clippings off the walkway and onto the lawn. A rose bush bloomed beside the porch.

The man who answered the doorbell had the flawless, chiseled facial features of a Roman god. Lean and strong, with his black hair brushed to perfection, Burke appeared as if he'd stepped out of a fitness magazine. He gave Chelsey a derisive stare.

"May I help you?"

Chelsey handed him a business card.

"I'm Chelsey Byrd with Wolf Lake Consulting. If you can spare a few minutes, I'm investigating Harmony Santos's disappearance."

Burke's eyes narrowed.

"Harmony vanished four years ago. You're a little late to the party."

"Please, Mr. Burke. I only have a few questions."

Instead of inviting her inside, Burke ordered Chelsey to meet him on his backyard deck. Then he closed the door in her face. She followed a red brick walkway to a picket fence gate, the north side of the house lined with green-leaved hostas. Burke awaited her on a cherry wood deck. He gestured for Chelsey to join him at the table. Burke held an iced tea with condensation dripping down the glass. He didn't offer Chelsey a drink. After she pulled up a chair, Burke spread his hands wide.

"I fail to see how I can help after so many years."

"I understand you dated Harmony Santos during college and remained close after."

"Harmony and I dated for almost three years."

"Did she break up with you? Or was it the other way around?"

Burke shifted his back.

"Consider it a mutual decision."

"Why?"

He shrugged.

"Lots of reasons, I suppose. Uncertainty about our futures and where we'd end up. Perhaps we'd grown apart."

"Yet you remained friends after the breakup."

"We did. Harmony and I kept in touch after college. I was thrilled she invited me to the wedding, though Lawrence never impressed me."

"You didn't approve of Harmony's spouse?"

"Harmony could have done better. She settled. That's a kinder way of saying she married down."

Chelsey made a mental note to dig into Burke's past. The man didn't mince words, and contempt twisted his mouth whenever he mentioned Lawrence Santos.

"What do you remember about the day Harmony disappeared?"

"You mean, where was I when it happened?"

"I'm not accusing you."

"The sheriff did," Burke said, tilting his head in remembrance. "Lawrence Santos put the idea in Sheriff Gray's head. But I was in Buffalo, attending a conference the day Harmony vanished, so the sheriff had no choice but to recuse me of wrongdoing."

"Will you write the conference name and who organized the event?"

Burke's eyebrows shot up.

"Aggressive, aren't we?" He huffed. "Fine. I'll provide you with the details, if you need to confirm my attendance. But you're wasting your time."

Chelsey handed Burke a sheet from her memo pad. He wrote the names and dates and slid the paper back to her. Before Chelsey asked another question, Burke held up a hand.

"I'm afraid I have an important engagement in an hour. This interview is over. If you have additional questions, make an appointment next time."

Burke rose without shaking hands. Chelsey wondered what Harmony saw in the man.

On her way back to the car, Chelsey studied the neighboring houses. Despite the privacy fences, the lots stood atop each other with small yards. Could Burke kidnap Harmony and murder her inside his house without drawing attention? Doubtful.

She slipped the key into the ignition. As the engine started, she noticed Burke watching her between the curtains.

12

Upon entering the county sheriff's department, Thomas stopped at Maggie's desk. In her early fifties, the administrative assistant wore her brownish-orange hair shoulder length and permed. Maggie had held her position for twenty years, overseeing three different sheriffs.

"Did Sheriff Gray arrive yet?"

Thomas had phoned Gray this morning, hoping the former sheriff would shed light on Father Fowler and his mysterious visitor.

"He arrived five minutes ago. I told him to help himself to a donut in the break room. Lambert has his ear."

"Thanks, Maggie."

When he passed Aguilar's desk, the diminutive deputy released an exaggerated sigh and glared at him from beneath a mountain of papers. He hated throwing paperwork at his most talented deputy. But the department had fallen behind, and she needed to stay busy, even though she wanted to headlock Thomas and toss him over her hip.

"Deputy," he said, touching his hat as he passed.

Aguilar grumbled something indiscernible.

Thomas found Sheriff Gray in the break room with Lambert. Both wore their smiles from ear to ear, Lambert finishing a joke as Thomas entered.

"Good to see you again, Sheriff Shepherd," Gray said, shaking Thomas's hand. "What's it been? Four days?"

Gray was a frequent guest at the cookouts beside the lake. He hadn't aged since retiring last year. Thomas thought Gray appeared five years younger. The former sheriff had shed fifteen pounds, and his eyes were no longer creased with the worries the position entailed.

"You'll join us again next Wednesday, I hope. We're grilling filet mignon."

"Wouldn't miss it for the world. What's up?"

"Follow me to my . . . your office."

"It's your office now, Thomas. I'm pretty sure I remember the way."

Thomas closed the door and motioned to the empty seat beside his desk. The role reversal struck a strange chord in Thomas. How many times had he sat in the visitor's chair with Gray behind the desk? Gray took in the room, his eyes soaking in memories.

"What's with the secrecy? The door is closed, so it must be important."

"It's about Father Josiah Fowler."

Gray flinched at the priest's name. He'd never given up believing Father Fowler drove Lana off the road.

"What's the serpent up to now?"

"You probably read about the body part left inside the church."

"It was in the newspaper. Nasty business. You suspect Fowler murdered your Jane Doe?"

Thomas folded his hands on the desk.

"Not exactly. And she's not a Jane Doe until her body

surfaces. Fowler claims a man visited during confession. This guy acted as if he knew Fowler from a long time ago. Before he departed, he left a wood box containing a woman's hand beneath the seat."

"And Fowler won't disclose the nature of the confession or the suspect's name."

"No."

Gray puffed out his mustache.

"He's hiding behind the sacramental seal. The question is, is Fowler protecting himself or the church?"

"That's what I'm wondering. Nobody at the church saw this guy. My guess is he timed his entrance to avoid the crowd, slipping in and out unnoticed."

"You visited the neighborhood and knocked on doors?"

"Lambert and I did. Nobody recalls seeing a stranger lingering outside the church, and we don't know what type of vehicle he drives. We're in the dark."

"What about security cameras? I don't suppose Fowler installed any."

"Nope."

Scratching his chin, Gray said, "I'm not surprised. He's crooked, and no criminal wants a camera recording his actions. I'll tell you one thing. This stranger made it personal when he left a hand inside the booth. Whoever he is, he has a huge issue with Fowler. Even more than I do." Gray tapped his fingers on the chair arm. "Figure out what Fowler is hiding, and you'll catch this guy."

"I considered bringing in the media. Maybe someone can find a link between Fowler and his visitor."

"I wouldn't recommend it. The media will turn the investigation into a circus. I'll call my old deputies. A few are still around. Someone might recall an accusation involving Fowler. But don't hold your breath. After Lana died, we turned over every stone and dug into Fowler's past. We found nothing."

"He's a slippery guy. I haven't trusted him since the Thea Barlow murders." Thomas regretted bringing up the Barlow investigation. The former sheriff had accused Father Fowler of the murders. Gray's embarrassment over the ordeal led to him stepping down. "Where should I start? Fowler holes up inside the church like a recluse, and he refuses to disclose anything the man said."

"Fowler will slip up and show his true colors. Even a snake needs to emerge from a hole to sun itself."

13

An ocean of dusk spread across the sky above Wolf Lake State Park. The season's first fireflies danced among the trees, and the campfire drove back the mosquitoes. Scout and LeVar toasted marshmallows on sticks as Darren and Raven readied the meeting area inside the ranger's cabin.

The camping season wouldn't hit full stride until schools let out for summer vacation. But a few campers enjoyed the mild night. The family of four watching LeVar and Scout from across the clearing couldn't have known they were amateur sleuths with a storied history of solving mysteries and catching criminals.

LeVar scanned the forest. The firelight bounced off the trees and reflected into the clearing as darkness thickened. Enjoying the peace inside the park, LeVar understood why Raven wanted to move in with Darren and sell her house to their mother. There was safety here. It was easy to put the day's troubles in the rear-view mirror and relax. No busy roadways, no exams or essays to write. As night deepened, an endless diamond mine of stars flickered.

Scout caught her breath and pointed.

"A shooting star. Did you see that?"

LeVar followed her outstretched arm to the western sky.

"I missed it."

"Keep watching. I bet there will be more."

"Don't burn your marshmallow," LeVar said as flames caught Scout's stick.

Scout had been too focused on the sky to pay attention to her dessert. She swept the stick through the air to douse the fire.

"Perfect," she said, blowing on the blackened treat before popping the marshmallow into her mouth. "I'm an expert marshmallow roaster, LeVar. You could learn a thing or two."

"First you profile armed robbers, then you flaunt your expertise with marshmallows. It's not easy living in your shadow."

"Yet you keep me around." Scout glanced at the cabin. "They're probably expecting us. We should head inside."

"*Aight*, but I still have half a bag of marshmallows left."

LeVar wheeled Scout into the cabin. Darren's log cabin sat a hundred feet from the welcome center. The interior was one large living space with thick curtains over the windows, a bed tucked against the far wall, a couch with two mismatched chairs, and a tiny kitchen off to the left. Darren served coffee while Raven fixed the throw pillows on the couch. After he set the coffee down, Darren dragged the chairs around to face the couch. When they were settled, Raven clicked her laptop and brought up a digital list of potential cases.

"And so begins another laugh-filled episode of the secret sleuth files," Raven said, invoking giggles from the others.

Though they made light of their amateur sleuthing activities, their research had helped solve multiple murder cases over the last year. They even located a lost girl named Skye Feron after a kidnapper held her captive on the outskirts of Wolf Lake.

"Let's get started," Darren said, sliding onto the couch beside

Raven. Before taking over the ranger position at Wolf Lake State Park, Darren worked as a police officer in Syracuse. "We're all busy, so we can only afford to take on one case. Choose carefully."

LeVar grabbed a notebook and tapped a pen against the open page.

"How about the Harmony Santos disappearance? Raven and I are already helping Chelsey with the investigation, so we'd have a head start."

They all shared uncertain looks.

"A four-year-old cold case?" Raven asked. "The chances of Wolf Lake Consulting recovering Harmony Santos alive are slim to none. What about the severed hand at St. Mary's?"

"I doubt Thomas wants us near his investigation," Darren said. "He's under enormous pressure. The media wants an answer, and Father Fowler's name evokes controversy."

"But what if there's another serial killer in Wolf Lake?" Scout asked. "We'd miss out if we blew the case off."

"It's difficult to cry *serial killer* when no women have gone missing in the last month," LeVar said.

"Well, the hand had to come from somebody. What if the killer snatches his victims around the country and brings them home to Wolf Lake?"

Darren sat forward.

"That's possible. But until the sheriff's department gathers evidence, we're in the dark. I say we hold off on the severed hand case until we have more information."

Raven and LeVar nodded. Scout shook her head in disappointment.

"There's a cat burglar in Barton Falls," LeVar said, drinking coffee.

Raven glanced at her brother.

"Where does the term cat burglar come from? They don't steal kittens. Why not just call him a burglar?"

"Cat burglars enter homes through upper floor windows, fool. They're nimble like cats, hence the name. Ya dig?"

"Look at you brimming with knowledge. You'd think you made dean's list this semester or something."

"There ain't no cat burglars in my text books, Sis. I'm dropping common knowledge."

"What about the Poplar Corners ghost?"

They all turned to Scout. She fidgeted under their glares.

"The Poplar Corners ghost?" LeVar brushed his hair back. "Halloween isn't until October, Scout, and you're a little old for make-believe horror stories."

"The ghost is just an internet legend," Raven said, drawing a nod from her brother.

"No, I don't think he's a legend," Darren said. "During my Syracuse PD days, I knew a trooper who looked into the case. There are dozens of complaints of some guy staring into people's windows at night. But nobody can catch him."

"So he's a Peeping Tom." LeVar waved the idea away. "I hope someone nails him, but it doesn't seem worth the effort."

Scout rolled over to Raven's computer and brought up a website devoted to catching the Poplar Corners ghost.

"Over two dozen sightings in the last year," Scout said, pointing at the dots covering the screen. "Hundreds more this decade. And check out this chart." She clicked the mouse. "The sightings are up fifty percent since last year."

"You know how that goes. One person claims the ghost stared into his window, and five more jump on board. They're all seeing their own reflections."

"I disagree. The increase in sightings suggests he's losing control."

"Scout's right. We should take the case," Darren said.

LeVar narrowed his gaze at Darren.

"Okay, convince us."

"Harmony Santos disappeared from Poplar Corners. What if the same guy peeking in everyone's windows kidnapped Harmony four years ago? We might solve two mysteries for the price of one."

Staring at the ceiling, LeVar pondered Darren's theory.

"It's not a stretch. A Peeping Tom might graduate to kidnapping."

"Or murder," Scout added.

"We can't prove the ghost kidnapped Harmony Santos, let alone killed her." LeVar turned his head to his sister. "What's your opinion?"

Raven extended her legs and crossed them at the ankles.

"Since we don't have a better option, I say we take the investigation. If it falls flat, we'll choose a different case next week."

Darren banged his fist against the coffee table like a gavel.

"So it's decided. I'm ready to begin tonight, if everyone is willing."

"No school tomorrow, so I can stay late," Scout said.

LeVar glanced at the window. Night pushed between the curtains and slipped inside the room.

"Nobody can find this guy," LeVar said, studying the sightings on the computer screen. "The Poplar Corners ghost avoids detection, so he's smart. Not your average criminal. We'll need a miracle to track him down."

14

B illowing clouds replaced the morning sun when James McKinney stopped his minivan in the parking lot. Beyond the gate, the Poplar Corners town park and its fields of green beckoned. A playground grew out of the ground with swings, slides, and monkey bars connecting two towers.

The park sparkled with children's laughter when James opened the sliding door. The second he unbuckled Lonnie, the four-year-old boy took off running.

"Slow down, Lonnie."

James reached for his son, but the boy was already halfway across the blacktop and sprinting toward the open gate. Releasing a frustrated sigh, James surveyed the parking lot. If another vehicle had driven through when Lonnie bolted out of the door . . .

There were only three vehicles besides his van. The sporty compact belonged to Trina, who lived two blocks from James and Lonnie. She must be here with her son, Martin, which explained why Lonnie couldn't wait to reach the park. Martin and Lonnie were best friends.

James turned sideways and slipped through the opening in

the gate. Surrounding the play area, benches sat upon mulch beds. After waving to Trina, James took an open bench between the slide and swing sets. He glanced around the playground. Where did Lonnie go? He turned left and right before Lonnie's excited voice pulled his eyes toward the towers. Lonnie and Martin climbed to the top and extended their arms toward the monkey bars. Both boys made it halfway across before their grips gave out. They fell laughing to the mulch, brushed off their knees, and ran back to the tower.

"Stay where I can see you," James said, meeting his son's eyes.

"Okay, Dad. Watch this."

Lonnie scrambled up the tower again and leapt to the monkey bars. He almost made it to the end this time. James clapped and hooted while Lonnie stared at his red, sore hands.

"You're getting closer. Pretty soon we'll need to find a longer set of bars."

"I'll make it next time."

James grinned. Lonnie and Martin ran to the swing set. Trina caught James's eye from across the park where she held court with two stay-at-home moms. They shared a wave. James turned his attention to Lonnie, never letting the boy out of his sight. After marrying his wife, Brooke, who died three years ago, James chose Poplar Corners for its promise of small-town safety. He'd made a mistake. After Lonnie came into his life, rumors of the Poplar Corners ghost exploded in frequency.

James didn't believe in ghosts. But creepers, kidnappers, and child molesters haunted the evening news. They were everywhere, and James refused to let his guard down. Let the gossiping townies weave stories about specters in the night. The real boogeymen were cancer, heart disease, and random blood clots buried deep inside the body like ticking time bombs. A freak stroke took Brooke at thirty-one. Lonnie had been one when Brooke died. James didn't want Lonnie to forget his mother, so he kept her picture beside Lonnie's bed. Every night they prayed for Brooke before turning off the light.

Sneakers scuffing through mulch pulled James's head around.

"Got the day off from work?" Trina asked, sitting beside James.

"I have two days of vacation time to burn before summer."

Trina bobbed her head in understanding, though the woman quit her job years ago after her uncle left Trina a generous inheritance. James wished he'd fall into money so he could care for Lonnie. Daycare providers were undependable.

"Lonnie and Martin sure are having a good time."

"They're inseparable."

"Sometimes I wish I was a kid again. Nothing to worry about but skinned knees and whatever make-believe aliens or bad guys you fought that day." Trina waved to a woman on the other side of the swing set. "Oh, that's Jana. I need to say hello. Call me later. We'd like to have you over for dinner."

James returned to his duty. Unlike the other parents, James never relaxed, always paranoid about Lonnie running off or a stranger slipping inside the park. A stranger like the wacko who stared into people's windows in the middle of the night. Martin pushed Lonnie on the swings, a little higher each time as Lonnie pumped his legs.

"Not too high, boys. You'll flip over the top."

James shook his head and laughed to himself. He sounded like his parents. Recalling his childhood, he failed to remember any kid flipping over the top of the swing and plummeting to his demise. Physics got in the way once a kid surpassed a ninety-degree angle. But James was an adult now, and adults worried. It was his job.

Speaking of his job, James's phone hummed. He read the

message and scowled. The firm where he worked had lost the Martinson account, and the boss wanted everyone to stay late tomorrow. Wonderful. James already promised Lonnie he'd take the boy to the mall after dinner. Now he needed a sitter. Hopefully Trina would babysit the boys for a few hours after school. While James replied to the message, Lonnie and Martin played with four children from the neighborhood. They ran circles around Trina and a woman James didn't recognize. Probably Jana.

The assistant manager, Phillip, replied to James's text. After four messages filled his mailbox, James sighed. He liked the people he worked with, but they never respected his time off. As the debate spun out of control, James lost track of Lonnie. Keeping up with messages and watching his son proved impossible. When he glanced up, Lonnie was gone.

He stood up from the bench and scanned the park. The boy had been in front of him ten seconds ago. No way he could have run off. The icy cold fear of losing Lonnie struck his chest and froze him to his core.

James exhaled when he heard Lonnie's voice from the other side of the playground equipment. Slumping against the bench, James stretched his tired legs.

"My birthday is in nine weeks, but Dad says I can have one of my presents sooner if I'm good."

Trina was great with Lonnie, and the boy loved talking with her. All the more reason James should ask Trina to do him a favor and babysit Lonnie for two hours tomorrow. James rolled his eyes as Lonnie talked her ear off. His gaze fell to the phone when Phillip sent another message. From the corner of his eye, James saw a woman chastising her son for roughhousing. His heart caught in his throat when he realized Trina was yelling at Martin for pushing another boy to the ground. The fallen boy wiped a tear from his eye while a consoling mother knelt in the grass. Who was Lonnie talking to?

James shot off the bench as though electrocuted.

"Lonnie? Where are you?"

No answer.

Pushing a swing aside, James ran beside the playground equipment to dead silence. He knew Lonnie wouldn't be there when he rounded the towers, that his worst fears would be realized. Breathless, he smacked his shoulder against the corner as he stumbled through the mulch.

"Lonnie!"

"I'm right here, Dad."

When James found his son, Lonnie was climbing up from the base of the slide, the boy's sneakers slipping on the slick metal. James glanced around. Across the park, Trina pulled Martin aside and lectured him on playground etiquette. The other parents watched their children play.

"Who were you talking to?"

Lonnie furrowed his brow. In that moment, James felt certain Lonnie had spoken to a pretend friend, as the boy liked to do. Sometimes he overheard Lonnie talking to Brooke, as if his mother was playing with him.

"There was a nice man in the park."

James knelt beside Lonnie and grabbed his arm when the boy tried to climb the slide again.

"What man?"

James didn't see anyone else in the park. Lonnie shrugged.

"He didn't say his name."

"You're not making this up. Right, Lonnie? It's okay if you're pretending."

"He was right here, Dad. Standing beside the slide like you."

James wanted to believe the stranger was a maintenance

worker from the parks department. The cold hand squeezing his chest told him otherwise.

"What did he say?"

"Not much. He asked me my name and if I enjoy playing in the park."

James rose to his feet.

"You didn't tell him your name, did you?"

Lonnie shook his head.

"Nope. I don't give strangers my name. Just like you taught me, Dad."

"Where did this man go?"

Lonnie pointed toward the trees bordering the park.

"That way."

James took Lonnie by the hand. He needed to warn Trina about the stranger. God help James if the man was a child predator.

"Let's talk to Martin's mother, okay? I want you to describe the man you saw."

15

"Anyone home? Thomas?"

Chelsey poked her head inside the sheriff's A-frame beside the lake. The keys dangled from one hand, Tigger's carrier from the other. Her voice hadn't finished echoing off the walls when a jingling chain announced Jack. The pup raced down the stairs, his nails slipping on the hardwood floors as he skittered across the lower landing.

"Easy, Jack," Chelsey said, holding the carrier above her belly so Jack didn't stick his nose through the grates. Tigger hissed and retreated to the dark corner of the carrier. "Tigger doesn't want to meet you. Not yet."

Chelsey's mouth went dry. The dog could swallow Tigger in one bite. So far, Jack seemed curious and excited. No hair-raising growls or warning barks as Chelsey carried Tigger to the dining room and set the crate on the table. A stack of bills lay on the counter beside a notepad where Thomas had scribbled his thoughts on the St. Mary's church mystery. Not wanting to pry, Chelsey ignored the notes and opened the sliding glass door to the deck.

"Do your business, buddy. I need to get back to the office in an hour."

Jack forgot Tigger and sprinted through the opening. While the dog relieved himself, Chelsey scanned the guest house windows. Today was LeVar's day off, but the lights were doused inside the house. Chelsey turned to Tigger and peered inside the crate. The tabby cowered at the back, afraid to emerge from hiding.

"It's okay, little guy. Jack's friendly." She squinted at the supposed Siberian Husky. "I think."

When Jack returned, tail wagging and slapping against the table legs, Chelsey closed the screen but left the sliding glass door open. A clean, refreshing breeze drifted off the lake and ventured around the dining room and kitchen. There wasn't a sound in the world except the water sloshing against the shoreline. She could get used to this.

And that pulled her mind back to Thomas's offer. If she accepted, her life would change forever. She appreciated her independence and having personal space. Plus, she worked as a private investigator. Sometimes private investigators bumped heads with law enforcement. Living under the same roof with the sheriff of Nightshade County might get awkward.

She glanced down at Jack, who stared up expectantly. His attention kept drifting between the crate and Chelsey, an obvious message that he wanted Chelsey to bring Tigger out. In her imagination, it had seemed so easy. She'd let Tigger out of the cage, observe Jack's interaction with the cat, and place the tabby inside the protective carrier if Jack threatened Tigger. Now that she was here, her pulse raced. If Jack turned on Tigger, could she stop him?

She needed to find out. If Chelsey moved in with Thomas, Jack and Tigger had to get along. No way would she give the tabby away.

"Here goes nothing," she said, lowering the carrier to the floor.

Jack pawed at the door, shaking the crate. He didn't display aggression, just curiosity.

"Give Tigger space, Jack. You'll be a good boy, won't you?"

Jack raised his eyes to Chelsey, the dog's tongue hanging out as he panted. The angry meow from inside the cage sounded doubtful. Tigger didn't trust Jack's smile.

Chelsey squatted beside the crate. Shielding the enclosure with her body, she opened the door and waited. Tigger didn't budge. Not that she blamed him. Two minutes passed with Jack lying on his stomach with his snout draped over the lip of the crate and Tigger hiding inside a blanket.

"All right, Jack. Take two steps back."

Jack didn't understand the command, so Chelsey moved the crate away and ordered Jack to stay put. Reaching inside, she pulled Tigger into her arms and cradled the tabby. As she stroked the cat behind his neck, Tigger stopped struggling and purred. Chelsey watched Jack with one eye. The dog never moved, but his gaze remained fixed on Tigger.

It took a long time for Chelsey to work up her courage. After Tigger relaxed, she placed the tabby on the floor. Jack started forward and Chelsey stopped him.

"Nuh-uh. Stay where you are, Jack."

The dog's tail thumped the floor. Chelsey petted Tigger, who crouched behind her leg and glared at the massive dog.

"Are you ready to meet Jack?"

More tail thumps.

"I suppose it's now or never. Okay, Jack. Time to meet your friend."

Jack trotted over to Tigger and nudged the cat with his nose. Every nerve in Chelsey's body was a live wire. She wasn't sure if Jack's excitement was for his new playmate or his next meal. She stayed on one knee and monitored the interaction. Tigger padded toward the living room, and Jack followed, nudging him again.

"Give him space."

Tigger let out a loud meow. Jack dropped to his stomach and grinned. A second later, they were chasing each other around the downstairs, leaping off Thomas's couch, scrambling beneath the dining room table, sliding around the kitchen. To Chelsey's relief, Tigger did most of the chasing. She shook her head in wonder before reality struck her. With Jack and Tigger best friends now, she was out of excuses. Thomas deserved an answer.

As she mulled over her decision, the doorbell rang. Jack froze. Tigger scrambled across the top of the couch, confused why the dog had stopped the chase. Glass covered most of the A-frame. Outside, a fit man wearing a gaudy Hawaiian shirt stood atop the handicap accessible ramp. A salesman? Jehovah's Witness?

"Who the heck is that?"

Jack cocked his head when the doorbell rang a second time. Chelsey gave the man another glance through the window. The mid-forties visitor appeared nonthreatening. Even if he caused trouble, she had the dog to protect her. Before the man could press the bell again, she whipped the door open. He opened his mouth and stared at her dumbstruck, expecting someone else.

"May I help you?"

The man raised on his tiptoes and peered into the downstairs as if searching for someone. When his eyes landed on Jack, the man took an involuntary step backward. He wore sandals on his feet, sunglasses pushed atop his head. A few flecks of gray dotted his dark hair.

"Sorry. I must have the wrong address. Is this Thomas Shepherd's house?"

"Yes, you're at the right place. He's working today."

"Oh, of course." He cleared his throat and reached into his pocket. After he didn't find what he was searching for, he dug into another pocket, gave Chelsey an embarrassed smile, and checked his shirt pocket. "Ah, here it is. My name is Neil Gardy. I'm an agent with the FBI Behavior Analysis Unit."

Gardy flicked open his wallet and displayed his credentials. The identification appeared legitimate. Thomas had FBI contacts?

"Chelsey Byrd," she said, offering her hand. "I'm Thomas's... friend. He should be home from work in three or four hours. Do you want to leave a message?"

"Uh, sure. Tell him Agent Gardy is in town and stopped by to say hello. Well, I'm not actually in town. I'm staying in Coral Lake."

"Are you investigating a case?"

"Just a pleasure trip. I always wanted to visit the Finger Lakes region." He sifted through his wallet and produced a business card. "I wrote the number for the inn on the back. Have him call me when he has a chance. I'd love to catch up."

"I'll tell him. Thomas will be sorry he missed you."

Gardy peeked his head around Chelsey's shoulder.

"Hey, doggy."

Jack growled. Gardy backed away.

"I won't take more of your time. Nice to meet you, Ms. Byrd."

The vacationing FBI agent descended the ramp and followed the walkway to his minivan, a humorous vehicle for an agent with the Behavior Analysis Unit. As he backed onto the lake road, he beeped the horn and waved. Chelsey waved back to the odd, yet friendly agent. She watched with curiosity as his vehicle vanished down the roadway.

16

Thomas narrowed his eyes at Chelsey's message as he navigated the cruiser around a bend. Agent Neil Gardy was in Coral Lake? Gardy never took vacations. The man worked twenty-four hours a day, seven days a week. Thomas pictured the agent in a Hawaiian shirt and laughed to himself.

There were no interstate routes near Coral Lake. Two rural roads meandered down the east and west sides of the long, narrow lake, the properties growing in grandeur as he approached the village. He repeated the address in his head and checked the GPS. If memory served correctly, the inn lay on the northern shore in the village center.

When he found the inn, Thomas parked the sheriff's cruiser at the rear of the lot. This wasn't his county, and he didn't wish to step on toes. When he found Gardy's room, he knocked twice and waited. The door opened to an unexpected sight: Agent Gardy in cargo shorts, sandals, and the Hawaiian shirt Chelsey mentioned. Her description failed to do the shirt justice. Thomas squinted at the bright colors.

Gardy's eyes widened in surprise.

"Sheriff Thomas Shepherd. I figured you'd call first."

"I had a few hours this afternoon and thought I'd drive over."

The FBI agent stood aside and motioned Thomas into the room.

"Come in, old friend."

Thomas wandered inside and took everything in. The resort suite featured a kitchenette, a generous living space, and a deck overlooking the lake. An overstuffed suitcase lay on the bed.

"I can see why you'd want to stay here. Very nice."

"Right? Come out to the deck. The dinner cruise is pulling out of port." There were two chairs on the deck. Thomas sat beside Gardy as a dinner boat filled with tourists drifted past the inn. "So you're the big cheese in Nightshade County now. What's it like being sheriff?"

Thomas shrugged.

"It's a dichotomy. I have jurisdiction over the county, so lots of responsibility. Yet the job is quiet. Most days, that is."

"I read about the Thea Barlow case. The murders drew national attention."

"Your profile was dead on," Thomas said, setting an ankle on his knee as he eyed the agent with skepticism. "I appreciate your help."

Gardy waved a hand through the air.

"Anytime. That's what we're there for."

Thomas studied the water. Coral Lake was as blue as the Caribbean when the sun began its afternoon descent. A slew of boats bobbed and motored across the water, one dragging a girl on an inner tube.

"You're a long way from Virginia, Gardy. What made you choose Coral Lake for a vacation spot?"

Gardy's lips moved in silence, as though he'd practiced his response.

"Agent Bell and I worked a case here a few years ago. I fell in love with the village and always planned to return." He opened his arms. "And here I am. Back in paradise."

"Speaking of Agent Bell, she corresponds with my neighbor."

A confused look fell over Gardy's face.

"Your neighbor?"

"Scout Mourning. She's a teenager with an interest in criminal profiling. Scout wrote Agent Bell and received a reply."

"That sounds like Bell. She has a soft spot for kids. Plus, the woman never stops blabbing about profiling."

"Since you're in the area, perhaps you'd be willing to sit with Scout before you leave and tell her about the job. She's as bright as they come, and she even helped me catch Jeremy Hyde last year."

"Absolutely. I have three more nights in Coral Lake. I'm happy to meet with Scout."

Thomas sat forward with his elbows on his knees and gave Gardy a wry smile.

"And maybe you'll tell me why you're really here."

Gardy swallowed.

"What?"

"How long have we known each other? Agent Gardy never takes a vacation."

The agent opened his mouth to protest and clamped it shut. He fell back in his chair, deflated.

"What gave it away?"

"The Hawaiian shirt. Laying it on a little thick, aren't we?"

"It is an unfortunate wardrobe choice. But I fit in with the locals."

"Then there's your suitcase. You packed for a few weeks, not for a few nights. And if I open the closet doors, I bet I'll find black suits on hangers."

Gardy wagged a finger at Thomas.

"Don't I always say you should be a profiler?"

"You're deflecting."

"Guilty as charged."

"So why are you in Coral Lake? This is about the woman's hand in the church, isn't it?"

Agent Gardy chewed his lip.

"Listen, Thomas. As far as the FBI is concerned, I *am* on vacation. It just so happens your case might be a part of something bigger."

"I'm all ears."

Gardy stood from his chair and leaned his hands on the railing. He looked over the lake, the humor gone from his face.

"A severed hand inside a confession booth. You got off easy. In Kalamazoo, he left a human leg on a kids' playground in the center of the city."

"You're certain it's the same guy?"

Gardy's silence spoke volumes.

"He's a phantom, Thomas. Over eight years, he's murdered twelve people, including four children. At least, those are the twelve I'm aware of. He's impossible to catch because he doesn't have a preferred victim type like most serial killers. Men, women, young or old. It doesn't matter with this guy. He just likes to kill, and he has a taste for it." Gardy gestured for Thomas to follow him inside. "Come with me. There's something I need to show you."

Agent Gardy opened his laptop case and set the computer on the desk. He slid his ID into the card reader and typed a password. After he passed the FBI welcome screen, he opened a folder and clicked on a map. Gardy tapped his finger on the screen.

"Not only does he change his victim type, he moves around. He's killed in Michigan, New England, Ohio, and various points around the Mid-Atlantic."

"Does he always leave a body part behind?"

"Not always. But when he does, he prefers to dump the body part in a populated area. Killers like our unsub love to grab the headlines. He dumped a teenage boy's head outside a busy restaurant in Annapolis. The bastard avoided the traffic cams. There must have been a hundred people inside that restaurant and just as many on the street, and nobody saw him."

"Does he ever kill in the same place?"

"Never."

"So why did you travel to Coral Lake? It appears he already murdered his victim and left a part of her behind. He won't strike again, right?"

"He might. Because it's personal this time."

Thomas pulled his chair closer to the computer.

"Why do you think it's personal?"

"Think about it. Leaving the hand inside a confession booth guaranteed only one person would see it."

"Father Fowler, the priest who received his confession."

"Exactly."

"Problem is, Father Fowler won't divulge the man's confession," Thomas said. "All Fowler told us is the man claimed to know him from years ago."

Gardy's eyes lit.

"That's a start. Honestly, that's the closest we've come to learning about his past. But there's a bigger problem." Gardy traced an invisible circle around the map with his finger. "See the pattern? Nightshade County lies in the center of the circle."

"This is his home base."

"And he's spinning out of control. I have a bad feeling about this guy, Thomas. He's just getting started."

Thomas tapped his foot.

"What do you need from me?"

"An invitation, if you're interested. You know the protocol.

The FBI won't send me in unless the locals make the call. We're like vampires. I'm not allowed to enter your home until you open the window."

"If what you say is true, I want the FBI in Nightshade County."

"Consider it done." Gardy dropped a hand on Thomas's shoulder. "Together again, Thomas. Just like Los Angeles. Let's catch this guy."

17

Deputy Aguilar gasped and bolted upright. She stared at the bedside clock with no clue where she was or if it was early or late. The bedroom seemed darker than normal, the ambient light blocked at the window by blackout curtains. Beside the bed, the alarm clock flashed the time, a signal the power had gone out, resetting the clock. She rubbed the grit from her eyes and fluffed the pillow, frustrated she was awake again in the middle of the night. Until the shooting, she'd slept like a baby. Eight hours every night without fail. Now she was lucky if she stole four hours from the sandman before she slogged into work.

She grabbed her phone to read the time, but the phone was dead. Hadn't she recharged it yesterday afternoon? Resting her head, she snagged a second pillow and dropped it over her face. Anything to block out the flashing alarm clock.

A knock on the front door sent a shock through her body. She sat up and listened, hands clutching the blanket. Nobody knocked on her door, let alone this late. The hairs rose on the back of her neck, her legs frozen and stiff as she willed the visitor to go away.

The knocks came again. Three insistent thuds that rattled the door.

Aguilar searched the gloom for her service weapon and found it beneath the bed stand. It was too dark to make out anything but vague shapes as she held the gun with a quivering hand. The deputy swung her legs off the bed. The floor felt cold against her bare feet, as though a sheet of ice lay beneath the carpet.

She crossed the hallway and approached the front door. Moonlight beamed into the living room, distorted by the shape of the man outside her door. Aguilar held her breath. Something about the misshapen shadow chilled her blood.

Aguilar opened her mouth and ordered the stranger to go away. No words escaped her lips. She swallowed, her throat parched and constricted, as if a snake wrapped around her larynx.

The man pounded three times again. Loud, booming thuds that caused the door to jiggle inside the jamb. She should call the sheriff's department. Except she'd forgotten to charge the phone.

She aimed the gun at the door and reached for the handle. When she pulled it open, the leering face of Officer Avery Neal smiled at her. Blood dripped down his face, his eyes hollow sockets. The officer lurched forward and wrapped his fingers around Aguilar's neck. Squeezing. Lifting her off the floor so her feet beat uselessly against his shins.

Neal drove her against the wall. The plaster crackled. A picture frame tumbled off the hanger and struck the bloody officer on the shoulder. And she kept repeating in her head, *This isn't Avery Neal. This is another attacker, some psycho or creep out of my past. I'm imagining Neal's face.*

He strangled the life out of Aguilar, slamming her head against the wall as the moon illuminated his gangling body from behind. She couldn't pull oxygen into her lungs. Her vision failed as the life seeped out of her body. His clawed hands released her throat as she fell to the floor. Then he vanished.

Aguilar screamed and yanked herself out of the nightmare. The deputy threw the covers off her legs. She clutched her neck, as if Neal's fingers dug into her skin. On the bedside table, the clock rolled over to midnight. Shivering, she curled into a ball and stared into the darkness. She was losing her mind.

SOMETHING AWOKE James McKinney after midnight. A sound outside. Or the sharp starlight washing against the windowpane.

He sat up and grabbed a glass of water off the floor. Sipping from the glass, he crept down the hallway and peeked in on Lonnie. The boy lay tucked beneath the covers, his chest rising and falling in gentle waves. James edged the door shut and moaned, accepting it would be hours before he fell asleep again. As he built a sandwich in the kitchen, he stared out the window. The night was silent, no cars moving through the neighborhood, nobody on the sidewalk.

He'd been a nervous wreck since the stranger spoke to Lonnie in the park. Was the man at the playground the Peeping Tom who stood outside his neighbors' windows late at night? Four years ago, a woman vanished from Poplar Corners. James recalled reading about the disappearance. Santos was her name. At the time, he believed she'd run off to escape her husband. But the newspaper articles painted her as a loving wife. James worried the same man who haunted the night, the so-called Poplar Corners ghost, kidnapped Santos. And if this kidnapper had approached Lonnie in the park, right under James's nose . . .

No. Driving himself crazy wouldn't keep his son safe. He shook off his trepidation and wiped the crumbs off the counter.

After James consumed half of his sandwich, he returned to the bedroom and sat with his back against the headboard. Outside the window, starlight frosted the neighbor's roof, making the night seem preternaturally frigid. He considered turning on the television but opted for a book instead. Three pages later, he hadn't comprehended a single word. James set the book down and yawned. He needed to wake up for work in five hours.

Certain he'd be up all night, James jolted with surprise when his eyes popped open. The clock told him he'd been asleep for two hours.

Yet something in the night had changed. The sounds were unfamiliar now. A secretive wind whispered around the house. In the distance, a car raced down a lonely stretch of highway.

He was about to pull the covers over his head when his son's voice shocked him out of his slumber.

"Are you cold? Come inside before you get sick."

Then the screech of Lonnie's windowpane sliding open.

"Lonnie!"

James leaped off the bed. His balance wavered as he stumbled down the hallway. Lonnie's bedroom door seemed so far away now. It appeared to drift away as James ran for the door.

James burst into his son's room. The blankets were tossed aside on the bed. Two child-size slippers lay on the floor.

The drapes danced with the night breeze, mocking James.

"No, no!"

He stuck his head through the open window. Lonnie was gone.

18

W hen Thomas stopped his truck outside James McKinney's ranch home, Lambert galloped across the yard to meet him. His deputy had received the call ten minutes before Thomas and beaten him to the scene. Thomas dropped from the cab and stared at the house. Every light shone inside. He could see Aguilar through the window as she spoke to a man in pajama bottoms and a sweatshirt. The lawn was a lunar minefield of starlight.

"Someone approached the four-year-old son's bedroom window around two in the morning," Lambert said, flicking his attention at the ranch. "James McKinney was awake. A sound knocked him out of sleep. McKinney heard his son, Lonnie, speaking to an unknown person outside. By the time the father ran to the bedroom, the window was open, and the boy was gone."

"Fingerprints on the pane?"

"Just the boy's. It's possible the kid opened the window."

"Or the kidnapper wore gloves."

"That's what I'm thinking too."

Thomas set his hands on his hips.

"Does the father have any clue who kidnapped the boy? A disgruntled spouse?"

"The wife died when the boy was a year old. But McKinney claims a man spoke to Lonnie in the town park two days ago."

"Did he give a description?"

"The kid told his father the stranger had blonde hair, but that's the only description we have. McKinney overheard the conversation and figured Lonnie was talking to another parent. The stranger disappeared before McKinney identified him."

"All right. I assume you checked for shoe impressions below the window."

"There weren't any. Grass is too thick."

"Grab a flashlight and search between the window and the road. This guy must have left a shoe print somewhere."

Lambert shifted his body to observe his fellow deputy through the window.

"There's something else, Sheriff. Aguilar shouldn't be here tonight."

"This is an emergency, and we need all hands on deck. The higher-ups won't count it against her."

"I'm not worried about the county. I mean, Aguilar shouldn't be on duty. At all. Something is wrong with her, Sheriff. I've never seen her like this. I doubt she's slept more than a few hours this week, her color is bad, and she's a jittery mess. This is none of my business, but have you heard anything about her therapy sessions?"

Thomas stared past the window. Inside the living room, Aguilar wrote on a notepad as McKinney spoke.

"Aguilar told me she enjoys therapy. I shouldn't say more than that."

"Understood. She claims she's getting a lot out of it. But not from where I stand. I never thought I'd say this about Aguilar, but she needs time away from the office."

"You're saying I should put her on leave?"

Lambert removed his hat and scratched his head.

"I'm not sure. All I can say is I'm worried about her. She's not herself. And she's missing stuff, Sheriff. Like yesterday, I went over her paperwork. She left multiple entries blank and forgot to sign four documents."

Thomas's jaw pulsed. Aguilar was meticulous. If she was messing up paperwork, Aguilar's head wasn't right.

"Anything else?"

"Before you arrived, Aguilar helped me dust in the bedroom. She worked for two minutes before she remembered to put on gloves. You ever recall her screwing up like that?"

"Thanks for telling me, Deputy. I'll keep an eye on her. Right now, I need you focused on this missing boy. Find me a print while the scene is still fresh."

Lambert swept the flashlight beam ahead of him as he rounded the house. Thomas took a breath and removed his phone. He needed Neil Gardy. With a child taken from his own bedroom, Thomas believed Gardy's theory about a serial killer living in Nightshade County had to be accurate. The agent was probably sound asleep at this time of night. Before he dialed the inn, Thomas's phone rang, and Gardy's name appeared on the screen.

"That was quick," Thomas said, moving away from the screen door so McKinney wouldn't overhear.

"The report came into the FBI five minutes ago. What can you tell me about the kidnapping?"

"Four-year-old boy. The father claims a stranger approached the child two days ago at the town park. No witnesses so far."

"Our unsub has a knack for avoiding detection. It has to be him, Thomas."

"That's what I'm afraid of."

"Agent Bell is flying into Syracuse at eight this morning. As soon as she arrives, she'll work up a profile. Remember, we followed this guy for eight years, so we have a head start."

"We'll need it, Gardy. I don't want to pick this kid's body parts out of a public place."

"We won't allow that to happen." Gardy paused. "I need to shower and change. Give me an hour to reach the scene."

"It's an hour's drive from Coral Lake during the day."

"I'm aware. Like I said, one hour."

The call ended, and Thomas opened the door and introduced himself to James McKinney. The man's hair stuck out in opposite directions, his pajama bottoms wrinkled. Deep red pooled in McKinney's eyes.

"Tell me everything about the incident in the park and what happened this morning."

"I got his statement, Sheriff," Aguilar said.

"Thank you, but I'd like to speak with Mr. McKinney. You checked the boy's bedroom?"

"Of course."

"Help Lambert outside. The FBI is on the way."

"FBI?"

Thomas turned to McKinney without replying. Aguilar wore a jilted expression as she strode away. Thomas felt horrible upsetting his lead deputy, but repeating questions was common procedure. Often, victims recalled important information when asked to repeat their stories. This time, McKinney didn't tell Thomas anything new.

"Is there anyone around town who paid too much attention to your son? Maybe someone you assumed was being kind."

McKinney's eyes darted around the room like bats caught in the light.

"Nobody."

"Anyone ever threaten you or your son?"

"Don't you think I'd tell you if someone had? What's

happening in this town? A child predator strolls through a playground with no one stopping him, then he steals my son through his bedroom window. What are you doing to find my boy?"

Thomas wanted nothing more than to find Lonnie McKinney. He pictured the withered hand inside the wooden box. In the sheriff's mind, a child's hand replaced the woman's. His stomach churned.

"As you probably overheard, the FBI is on the way and will help us find your son."

"Can you look me in the eye and promise you'll bring Lonnie back alive?"

"There's an AMBER Alert out on Lonnie. The state police are checking vehicles, and Lonnie's face will be on every news report today. We'll find your boy."

19

Purple and magenta bruised the eastern sky when Deputy Aguilar left the McKinney ranch and drove home. She was due back at work by four this afternoon, but Thomas had given her the day off.

"Rest up, and return when you feel better," he'd said, hiding his disappointment.

She'd almost blown the investigation by contaminating the crime scene. While she dusted, the gloves hung out of her back pocket. She never forgot to wear gloves. If Lambert hadn't said something, she might have worked another hour before she remembered. She struck the steering wheel with her palm.

Lights turned on inside houses as people rose for the new day. Many were just learning of Lonnie McKinney's kidnapping. Children held a special place in Aguilar's heart. Whenever harm came to a child, it tore her to shreds. She wanted to bring Lonnie home to his father. Though she recognized her convoluted logic, she believed saving Lonnie would redeem her.

For what? For shooting a murderer disguised as a cop?

As Aguilar turned out of Poplar Corners, she followed an unlit road along a rocky creek. She repeated Dr. Mandal's words in her head. This wasn't her fault. She'd done the right thing by firing at Avery Neal. She might have saved Lambert and Trooper Fitzgerald, as both were pinned beneath Neal's gunfire when her bullets struck the murderer and whipped him against his vehicle, blood spurting from his chest and shoulder before he crumbled to the blacktop.

Trees grew thick along the creek bed. What little ambient light existed on the horizon vanished inside the tree tunnel. She turned on the high beams and took a deep breath, one hand fiddling with the FM radio, muscles taut as she worried about deer bolting out of the brush and running in front of her cruiser.

The dispatcher's voice crackled over the police band. He asked for her position. Aguilar muttered to herself. This was Thomas's doing. The sheriff had offered to follow Aguilar home after they wrapped up the investigation, afraid she'd fall asleep at the wheel and wreck. He hadn't said as much, but she'd read it on his face. She cleared her voice and reached for the radio.

"Unit two here. I'm five miles west of the highway. Estimated time of arrival in Wolf Creek is six o'clock."

Dispatch acknowledged receipt. She turned the music louder, drowning out the infernal quiet creeping around the cruiser. Aguilar took her eyes off the road for a half-second. When her head snapped up, the man was standing on the centerline.

She slammed her foot on the brakes, the front end pulling left as the rear wheels fishtailed toward a ditch. The shriek of rubber against macadam deafened Aguilar. Trees whipped by. Then she saw the creek in the windshield, the centerline zipping past her vision, as the steering wheel pulsed and rattled beneath her failing grip.

The cruiser screeched to a halt on the shoulder. The rear tire on the passenger side dropped into the ditch with a heavy thunk and a crunch of metal. Her heart slammed. She killed the motor and stared at the empty road, searching for the man. When she didn't find him, she twisted around in the seat, terrified his mangled body would lie behind the cruiser. The blacktop merged with the darkness.

Trembling, Aguilar dragged herself from the vehicle and stumbled back the way she'd come, afraid to turn on the flashlight. She didn't want to see his body.

But when Aguilar aimed the beam down the road, there was no one on the road except her.

"What the hell?"

She swept the light over the ditch, then back toward the creek. Nothing. No crumpled body. No injured man moaning from the tall grass. She'd imagined him.

"No, this is impossible."

She rubbed her eyes and blinked. The scene remained the same. Just an empty rural road with the peepers shrilling from the creek bed. Aguilar slapped at a mosquito. Her brain fumbled to decipher the last minute of her life. She pictured the man in the road, the way he'd stared straight into the cruiser's headlights without shielding his eyes. And she suddenly recognized the man she'd seen.

Shit.

Officer Avery Neal.

Aguilar bent over and screamed into the crook of her arm. Her stomach lurched as she set her hands on her knees and waited for last evening's dinner to reemerge. It didn't, though sour acid seared her throat. With her fingers interlocked behind her head, she staggered back to the cruiser to assess the damage. As she feared, the back wheel hung uselessly into the ditch, the cruiser's bottom flush against the road. How the heck would she get the vehicle back on the road? Radioing dispatch was a last resort. She'd only confirm their beliefs that she wasn't fit for the job.

And they were right.

Aguilar leaned on the trunk and bit back a sob. Since she was a child, she'd wanted to help people. Law enforcement was her life, but she wasn't cut out for the job. One shooting, and she was a mess. She couldn't picture herself in another career or working an office job.

To hell with therapy and reinstatement. When the time was right, she'd break the news to Thomas and resign. Just imagining her words tightened her throat.

She dropped into the ditch and pushed on the bumper. The cruiser wouldn't budge. She was stuck here and couldn't bear the humiliation of admitting she'd driven off the road. Maybe she'd claim a deer ran in front of her. Anything but the truth.

As she threw her shoulder against the bumper and lifted, a branch snapped in the darkness. She spun around and aimed the flashlight into the shadows.

"Hello?"

The peepers continued to sing. After a moment, she struggled with the cruiser again. In the gym, she squatted two-hundred-fifty pounds. The cruiser was a helluva lot heavier than that. She needed leverage. Shifting the cruiser into neutral, she returned to the back tire. With a grunt, she lifted and shoved, rocking the vehicle until the front tires drifted forward. Aguilar was so relieved, she almost cried.

On tired legs, she climbed out of the ditch and sat behind the wheel. Now she wanted to go home. Even if she drove at twice the speed limit, she wouldn't reach Wolf Lake before six. Thomas had ordered her to check in when she arrived, and she needed an excuse for being late.

Aguilar inhaled and steadied her voice, hiding the embarrassing quiver. She radioed dispatch.

"Be advised, unit two is stopping at a roadside diner for coffee and breakfast. It's been a long night."

"I hear you, unit two. Pancakes and eggs sound good right about now. Let us know when you reach Wolf Lake."

Aguilar promised she would. She shifted into drive and allowed the cruiser to roll on its own momentum before she touched the gas. Her hands refused to sit still, and her eyes swept the shadows for another vision of Avery Neal.

Even on the highway, she never drove faster than forty. Tractor trailers roared past, the drivers shooting her concerned glares, worried there was something wrong with the cruiser. She waved each time and gave a thumbs up.

She couldn't wait to reach Wolf Lake and put the night behind her. But when the village appeared before her windshield, it only reminded the deputy of her failures. Aguilar returned the cruiser to the station and switched to her own vehicle, a red Rav4 with a scratch on the driver's side door.

She fell into bed face-down and lay there. Breathing and thinking. Aguilar couldn't do this another day. She'd announce her resignation this afternoon.

20

Thomas awakened to Jack licking his face. He worked the sand out of his eyes and squinted at the clock. Ten-thirty.

Giving the dog a pat on the head, Thomas sat up and lowered his eyes as sunlight burned through the windows. His head throbbed. Though he'd taken Aguilar's advice and switched to green tea, he needed coffee this morning. He doubted he could function without a caffeine influx.

Jack followed at his heels until Thomas let him outside. LeVar's Chrysler Limited was gone from the driveway, and the lights were off inside the Mourning house next door. Everybody was up and going about their days except Thomas. Realizing he was running low on breakfast food, he fed the dog and sliced a cantaloupe. While the coffee brewed, he checked his messages. According to dispatch, Deputy Aguilar made it home before seven. He wondered what took her so long. A text from Agent Gardy confirmed Scarlett Bell had landed in Syracuse at eight o'clock. The FBI requested a station meeting at the sheriff's office at two. Agent Bell would reveal her preliminary profile.

Everyone seemed eager to catch the man who'd evaded the BAU for eight years.

Thomas sifted through his notes as he ate. The coffee twisted his lips. Though he appreciated the jolt of energy, he'd lost his taste for morning brew. After showering, he dressed for work and radioed the office. He had a few stops to make and planned to arrive an hour before the station meeting. Before leaving the house, he'd called and confirmed Chelsey was at Wolf Lake Consulting this morning. After the last week's horrors, he needed to be around friends. He was in luck. Darren, Raven, and LeVar were also at the private investigation firm.

As he drove the F-150 through the village center, his thoughts returned to the elusive killer. What made the murderer tick? The psychopath didn't have a preferred victim type, making him difficult to catch. But all criminals displayed tendencies. Humiliation and mutilation drove the unsub. He goaded the FBI and police by placing body parts in populated areas. Whoever the killer was, he needed attention. More so, he wanted to shock and terrorize the public. And he must have a massive ego to take so many risks.

Chelsey met him at the door with a hug. Thomas didn't let go for a long time. Her presence grounded him.

In the hallway, LeVar slapped him on the back.

"Glad you made it, Shep Dawg. You need a pick-me-up, and we're just about to eat lunch."

Chelsey gave Thomas a concerned look.

"Did you eat anything today?"

"Half a cantaloupe."

She rolled her eyes.

"Come on. I'll make you something healthy."

Darren and Raven worked at the kitchen counter as LeVar removed plates from the cupboard.

"Long night?" Darren asked with a knowing glance.

"Or an early morning. Days and nights blend after a while."

Darren, who'd worked shifts as a police officer, appreciated the effects long nights and inconsistent hours had on a body.

"I remember it all too well. What do you prefer: ham or roast beef?"

"Eat, Darren. I'll take care of Thomas," Chelsey said, slicing a roll. "Honey mustard?"

"Sounds perfect," Thomas said.

Making himself useful, Thomas pulled glasses from the cupboard and poured drinks. They pulled their chairs around the table and sat down for lunch. Chelsey placed a bag of potato chips in the center of the table and told everyone to help themselves.

Raven gestured at Thomas with a ham sandwich, something Thomas found amusing.

"Chelsey says the FBI is coming to Wolf Lake. Is that true?"

"They're already here. Neil Gardy, an agent I worked with on joint task forces in Los Angeles, is staying in Coral Lake this week. His partner, Scarlett Bell, flew into Syracuse this morning."

"Scarlett Bell." Darren raised his eyes to the ceiling and rubbed his chin. "I read about her. She profiles serial killers, right?"

"The national magazines have an infatuation with Agent Bell. Besides her track record of success, she has an interesting background. Heartbreaking, really."

"What happened to her?"

Thomas finished chewing and set his sandwich down.

"When she was a child, a serial killer abducted her friend. The two girls had been playing near the river behind Bell's house."

LeVar leaned forward and asked, "Did the police find the girl?"

"Not alive." The others became quiet as Thomas recalled the story. "Eventually, the killer tried to kidnap Bell. But she escaped. Agent Bell blocked out the kidnapping until a few years ago when the murderer resurfaced. Bell killed him steps from where he'd kidnapped her friend."

"That's insane. I'm surprised someone hasn't made a movie out of that story."

Thomas slumped back in his chair.

"According to Agent Gardy, the attention embarrasses Bell. She has the looks and the charisma of a star when she's on camera, but she prefers to keep to herself." Thomas sipped his water. "Anyhow, she's our best bet to catch Lonnie McKinney's kidnapper."

Darren shifted his chair closer to the table.

"Raven and I hosted Scout and LeVar at the cabin recently."

"Another super-secret investigations meeting?"

"Something like that. We settled on a case, and I think we're crossing paths with your investigation."

"Tell me about it."

"Have you ever heard of the Poplar Corners ghost?" Raven asked before she popped a chip into her mouth.

"Sounds like some script John Carpenter turned down."

"Scout brought him up," LeVar said. "There's a website devoted to the ghost. For the last several years, some Peeping Tom has crept around Poplar Corners, staring through people's windows at night."

Thomas straightened his back. That sounded too much like James McKinney's story.

"But he never kidnapped someone before."

"Maybe he decided peeping wasn't enough."

"It made me wonder after I read about this morning's kidnapping," Darren said. "Four years ago, a woman went missing from Poplar Corners."

"Harmony Santos," Chelsey said, covering her mouth. "That's my latest case. Her husband hired me to track her down."

"What if we're all searching for the same guy?"

Thomas set his forearms on the table.

"Are you suggesting Lonnie McKinney's abductor kidnapped Harmony Santos four years ago and spent the better part of the last decade peeping through windows?"

"It's possible." Darren set his plate aside. "All I'm saying is we should put our heads together. While you investigate the kidnapping with the FBI, Chelsey can search for clues on the Harmony Santos disappearance. We'll interview neighbors and track down this supposed ghost. If my intuition is correct, we'll zero in on the same guy."

Pressing his lips together, Thomas glanced around the table.

"There's something you should know. Bell and Gardy involved themselves with my case because they believe this guy murdered a dozen people."

Raven shared a look with Chelsey.

"A serial killer?" Raven asked.

"This information doesn't leave the table, understood?" Thomas waited until they nodded. "The FBI mapped the murders—Ohio, Michigan, the Mid Atlantic, New England. Even two unexplained disappearances in Ontario Province. If you draw a circle connecting the murders, Nightshade County falls in the center. If Agent Gardy is right, the same man who left the woman's hand inside St. Mary's church abducted Lonnie McKinney."

"And murdered a dozen people around the northeast," LeVar said, bobbing his head in understanding.

"I'll learn more this afternoon when Agent Bell presents her profile."

"Wish I could be a fly on the wall for that meeting," Chelsey said, drawing mutters of agreement.

Thomas steepled his hands and swept his gaze across the table.

"The possibility we're all searching for the same person raises the danger level. We need open lines of communication, and I don't want anybody encountering a suspect alone. Do we agree?"

They did.

"Good. Learn everything you can about the Peeping Tom." Thomas turned to Chelsey. "Find a connection between Harmony Santos and Father Fowler. There must be a reason the killer targeted the confession booth inside St. Mary's." Chelsey scribbled a note. Thomas glanced at the clock. "I prefer spending the afternoon with friends, but I'm running late."

"Shep, you'll share the profile with us?" LeVar asked.

"As soon as it's available."

21

"Your compositions are sound, Ms. Schneider. But your writing is third-grade level and a black mark on the department."

Justice Thorin slid the essay across the desk. The girl glared at the red D drawn atop the essay. She rolled the paper into a cone shape and shoved it inside her book bag. The girl swung her fury to the professor.

"But this is a photography class. Why are we writing essays at all?"

"No matter your talent as an artist, you won't get far in life if you can't express yourself on paper. Words carry weight, Ms. Schneider. At their finest, they convey emotion and sway opinion. In your case, I only wish for proper grammar and a coherent thought."

"At least let me correct the mistakes."

"Your grade is final. If I allowed my students to rewrite their papers, I'd bury myself under a mountain of work. Now, if you'll be so kind, I have a pressing engagement."

She cocked her head, ready for another argument before he waved her toward the door, as if batting away a bothersome fly.

He blew out a breath when the door closed. Students these days wanted everything handed to them—high grades, simple assignments, a job gifted to them after college. Ms. Schneider would learn the hard way after she graduated. The world was a cruel, unforgiving place. There were no second chances, no grading on a curve in the real world. Either you kept pace with your peers, or you lost the race. And Ms. Schneider was a loathsome tortoise running against hares.

Thorin checked his watch. Dammit. The banquet began in fifteen minutes.

He removed a handheld mirror from his desk drawer and studied his reflection. Outside his room, shoes and sneakers shuffled by as students lumbered to their classes. Thorin licked his fingers and sculpted his hair until no strands were out of place. Icy blue eyes, the color of sapphire resting on the bottom of a pool, stared back at him. His smile faded when he remembered the banquet. What a waste of time.

On his way out the door, Thorin grabbed his jacket and hung it over his shoulder. A boy called to him as he descended the stairway. He held up a hand without looking back.

Sunlight blinded Thorin on the concrete steps outside the Arts Building. He shoved sunglasses over his eyes and crossed the quad, his eyes flicking over three Kane Grove University students sitting cross-legged on the lawn. Two girls, one boy. It was the girl in the flower-print skirt who caught his attention. She was a freshman in Bennet Dean's Intro to Graphic Arts class. Thorin snickered. The girl wouldn't learn anything from an uncreative slug like Dean. But he could teach her a thing or two. Thorin's tongue slid across his lips as he passed. The other girl, a pudgy sloth with a nose ring, waved to Thorin. He smiled, his hidden eyes fixed on her freshman friend. The professor couldn't say what attracted him to the freshman, just that she pulled his attention. She'd make a fine pet.

The banquet hall sat in the Kitterly Building on the east side of the quad. The second he entered the building, Felicia Armstrong converged on Thorin. Her black, permed hair clung to her shoulders, and her heels clicked and echoed off the polished floor. She wore a gray pant suit and carried a leather briefcase that was nothing but a purse made to appear masculine. If Thorin snatched the briefcase from her hand and whipped it open, he'd spill makeup, lipstick, and car keys. Felicia didn't fool him with the professional attire.

"I didn't think you'd make it."

"You doubted me, Felicia?"

He never broke stride as he angled toward the banquet hall. Felicia hustled to keep up.

"It's just that you acted like you didn't want to attend."

"Then you assumed wrong. I set aside two meetings for this . . . engagement. Now, where is the man of the hour?"

Walking alongside Thorin, Felicia gave him a doubtful glance. A teenager with pink hair held the banquet hall door open.

"Good afternoon, Professor Armstrong," the girl said. Felicia doted over the girl. Thorin rolled his eyes. "And good afternoon to you, Professor Thorin."

Thorin put on his best smile, the one that concealed the wolf's fangs.

Ten tables covered by white cloths sat at regular intervals inside the banquet hall. Felicia hooked elbows with Thorin and pointed at a table near the front. He groaned. A table near the back would have provided a quick exit. Now Dr. Cooke or Professor Mills would pull him into a conversation after the banquet ended, and Thorin would never leave.

Felicia scooted her chair forward. Thorin took the seat beside her. The banquet hall stank of beef and some vegetable medley that probably came from a plastic bag. When the server set lunch in front of them, Felicia thanked the girl as if the server had handed her a diamond necklace. While Felicia forked food into her mouth, Thorin glared at the colorless meal. He'd expected mediocrity, but this was an embarrassment. Dr. Cooke appeared with a wine glass. From the way Cooke's legs wobbled, Thorin assumed this wasn't the doctor's first drink. Cooke raised the glass.

"A wonderful honor for Professor Dean, don't you agree, Justice?"

"No one deserves it more," Thorin said, chewing the inside of his cheek until he bled.

"After the banquet, I'd like to discuss this year's scholarship awards."

"So soon? Perhaps we should table the discussion for another time. I have class at two o'clock."

"No worries, Justice. I won't keep you long."

Before Thorin could protest, Cooke gave a boisterous shout and waddled to the next table. Wonderful. Cooke would talk Thorin's ear off about his glowing prodigies. None would amount to anything upon graduating, Thorin thought. But let them have their moment in the sun before life knocked them down a peg.

Felicia stabbed an olive with her fork and pointed it at Thorin.

"Lighten up, Thorin. This is the most talented class of artists I've seen since—"

Two taps on the microphone cut Felicia off. Thorin wiped his mouth on his napkin and set the cloth on his lap. The crowd turned their attention to Dr. Cooke at the podium. He lowered the microphone to his mouth. Feedback shrieked through the hall, inciting a round of laughter.

"We are gathered here today to honor Professor Dean for advances in the photographic arts."

Polite applause followed. For the next five minutes, Thorin forked salad and beef into his mouth while Cooke droned on and on about Bennett Dean. Standing at the side of the stage, Dean beamed with fake humility. When Cooke invited Dean on stage and presented him with his award, Thorin applauded. Felicia raised an eyebrow, questioning his sincerity.

"Please," Thorin said, staring at her through the tops of his eyes. "Who do you think gave Dean the idea for his thesis?"

"You?"

Thorin winked and turned back to the stage where Dean and Cooke shook hands and posed for pictures. After the dog and pony show ended, Thorin tossed his napkin on the table and pushed his chair back, hoping to escape before Cooke cornered him again. He leaned close to Felicia and whispered in her ear, close enough to smell her perfume.

"Stick with me, Felicia. The Cookes and Deans come and go. But I'll be running this department in five years."

Her mouth hanging open, Felicia stared at Thorin as he pushed through the crowd.

22

The Nightshade County Sheriff's Department didn't have space for a conference room. Instead, Thomas chose the interview room for the FBI briefing. The computer rested on a wobbly desk at the front of the room. A long table took up most of the floor space, and there weren't enough chairs to accommodate his deputies, the FBI agents, and the handful of New York State Troopers who attended. Thomas nodded across the room at Trooper Fitzgerald, Darren Holt's friend.

The sixty-inch television on the wall displayed the FBI logo. At the front of the room, a striking woman with blonde hair hanging past her shoulders conferred with Agent Gardy. Thomas had seen pictures of Agent Scarlett Bell in magazine articles. He never appreciated the woman's beauty until now. Piercing, interrogative intelligence swam in Agent Bell's eyes as she took in the troopers and deputies. Thomas doubted anyone could hide a secret from Bell. When her eyes landed on him, it was as if she stared into his soul.

Thomas weaved through the crowd, accepting handshakes along the way. He raised his hands to quiet the chatter.

"We're privileged to have Agents Bell and Gardy from the FBI Behavioral Analysis Unit with us today. With their help, we'll find Lonnie McKinney and capture the man who kidnapped him." He turned to Bell and offered her a microphone. She held up a hand, a signal she didn't need one. "I'll turn the presentation over to the FBI."

All eyes settled on Agent Bell at the front of the room. She clicked a wireless mouse and moved the presentation forward.

"Thank you for inviting us to Nightshade County. As you're aware, an unknown individual kidnapped four-year-old Lonnie McKinney from his home in Poplar Corners, New York, a little after two o'clock this morning. We believe the same man, who we refer to as our unsub, or unknown subject, left a woman's hand inside St. Mary's church in Wolf Lake."

Mutters moved through the crowd. For many, this was the first they'd learned of the link between the kidnapping and the severed hand.

"Our unsub has been busy the last eight years. He's murdered at least twelve people around the Great Lakes, Ohio Valley, New England, and Mid-Atlantic region, including four children."

Bell had their attention now. A pall fell over the room as the agent displayed a map of the murders.

"Notice the center of the circle falls over Nightshade County. Given the recent uptick of criminal activity in your region, I'm convinced the killer lives among us, possibly in Wolf Lake or Poplar Corners."

The grumble of conversation halted when Agent Bell displayed a picture of Dennis Rader, the BTK killer.

"Not every serial killer is insane in the manner Hollywood paints them. Many are cunning, intelligent, and aware of their actions. It's my hope this profile will help you catch this man."

She paged forward. A bloody stump of a leg lay in the grass. Playground equipment climbed out of the ground in the background. An atrocity among a child's paradise.

"This is Kalamazoo, Michigan, four years ago. A mother pushing a stroller through the park spotted a human leg on the lawn, steps from the playground equipment. An hour later, and the park would have been filled with children."

Next slide. A heavyset trooper in the front row moaned and covered his mouth.

"And this is Annapolis last spring. Our unsub murdered sixteen-year-old Troy Cullip and left his head outside Barry's Fish Market, a popular restaurant along the water. He murders the young and old, male and female, with no discernible tendency toward victim type. The unsub strikes in the middle of the day and in the dead of night. His range stretches several hundred miles. This makes him very difficult to catch."

Agent Bell paused and held their eyes.

"This morning, a call came into the Kane Grove Police Department. A twenty-one-year-old college student named Scott Rehbein went missing three nights ago. His roommates assumed he'd driven home to visit his parents and hadn't reported Rehbein missing until this morning. The disappearance might be a coincidence. But I don't think so. Kane Grove is a thirty-minute drive from Poplar Corners. Our unsub is escalating."

Now a picture of Ted Bundy.

"We're not searching for a deranged recluse. We're searching for a man who passes for a friend, a colleague, a pillar of the community. Our unsub is an organized killer, which means he plans his attacks and possesses average to above-average intelligence. I lean toward the latter, given his ability to evade the authorities for almost a decade. He's educated, employed, and engaging, though he displays antisocial tendencies such as arrogance, obnoxious behavior, and contempt for others. He places himself on a pedestal and considers himself better than those around him, deserving of their adoration. The unsub might be married or dating. He's what we call a malignant narcissist. Don't underestimate him. Our unsub is skilled, an expert murderer. Despite his antisocial behavior, he's charming when he wants to be. This ability helps him win his victim's trust. He's capable of luring his targets, skilled at seducing victims into being captured."

Agent Bell propped herself on the corner of the desk and held their gazes.

"He's motivated by mutilation and a desire to terrorize. That's why he showed himself in the town park before he captured Lonnie McKinney. Despite the risk, he wanted James McKinney and the other parents to fear him before he struck. It's why he leaves body parts in public places. But this insatiable need to taunt the police and frighten the public may be his downfall. This is how we'll catch him. Let's get granular with the profile."

The next slide listed the killer's traits. The black letters stood in sharp contrast to the white background, like leafless trees against a washed-out sky.

"We're looking for an attractive white male in his early thirties to late-forties. He's a chameleon. Though he prefers a solitary life, he blends with his surroundings and displays social grace when the situation calls for charm. Based on his confession booth visit, we assume he grew up in this area and crossed paths with Father Josiah Fowler of St. Mary's church."

The heavyset trooper in the front row raised his hand.

"Yes, officer?"

"Does sex motivate the unsub?" The trooper twisted his mouth. "He takes kids."

Bell tucked a loose strand of hair behind her ear.

"Doubtful. Our unsub prefers control and humiliation. When he takes a child, he strikes fear into the hearts of every parent in the state. It's probable he watches the news after a kidnapping. He might archive the footage so he can relive the terror he invokes."

Bell's words didn't comfort the trooper. As the man peered behind him, Deputy Lambert stuck his hand in the air.

"Go ahead, Deputy."

"About this man visiting Father Fowler. Does his confession suggest the killer is experiencing remorse and wants to stop?"

The others stared at Lambert, then turned to Agent Bell, hoping for the affirmative. The agent shook her head.

"No. The visit to the confession booth feels personal to me. It's why I'm convinced this man had a past relationship with Father Josiah Fowler, though Fowler may not remember him after so many years. I advise you to pursue Fowler and convince him to divulge anything he knows about the unsub."

After the presentation, Thomas rose from his chair and met Bell and Gardy by the door.

"Excellent presentation, Agent Bell. Your profile troubles me, but we finally have a road map for finding this guy."

When Bell turned her eyes on him, Thomas thought of Dr. Mandal. That knowing glare that uncovered hidden truths.

"You're perfectly capable of building profiles, Sheriff Shepherd. The BAU knows all about the cases you solved—Jeremy Hyde, Thea Barlow, Avery Neal."

Thomas's face scrunched with discomfort.

"I never learned Avery Neal was the killer until he threw me into a gorge."

"You believed it was a police officer, and your deputy caught Neal. Sometimes, close enough is the best we can hope for."

As the troopers and deputies mingled, Thomas touched Gardy's shoulder.

"I'd appreciate five minutes alone with both of you, somewhere out of earshot."

Gardy lowered his voice.

"Is there a problem?"

"No problem. Follow me."

Bell and Gardy trailed Thomas out of the conference room. As he motioned them down the hall to his office, he spotted Deputy Aguilar slipping into the break room to avoid being seen. He'd told her to take the day off and wondered why she was here. Had she skipped the briefing? Thomas filed away his suspicion for another time and closed the door.

Gardy and Bell glanced at each other in question.

"I work closely with a private investigator in town. A woman named Chelsey Byrd. She runs Wolf Lake Consulting." Thomas wrung his hands. "In full disclosure, we're dating."

Gardy folded his arms.

"Congratulations, Casanova. But what does this have to do with the investigation?"

"Last week, a man named Lawrence Santos walked into Wolf Lake Consulting and hired Chelsey to investigate his missing wife. Harmony Santos vanished four years ago. From Poplar Corners."

The agents raised their eyebrows.

"Why haven't we heard about this until now?" Bell asked.

"Before this morning, I had no reason to link Harmony Santos to the woman's hand. Then Lonnie McKinney vanished from Poplar Corners shortly after Agent Gardy conveyed your theories about a killer living in Nightshade County." Thomas blew out a breath. "There's also a Peeping Tom in Poplar Corners. Maybe it's unrelated to our case. But in a town the size of Poplar Corners, I wonder if we're chasing the same guy."

Gardy scratched his head and turned to Bell.

"Could be the unsub is escalating. He begins with voyeurism and fantasies, then he graduates to kidnapping and murder."

Bell clicked her tongue against the roof of her mouth.

"Or he's hunting."

23

Aguilar ducked inside the break room when she spotted Thomas with the FBI agents. She hid behind the corner and waited until they passed, her teeth clenched. When the sheriff closed his door, Aguilar relaxed her shoulders. She shouldn't be here. Her decision to quit the department could wait another day or two. Looking Thomas in the face seemed impossible.

Down the hallway, the door to the interview room opened. Voices carried. She recognized two of them—Trooper Fitzgerald was chatting with Deputy Lambert. They bantered about last night's baseball game, searching for an escape after Agent Bell profiled the serial killer. During the briefing, Aguilar had sat in the back, away from the others, until the presentation overwhelmed her. She kept picturing body parts strewn across parks, parents weeping over lost children, a killer stalking the shadows and picking off unsuspecting victims.

And she wanted to stop this psychopath. God, how she wanted to take him down. Yet she was no longer fit for the job. Not since the Avery Neal shooting. Or maybe she'd never been fit for a career in law enforcement. This was her first test as a sheriff's deputy, and she'd failed. Miserably.

As she reached for the teakettle, a gunshot blasted down the corridor. She threw herself against the wall and reached for her service weapon.

Except she'd turned her service weapon over to Thomas while she completed therapy. Sweat poured down her brow. An active shooter was loose inside the department. Why didn't she hear shouting and return gunfire?

The sound came again. A thunderous pop that made her flinch and cower in the corner.

Not a gunshot. Deputy Lambert had clapped his hands together as he laughed at Trooper Fitzgerald's joke. She clamped her eyes shut and leaned against the wall, concentrating on her breathing until her heart rate normalized. Last week, a car backfired near her house. She'd ducked below the couch and huddled until she was certain nobody was running through the neighborhood with a firearm. When she closed her eyes at night, deafening explosions like bombs filled her thoughts.

"Aguilar, you all right?"

Lambert stood in the doorway with a perplexed expression. She exhaled and wiped her sweaty palms on her shirt.

"No problem. Just exhausted after the long night."

"Shouldn't you be home, resting?"

Aguilar wished he'd leave her alone. She liked Lambert, but he was always in her business. If everyone would just leave her alone, she'd overcome her trauma. But everyone wanted a piece of her—the county, Dr. Mandal, Thomas, Lambert. What did they expect from her? Avery Neal had given her no choice. The corrupt officer had aimed his gun at them and—

"Aguilar?"

She shook the cobwebs from her head in the manner a dog does when he emerges from swimming.

"You're right. I should be in bed."

Lambert glanced down the corridor. Conversation filled the corridor.

"Why don't you hang out at your desk while I clear the hall-way. It's overwhelming with all these people crowding each other."

She chewed a nail. Lambert wanted to shield Aguilar from the others so she didn't embarrass herself. One look at her, and they'd all know she'd lost her mind.

"Give me a few minutes, okay? I'll be fine."

The teakettle whistled. Aguilar's eyes flew to the kettle in alarm. She turned her back so he wouldn't notice her trembling hands as she poured steaming water into her cup, the container jostling dangerously in her grip. She sensed Lambert's stare. Then nothing as he left the break room and returned to the officers.

Water sloshed over the cup and singed her hand. She cursed and stuck her burned thumb into her mouth as she wiped the spill with a paper towel. Her reflection stared back from the stainless-steel faucet, warped and stretched like a funhouse mirror effect. The color had drained from her face. Aguilar fixed her hair. She grabbed her cup and hurried across the hallway to her desk, intent on grabbing her keys and running for the door. Officers clogged the corridor. They glared in her direction.

With a huff, she turned the corner and escaped their prying eyes. Her breaths came too fast as she entered the supply room and locked the door. Above her head, the cooling system hissed through the vents. Boxes of pens, ink toner, copy paper, and various office supplies filled the shelves. The white noise drowned out the hallway conversations. As she leaned against the frame, the metal shelving chilled her shoulders. After she stood still for a minute, the automatic sensor shut off the lights and plunged her into absolute darkness. Yet the sudden loss of light didn't frighten her. The dark felt warm somehow. Comforting. As if impenetrable walls guarded her from an attack. Given enough time alone, she would heal. But people refused to leave her be.

The second she moved, the automatic sensor flicked the lights on. She squinted and turned away from the harsh glare. Footsteps moved down the hallway and paused outside the door. She stood on tiptoe and grabbed a box of paper. If anyone knocked and asked what she was doing, she'd claim the copy machine was low on paper.

When was the last time she'd fulfilled her duty and protected the public? Who was she defending? Aguilar couldn't care for herself, let alone save others.

With a sigh, she set the box on the shelf and walked to the door. When she exited the supply room, she bumped into Thomas. He gave her a surprised look.

"Aguilar, I wanted to speak with you. Why were you—"

"I think I'm getting sick," Aguilar said as her eyes darted down the crowded hallway. "I should head home and catch up on sleep."

"If there's something you want to talk about, I'm here for you."

Aguilar held up a hand.

"No, I just want people to give me space. Nothing personal, Sheriff. I need to go."

24

The ancient florescent strip lighting buzzed and flickered inside the bowels of St. Mary's church. The colorless, dull glow flattened every shadow and revealed hidden secrets.

Father Josiah Fowler clutched his robe together and hurried from his office to the basement corridor. To his left, the laughter of children swelled from the church school room. A child called his name. He nodded without looking and hustled toward the staircase as sweat poured from his armpits.

At the top of the stairs, he stood against the wall and breathed. The vestibule was empty. Yet he sensed he wasn't alone.

He crossed between the pews. Each footfall reverberated off the ceiling like gunshots in a cavern. He didn't slow his pace until he reached the confession booth.

Inside the booth, the familiar leather scents returned to him. Though the floor muffled their voices, Fowler could still hear the children below. Giggling. Taunting. He'd been so weak when he first arrived at St. Mary's. Prone to make mistakes. To sin. He closed his eyes and leaned his head against the wall. Before he quieted his nerves, his eyes snapped open. Someone was coming.

The door in the opposite booth opened. He exhaled upon seeing the stooped over figure. Fowler recognized Mrs. Dolton's voice immediately, though he continued the anonymity charade as she confessed her sins. Ten minutes later, Mrs. Dolton waddled down the aisle and exited through the vestibule, leaving Fowler with the echoes of his guilt.

Nobody took her place. He usually listened to confessions for two consecutive hours during weekend sessions. Another minute passed in utter silence.

Then someone started down the aisle. Fowler's heart quickened as the steps grew closer. The door opened, and a black shadow crossed over the grates. His visitor had returned.

Fowler squirmed in his chair. He couldn't put enough room between him and the beast beyond the curtain. A squeal came from the other booth as the stranger settled into his seat.

"Good morning, Father. I trust you've thought a great deal about me since our last visit."

"What is your confession, my . . . sir?" Fowler's voice cracked.

"Too many sins to list in one session. Perhaps we should increase the frequency of our meetings."

"If you've nothing to confess today, I must ask you to leave. There are others waiting."

"No, we are alone, Father. Don't you know who I am?"

"The sacramental seal binds me from knowing your identity."

"Enough with the sanctimonious drivel, shaman. A dusty curtain and ten tiny holes separate us. You recognize my voice, and you must remember. Do you not?"

"I don't recognize your voice, sir. And even if I did—"

"Yes, yes. The sacramental seal. You tire me."

Father Fowler adjusted his robe until it draped over his knees.

"I'll ask you again. What is your confession?"

"Don't you wish to ask me about the gift I left you? Would her name interest you, or how she parted with her hand?"

"If murder is your sin, turn yourself over to the authorities and ask God for forgiveness."

"And will you turn yourself in too, Father? I did this for you. Don't pretend you've forgotten me."

The priest swallowed. His throat made a clicking sound. Beyond the divider, the stranger emitted a tired groan.

"You annoy me, pretend priest. And you give me no choice. If you won't acknowledge our past, I'll bring you another gift. A child, this time. Nothing is purer than the blood of innocence."

Fowler drew in a breath.

"You're the man on the news. The monster who kidnapped the boy in Poplar Corners."

"Behold the power of one who can move through a public park filled with adults and children and avoid detection."

"I beg you, don't harm the child."

Laughter followed.

"Why not? The boy needs to experience the harsh realities of life. You taught me well, shaman. I'm out of time, but we'll meet again. Soon."

"Please. Confess your sins in the house of God. You still have time to make amends."

"*I* am your God."

The door opened and swung shut. Fowler wrestled with indecision. He wanted to throw his door open and identify the man. Shouldn't he? Though his oath prevented him from breaking the man's trust, a child's life hung in the balance.

Fowler shoved his shoulder against the door and stumbled into the aisle. The stranger was gone.

A DOZEN CHILDREN watched from the church steps as Thomas and Lambert climbed out of the cruiser, trailed by two FBI agents dressed in black. Parents clutched their children to their hips. So many kids had been inside the church when the stranger returned. Thomas's skin crawled.

This version of Father Fowler appeared even older. His face was drawn, the blood drained from his body. His hands wouldn't sit still, fingers grabbing at his robe as his eyes darted around the church. Fowler stared at the agents.

"Who are these people?"

"You know who they are," Thomas said, hooking elbows with Fowler inside the vestibule and leading him toward the staircase. "The FBI is in Wolf Lake, and they're searching for your visitor."

"Where are you taking me?"

Gardy and Lambert split off to investigate the confession booth and question the people outside. Thomas and Bell clomped down the stairs with Fowler.

"Perhaps speaking in your office will loosen your lips." Thomas stood beside Agent Bell as Fowler slumped into his chair. The sheriff peeked around the basement and shut the door. "Repeat for me what your visitor told you."

"He said he'd bring me a child."

"Lonnie McKinney?"

The priest swallowed.

"I'm breaking my oath. You don't understand the position I'm in."

"I'm going out on a limb. But I believe God is more interested in protecting a child's welfare than maintaining confession secrecy. Did he mention Lonnie McKinney by name?"

Father Fowler shook his head.

"I brought up the kidnapped boy in Poplar Corners. He didn't deny taking him."

Agent Bell fixed Fowler with a glare and said, "It's possible your visitor read about Lonnie McKinney in the newspaper or saw the story on television. Did he say anything that proves he took the child?"

Fowler shook his head and stopped.

"He mentioned something about a public park. The park was filled with children and adults, and nobody saw him."

Bell glanced at Thomas.

"The kidnapper spoke to Lonnie at the playground."

"You're hiding something," Thomas told Fowler, sitting forward. "Why is this man interested in you?"

Fowler dropped his head.

"I have no idea."

"You're lying."

"I can't see him through the grates. All I hear is his voice. When he speaks, he does so in a roundabout fashion. It's as if he's only interested in taunting me."

Thomas and Bell spent fifteen minutes interrogating Fowler in the basement office. After, they met Gardy outside the confession booth while Lambert interviewed potential witnesses outside. Bell swung around to face Thomas.

"How long has Fowler been a priest at St. Mary's?"

"Since I was a child. Two decades or more."

"During that time, was there ever a scandal inside the church?"

"You mean child molestation."

"The idea crossed my mind."

"Never. A story like that would garner regional attention."

Bell leaned against a pew and tapped a finger against her chin.

"Many times, victims don't come forward."

"You're assuming Fowler sexually abused a child, and now the victim wants revenge."

"It's only a theory. The man claims he knew the priest years ago. Whatever Fowler did to him, it must have been traumatic. Why else would he target Fowler and leave body parts in the church?"

Gardy lifted his chin at Thomas.

"The forensics team is en route. I spoke with the staff. Nobody saw the man enter the church."

"Not surprised. This guy avoids detection. He's careful."

Bell folded her arms.

"With the basement packed with kids for church school and vehicles lining up outside, the unsub must have watched the church before he approached."

Thomas nodded.

"Lambert and I will canvass the neighborhood again."

"I want security cameras on the front door and aisle. No one approaches the confession booth without the camera catching him. If Fowler refuses, press him until he comes to his senses."

"My pleasure."

25

L eVar waited behind Scout with his arms folded over his chest. A digital map filled the computer screen. Coffee aromas wafted through the guest house as Raven carried two mugs into the front room.

"Two more Peeping Tom complaints," Scout said.

Raven leaned over Scout's shoulder for a better look at the screen. Outside, the morning sun sparkled off Wolf Lake.

"From last night?" asked LeVar.

"The sightings are already on the digital map. The Poplar Corners ghost is getting active again."

Raven threw up her hands.

"How does someone stalk his neighbors for the better part of a decade and get away with it?"

"Whoever he is, we need to catch him."

"What do you suggest?"

"I say we drive to Poplar Corners and interview more witnesses. What's Darren doing today?"

"He's busy until sunset. Darren found erosion on the trail below Lucifer Falls, so he's diverting the path until it's safe for hikers."

"So it's just the three of us."

Scout gave LeVar a bewildered stare.

"You really intend to push me from door to door while you interview people?"

"Why not?"

"It's too much hassle, LeVar. It means a lot that you want to include me. But I can work from here. Let me poke around the map. Maybe there's a pattern I haven't recognized."

"If you're sure. We'll keep in touch by phone." LeVar turned to his sister. "Chelsey expects us at work in an hour."

"We'll stop by the office and let her know our intentions," Raven said. "She's on board with the possibility that the Poplar Corners ghost and Harmony Santos's kidnapper are one and the same."

"Bet." LeVar turned to Scout, who leaned forward in her wheelchair and studied the screen. "You're sure you don't want to come with us? It's no problem."

"The last time you took me into the field, you channeled Batman and attacked a jogger with a gun."

He laughed.

"True. But don't say I didn't ask." LeVar glanced toward Scout's house. "Your mom home today?"

"She goes to work at ten. Don't worry. She knows I'm here."

"Cool." He started toward the door and spun back. "Keep the door locked."

"I will."

"And no parties."

LeVar double-checked the lock before he followed Raven through the backyard.

"She'll be fine," Raven said, reading his thoughts.

"Yeah, I suppose. It's just that I'm responsible for Scout when she's at the guest house. Ever since that surveillance fiasco, I've become a little overprotective."

Raven giggled.

"You'll make a fine father to some tortured teenager one day."

"Stop."

"I'm serious. You're caring and responsible. Don't push too hard. Scout can take care of herself."

When they arrived at the office, Tigger was padding down the hallway with his tail curled into a corkscrew. Lately, Chelsey brought the tabby to work, so the cat didn't spend eight hours alone every day. LeVar leaned over with his hands on his knees.

"Hey, Tigger. Where's Piglet?" The cat meowed and scampered into the bathroom. LeVar straightened. "That cat hates me."

"Must be the dreadlocks."

"Uh, he likes you."

Raven pushed her hair off her shoulder.

"My hair is beaded and pretty. Your dreads are a cross between Bob Marley and the alien from *Predator*."

"Aren't you funny?"

They found Chelsey in the kitchen, still wearing jogging shorts and a tank top as she nursed a tea. She leaned against the counter and read a folded newspaper.

"You two seem especially chipper this morning," Chelsey said over her mug.

"Scout found two more Peeping Tom sightings to investigate," Raven said. "Is it okay if we drive to Poplar Corners and poke around?"

"Sure thing. Mind sticking around until I finish showering? I don't want to leave the place unattended."

"That's fine. I have a case file to close out."

"Appreciate it. Help yourself to breakfast. The pull date on the eggs is next Monday, so finish them." Chelsey set the mug in the sink. "Be back in a jiffy."

After the bathroom door closed, LeVar glanced at Raven.

"She's still worried about being alone in the office."

Raven removed the frying pan from the cupboard and placed it on the burner.

"After all she went through over the last year, I understand." Raven shuddered. "Even before Mark Benson escaped prison, I couldn't sleep for weeks. Moving in with Darren helped a ton. But Chelsey doesn't have anyone to watch her back."

"What about Thomas?"

Raven tossed a slice of butter on the pan and fired up the burner.

"Only if she accepts his offer and moves in."

LeVar's mouth fell open.

"Shep Dawg asked Chelsey to move into the A-frame?"

"That's between us. She'd slap me silly if she knew I told you."

"Damn. That would be awkward with my boss living behind me."

"I thought you liked Chelsey."

"I do. She's cool." LeVar stuck his hands inside his pockets and stared up at the lights. "It would be nice having an extra set of eyes on Scout and Naomi."

"As you always say, *bet*." Raven huffed and pointed at the egg carton. "Why am I making your breakfast? I ain't your momma."

26

Five minutes after Raven and LeVar left Wolf Lake Consulting and drove to Poplar Corners, the front door to the office opened. Chelsey glanced up from her desk as someone moved down the hall. Her business was open to the public, but it still unsettled her whenever a stranger entered while she was alone.

Lawrence Santos, Harmony's husband, rounded the corner.

"Mr. Santos," Chelsey said, standing. "Did you schedule an appointment this afternoon?"

"No appointment, but I happened to be in the area. Where are you in Harmony's investigation?"

Chelsey slid the desk drawer open and removed the case file.

"We're making progress."

"But you still haven't found her."

"Not yet."

Santos rapped his knuckles on her desk.

"What about Gerald Burke? Did you investigate Harmony's old boyfriend?"

"I spoke with Mr. Burke. He claims he was at a conference in

Buffalo the day Harmony disappeared. The conference was at a hotel in the city."

The man scoffed.

"And you believe him? Burke is a liar and a cheat. I never should have allowed Harmony to invite Burke to our wedding."

"He's listed among the paid attendees. But I can't prove he was at the conference. It's possible he paid for his ticket and never attended."

"What about the hotel? They must keep records."

Chelsey sighed.

"The hotel's records don't go back four years, and I can't access Burke's credit card history without sufficient evidence he committed a crime."

Santos dropped his face into his hands.

"Then I'll never find her. I'm certain Burke kidnapped Harmony. Burke was obsessed, and that was the only way he'd get close to my wife."

Chelsey chewed on the end of a pen. The possibility that a serial killer had taken Harmony left a hollow pit in Chelsey's stomach. She didn't want to worry Santos without proof. Perhaps she could link Santos to the kidnapped boy.

"Mr. Santos, do you have many friends in Poplar Corners?"

He shrugged.

"My neighbors. A few people from work. Why do you ask?"

"Do the names Lonnie and James McKinney mean anything to you?"

"Should they?" Santos scrunched his face in contemplation. His eyes snapped to Chelsey's. "Wait, those names are familiar. Lonnie McKinney is the boy from the news, right? The kidnapped child."

"And James is his father. They live two miles from your neighborhood."

"The FBI is in Nightshade County. I saw it on the television. What's happening here?"

"The FBI is helping the sheriff's department search for Lonnie McKinney."

"The FBI can't respond to every missing child. There's something larger going on. Do they suspect a serial killer? Does this have something to do with that woman's hand the priest found in St. Mary's church?" Santos rubbed his eyes. "It's unfathomable a kidnapping could happen in our town. I feel terrible for the father, but I understand what he's going through."

"You've never met them? At church, perhaps?"

"I'm not religious."

"What about the Poplar Corners ghost? Are you aware of the story?"

The man fell back in his chair and glared at Chelsey.

"You can't be serious. That's just a scary story kids tell each other at slumber parties."

"You don't believe there's a Peeping Tom in Poplar Corners?"

"Some creep probably stared through a few windows over the years. Once the rumors started, the town blew it out of proportion. No, there's no Poplar Corners ghost. Tell me you aren't going down this path."

"It's my job to turn over every stone."

"I expected more from you, Ms. Byrd. No one in this region matches your reputation. Yet you're asking me about ghost stories."

Chelsey set the pen aside.

"It's curious, Mr. Santos. A missing woman, a kidnapped child, and a Peeping Tom in the same town. Is it all a coincidence?"

His eyes lit with understanding.

"Are you suggesting the same guy who took Harmony kidnapped Lonnie McKinney?"

"Think hard. Do you have a friend who knows the McKinney family?"

"It's a small town. If I dig deep enough, I'm certain I'll find an acquaintance who knows James McKinney."

"I'm interested in anyone who knew Harmony and the McKinney family."

Santos squinted his eyes in concentration.

"I can't imagine Gerald Burke kidnapped that boy. He's a sicko, and I'm sure he took Harmony. But a child predator? Are you certain the cases are related?"

Chelsey opened the case file and read through her notes.

"I did some digging. This man, Kit, who showed up at your wedding."

Lawrence Santos sat forward.

"What about him?"

"I didn't find Kit in your photos. But people who attended the reception remembered him. From all I can gather, he was friendly, and he hogged the buffet."

"I recall that, yes."

"Kit, if that's his real name, also took selfies at the reception. I have a witness who watched him snapping photos of himself."

"What does that prove?"

Chelsey dropped the folder on the desk.

"A kidnapper would avoid the camera, not take pictures of himself." When Santos failed to understand, Chelsey set her forearms on her desk. "He was showing off. Kit crashed your wedding and chronicled the fiasco on camera. He's a jerk, but he's harmless."

Santos touched his forehead.

"What an asshole."

"He probably yucked it up with his friends and plastered the photos all over social media. Kit didn't take your wife, Mr. Santos."

"I can't believe I wasted four years trying to figure out who he was."

"You did the right thing."

"No, I wasted time. If I'd realized he didn't take Harmony ..."

The man's words faded into a mutter. Chelsey waited until he refocused.

"Let's start at the beginning. Did anyone pay too much attention to Harmony around the time of your wedding?"

"Harmony is a beautiful woman. Guys looked. Not much I could do about it. If Harmony went out with her girlfriends, guys offered to buy her drinks. She turned them down."

"Were you ever with Harmony when this happened?"

"Never."

"Perhaps you were at a restaurant together, or walking through the town park, and some guy followed you around."

"Nothing like that ever happened."

"What about calls in the middle of the night? Did anyone harass Harmony or call her number without speaking?"

"Harmony would have told me."

Chelsey pinched the bridge of her nose. This was going nowhere. What if the serial killer chose Harmony by random chance?

"Before Harmony disappeared, do you recall a strange vehicle outside your house or nearby in the neighborhood?"

"Define strange."

"It's a small town. If your neighbor has visitors from out of town, you probably hear about it. I'm talking about a vehicle that didn't belong."

Santos set his chin on his hand and pondered the question. Chelsey was certain she'd reached another dead end when Santos looked up.

"Now that you mention it, there was a red Camaro convertible parked up the street from our house a week after our wedding."

Chelsey tore off a sheet of notebook paper and grabbed her pen.

"What made you recall the Camaro?"

"Because it's Poplar Corners. Nobody in town drives a Camaro, especially a convertible. It's a waste to buy a car like that in New York. The warm season is too short, and the salt and snow would be murder on the undercarriage."

"Did you get the license plate number?"

"You're kidding, right? That was four years ago. Harmony made a remark about the Camaro and wondered who it belonged to. I had no reason to suspect anything. It was just an unusual car to see in our neighborhood. Afterward, we asked the Jeromes if the car belonged to a friend or family member, because it was parked outside their house. They'd never seen the car before."

"You never spotted the Camaro around town after that?"

"I asked about it at work, only because I wondered who would drive a hotrod in Poplar Corners. Mike at the office claimed he'd seen a red Camaro convertible buzz past his place. But nothing since. I figured it had to be someone visiting from out of town." Chelsey noted the color and make of the convertible. Thomas could search the database for anyone in Nightshade County who owned such a vehicle. "Does the red Camaro have something to do with Harmony's disappearance?"

"Possibly. If you spot the vehicle again, call me. And take pictures."

27

Traffic clogged the thoroughfare between Kane Grove University and the highway. Justice Thorin drummed his fingers on the steering wheel as the air conditioner blasted against his face. The sun was a blowtorch at dinnertime, heat waves rippling off the pavement like a strange dream sequence. The light turned green, and still the traffic didn't budge.

He pressed his horn. The damn ramp to the highway lay a hundred feet to his right. He was tempted to swing the Tesla onto the shoulder and drive around everyone, but there was a traffic camera at the light. If bored, he could watch live footage of the intersection over the internet.

When the light cycled again, the glut unclogged. A woman in the left lane signaled her intent to merge. Tough luck. He was here first. Thorin gave her a few feet of space, but when she started to merge, he punched the gas and blew past her. The driver, an Asian woman wearing sunglasses, honked her horn and lifted her middle finger. Blood boiling, he glared at her through the mirror, their eyes hidden behind sunglasses, yet interminably locked. He grinned when she trailed him onto the entrance ramp, and when they reached the highway, he slowed to a crawl and forced her to pass. She laid heavy on the horn as she flew by.

He followed her.

A mile up the highway, he pushed the Tesla to eighty and drove inches from her bumper. He savored the alarm on her face, sensed her rising anxiety like ozone before a storm. At the next exit, she turned off. He clung to her bumper.

It occurred to him how easy it would be to find where she lived and take her. He'd never captured anyone out of anger. Undefinable needs had always provoked him. Now he only wanted to torture, maim, and tear the woman to shreds with his hands. To hell with her for challenging him.

A red light stopped them at the bottom of the ramp. His grille almost kissed the car's bumper. She glanced at him in the mirror and averted her eyes. A frightened mouse cornered by a feral cat.

Through the unfamiliar village—some rundown burg he'd passed a thousand times on the highway without a second thought—he followed her car. Past the shopping plaza and hair salon. Through the restaurant district to the suburbs. Twice, she took sharp turns without signaling to shake him. He remained inches behind with a cruel smile on his lips.

The woman pulled into a driveway beside a two-story duplex. Two men leaned on the porch rail and nursed beer cans. He doubted the woman lived here. In her panic, she'd sought help from complete strangers. He gave a friendly toot of his horn as he motored past.

Thorin circled the neighborhood and found his way back to the highway. His pulse eased as he put the unknown town behind him. He assumed the woman worked in Kane Grove. The possibility she worked at the university pushed energy through his body. How he'd love to encounter her again.

It was after six when Thorin pulled the Tesla into his garage. He unlocked the house and started dinner. His guests needed to eat.

He hummed while he worked. Thorin was most relaxed while he cooked a fine meal. Forty-five minutes later, the chicken Marsala looked divine. Such a shame to waste it on pets.

Thorin plated the meal for the child. He required food if he was to survive the week. Scott had challenged Thorin too many times since joining the family. Though the college student didn't deserve a meal, Thorin would fix him a dish if he cooperated.

Instead of descending the basement steps, Thorin exited through the back door and strode across the lawn. Eight years ago, he'd installed a trap door into the cells. It gave him an escape route should the authorities find him. Not that they ever would. He'd stalked his neighbors for years and never been caught. Most of all, he relished the secret entrance because only he knew of it. A lone sunflower poked up from the lawn, dancing and swaying to the whim of the wind. The handle to the entrance lay flush with the ground, impossible to locate without the sunflower. Without the marker, Thorin worried he'd strike the handle with the lawn mower.

Beside the trapdoor, he crouched and fit the key into the lock. Grabbing the handle, he yanked up. Musty air rose to his nostrils. The sudden shaft of fading light must have frightened his captives, who'd spent the day in perpetual darkness. He enjoyed that they never knew the time. It kept him in control.

They stirred as he descended the ladder and dropped into the enclosure. He pulled the string on the light bulb and threw harsh illumination into the cells.

Lonnie curled into a fetal position, shivering. Goosebumps and bug bites covered his flesh. The child protected his eyes with his hand and moaned. In the next cage, Scott grumbled and rolled over. The college student blinked twice and stared at

Thorin. The reality he remained a prisoner in this subterranean hell blanched his face.

"Wake up, my child. I brought you dinner."

Thorin set the insulated bag on the ground and unzipped the top. The dinner scents made his mouth water. From the bag, Thorin removed a fork and napkin. Instead of thanking Thorin for the fine cuisine, the boy wept and bleated.

"I want my daddy."

"Your daddy can't help you anymore, Lonnie. It's time you stood on your own two feet and became a man."

"Let me go. I don't like you."

"You'll learn to love me in time. Now, eat your food while its fresh and warm. You don't wish to spoil dinner by eating it cold."

Thorin slid the plate through the tiny entrance at the bottom of the cell.

"I don't want it."

"You'll do what I say. Eat your food like a good boy."

Scott rattled the cage.

"Why don't you leave him alone?"

Thorin swung his eyes to Scott, who stood naked in the cell with his hands wrapped around the bars. Scott's eyes fogged over. They hadn't adjusted to the light yet.

"I see you're finally awake, lazy boy. Perhaps you'll behave tonight and join us for dinner."

"Let the boy go," Scott said, yanking on the bars. "You don't need him."

Thorin raised an eyebrow.

"Full of vigor, aren't we? Lower your voice. You'll upset the child."

"What's wrong with you? You kidnap people and lock them underground. For what purpose?"

"Don't question me, Scott."

"That's another thing. How the hell do you know my name?

I've never met you." Understanding fell over Scott's face. "Ah. You stole my wallet and read my license. How much did you charge to my credit card?"

"I'm not a thief. Rest assured, I didn't steal your money."

Scott laughed.

"Is that supposed to make me feel better? You're sick."

"Shut your mouth and let the boy eat his dinner."

Lonnie shoved the plate back to Thorin.

"You haven't touched your food, Lonnie."

"I'm not hungry."

"You'll fall ill if you don't eat. And you'll make your daddy angry."

"You're not my daddy."

"I am now."

A rock plunked Thorin in the head. It was small, but it left a red welt on his cheek. He turned to face Scott, who grinned through the bars.

"Don't test me," Thorin said, grinding his teeth.

"You're a piece of shit coward who attacks people from behind and kidnaps children."

"Are you challenging me, Scott? I could take you apart with my bare hands."

Scott leaned his head back and laughed.

"You? Give me a break. If I ever get out of this cage, I'll—"

"You'll what?" Thorin walked to the cage and stood face to face with the instigator, the iron bars keeping them apart. For now. "Tell me what you'd do to me, Scott?"

"Open the cage and I'll show you, creep."

Thorin's mouth twitched. His hand brushed his pants pocket. The key lay against his thigh, warm and ready for use. Oh, how he wished to teach Scott a cruel lesson.

Thorin chuckled.

"Careful who you cross, boy."

28

Thomas watched the media gather through the windows. He'd requested the press conference hours ago and still wasn't sure he'd made the right decision. This was a gamble. A roll of the dice to save Lonnie McKinney and prod the killer out of hiding. It might backfire. Behind him, Agents Gardy and Bell stared with curiosity. Thomas nodded he was ready and stepped outdoors, the FBI agents remaining behind as the late-day sun blinded his eyes.

The reporter for *The Bluewater Tribune* wore a handlebar mustache. He fought for position outside the Nightshade County Sheriff's Department as a lumbering man with a television camera on his shoulder crowded him off the sidewalk. The reporter from the Syracuse television station had braided chestnut hair and a pleated skirt that showed plenty of leg. She pointed the microphone at Thomas, who stood outside the entryway in his uniform, one hand atop his hat to prevent the wind from blowing it away.

The newspaper reporter jabbed a digital recorder at Thomas's face.

"How long has the FBI been working with your department?"

"Since Lonnie McKinney's kidnapping."

"Is a serial killer responsible for capturing Lonnie McKinney? Should the public worry?"

"While there's no reason to panic, everyone in Nightshade County should exercise caution, lock their doors, and be vigilant of strangers. The FBI and Nightshade County Sheriff's Department believe the man who kidnapped Lonnie McKinney is the same man who left a woman's hand inside St. Mary's church."

"Can you prove this theory?"

Thomas paused.

"Not yet."

"Sheriff," the chestnut-haired woman said, stepping in front of the newspaper reporter. "What can you tell us about the kidnapper? Did he abduct Scott Rehbein too?"

"We're working hard to link the two cases. But yes, it's possible the same man is responsible."

"Is the kidnapper a pedophile?"

"There's no evidence he's a pedophile. The man we're searching for is incapable of sexual intercourse. He's uncomfortable in his skin and too shy to speak to women. Which is why he captures and kills them."

"But he also takes men and young boys. Is the murderer bisexual?"

"He's all about control, manipulation, and humiliation. This branches back to the killer's low self-esteem and fear of society. He kills what frightens him. This man is a coward, and we'll catch him. I promise you that."

Emboldened by the sheriff's willingness to speak openly about the murderer, the press fired questions at Thomas for ten minutes. The Syracuse news televised the press conference live, breaking in during a sports program that garnered high ratings.

When the press conference concluded, Thomas's stomach roiled with anxiousness. He'd know within hours if his plan worked.

The reporters dispersed after Thomas entered the building. Inside, Gardy and Bell awaited him. They'd viewed the press conference on a wall-mounted television.

"I hope you know what you're doing," Gardy said.

"It's a gamble, but I believe it will work."

As Thomas walked toward his office, Agent Bell shifted to block him.

"Sheriff, you'll provoke the killer and draw him to you."

"That's my intention."

LEVAR TURNED the car into Poplar Corners with Scout seated beside him and their mothers in the backseat. Intrigued by their children's interest in investigating criminals and cold cases, Naomi Mourning and Serena Hopkins joined LeVar and Scout this evening. LeVar assumed Naomi wanted to ensure Scout stayed safe and there wasn't a repeat of the robbery fiasco. It was almost sundown. An orange glow wrapped around the buildings as LeVar drove toward the westering sun.

"Tell me who we're searching for again?" Naomi asked.

"The Poplar Corners ghost," Scout said, studying a sightings map on her phone.

Serena tutted.

"Sounds like a made-for-TV mystery. Why the interest in a Peeping Tom?"

LeVar sighed.

"Because the same guy kidnapped Harmony Santos and Lonnie McKinney."

"And dropped the woman's hand inside the church," Scout added.

LeVar glanced across the seat at Scout.

"Where should we check first?"

As Scout studied the map, she furrowed her brow.

"The sightings seem random, but if I filter the cases, they cluster on the south end of Poplar Corners over the last year." Scout turned the screen toward LeVar. "Check this out."

"Keep your eyes on the road, fool," Serena said.

LeVar met his mother's glare in the mirror.

They passed through a neighborhood. Tall trees girded the road as shadows lengthened. By the time LeVar reached Durant Street on the south side of town, a veil of darkness spread down from the sky. Scout pointed out the window.

"Stop the car. That's where Harmony Santos lived."

LeVar hit the brakes and idled. The quaint yellow two-story had green trim. Grass and weeds overtook the garden, choking out where a flower bed once stood. An American flag flew from the porch. LeVar opened his palm.

"Let me check that map again." After Scout handed him her phone, he tapped his free hand against his thigh. "The sightings cluster between this residence and a cul-de-sac west of here."

"Lots of meadow and forest in between. It would be easy to move around unseen and hide if someone called the police."

Inside the Santos residence, a silhouette passed over the curtain.

"I can't imagine what it's like to lose someone you love. If it was a disease or a car accident, you'd come to grips and understand what happened after a while. But to never know if your spouse was alive."

He left the rest unsaid as the shape vanished from the window. LeVar's words humanized the case and left a somber tone inside the car. Naomi studied a road map on her phone.

"There's an access road a half-mile straight ahead. It curves toward the meadow. The utility companies probably use it."

LeVar leaned his head over the seat.

"Is there a place to park?"

"Hold on a second." Naomi enlarged the map. "There's a turnoff at the end of the road."

"That will do. Let's check it out."

Once they left the neighborhood, there were no streetlights to ward against the coming darkness. Branches dangled over the road and scraped the top of the car as they jounced over the rutted path. The further they traveled, the more LeVar felt cut off from the world, as if a black wall stood between him and civilization. Crickets sang from the meadow, and bats darted out of the trees.

"This appears straight out of a horror movie," LeVar said, straining his eyes to penetrate the gloom. Even with the brights on, the thick foliage swallowed the headlights. "All we lack is a psycho in a hockey mask running around with a machete."

Naomi shivered.

"I wish you hadn't said that."

Tire marks cut through the soil at the turnoff, marking where a utility truck had parked. LeVar stopped the car and glanced over his shoulder.

"Stay in the car while I snoop around."

Serena cocked an eyebrow.

"You sneak through the wrong person's yard, and someone will shoot your backside with buckshot."

"I can be quiet when I need to be. Nobody will know I'm here." LeVar tossed the car keys to Serena. "If anything happens before I return, drive back to the neighborhood and phone the sheriff's department. Don't worry about me."

"I'm not abandoning my son."

"Your job is to keep Scout and Mrs. Mourning safe."

Serena glanced at Naomi, who shrugged her shoulders. Before LeVar climbed out of the car, Scout grabbed his forearm.

"No joke this time, LeVar. Be careful."

LeVar nodded.

"Keep your radio on. I'll contact you if there's trouble."

The grass grew up to LeVar's knees along the access road. Beyond the meadow, lights shone from the cul-de-sac. Somewhere, a family burned a fire in their backyard. He recalled roasting marshmallows at the state park and wished he was there, instead of crawling through the wilderness and dodging mosquitoes.

LeVar fought through the meadow and lost sight of the car. A creek gurgled through the clearing, and the first stars flared on the horizon. Animals scurried through the brush as he high-stepped through burdock. His mother's warning rattled inside his head. Sneaking through a stranger's backyard brought back unwanted memories from his time with the Harmon Kings gang. How many times had he scouted a rival gang's territory or walked through the wrong section of town, always wondering if someone centered crosshairs on his head?

The cul-de-sac lay beyond the meadow. It occurred to LeVar how easy it was to spy on neighbors from here. With a pair of binoculars, it was possible for the ghost to peer into houses and avoid detection. The trees provided a hiding place if someone spotted the Peeping Tom. But there had to be another escape route. A way for the Poplar Corners ghost to vanish.

LeVar passed behind a Cape Cod with a tall privacy fence. He wasn't alone in the night.

The teenager paused and listened to the night sounds. He sensed eyes on his back and swung around. The meadow sprawled before him and stretched toward a patch of forest. LeVar crouched below a shrub, grabbed the radio, and lowered his voice.

"Someone is out here. You see anybody, Scout?"

"That's a negative."

LeVar squinted into the dark. His arms prickled a moment before a branch snapped in the forest. It could have been a deer. Or a limb breaking off a tree. Or a Peeping Tom watching him from the woods.

He bent low and moved through the meadow, his footsteps silent on the soft ground. The closer he walked to the tree line, the more convinced he'd become that someone stood among the trees.

LeVar slipped into the thicket and stared into the impenetrable dark. A man had been here. He was sure of it.

Scout's voice came over the radio.

"Someone just crossed the access road."

LeVar heard the alarmed voices of Naomi and Serena in the background.

"Get out of there, Scout. Tell my mother to drive."

A second later, the engine fired on LeVar's Chrysler Limited. He sprinted toward the sound, the headlights a beacon guiding him out of the meadow. Scout's eyes widened in alarm as he burst out of hiding. Serena braked, the car skidding to a halt as Naomi threw the door open. LeVar piled into the backseat. He peeked behind him. A shadow approached the car from behind.

"Get us out of here."

LeVar didn't have to ask his mother twice.

29

Scott walked along the bars. His pupils dilated against the absolute darkness. For the last hour, he'd paced the cage so many times he'd memorized the length and width, sensed the bars before his outstretched hands touched the cold iron. The damp ground chilled his feet. At least the exertion kept the shivers at bay.

Without a window to the outside world, he didn't know if it was day or night unless the sicko opened the trapdoor and descended into the subterranean cell. Sometimes, when his abductor entered through the basement, Scott estimated the time of day by the gray light spilling through the entryway.

His blood boiled. Every eight to twelve hours, the kidnapper visited with food and water. No ransom demands, no promise of release. Scott's only choice was to relieve himself in a bucket, which he passed beneath the enclosure for disposal. His kidnapper had reduced Scott to an animal.

The child moaned in the neighboring cell. Scott set his rage aside. Keeping Lonnie safe was his priority.

"I'm right here, Lonnie. Can you hear my voice?"

He sensed the boy nodding. The prisoners had bonded during their stay, though Scott didn't know how long he'd spent inside the cage. One day blended with the next until time lost all meaning. If his captor claimed Scott had been here a month, he'd believe it.

"I wanna go home."

"I know you do, buddy. You will. I promise." Somewhere in the dark, Lonnie sniffled. Scott reached his hands through the bars into the boy's cage. "Follow my voice and grab hold of my hands."

He flinched with surprise when the boy's dirt-crusted hands closed over his palms. Scott gave them a gentle squeeze as the boy sobbed.

"I miss my daddy."

"I'm sure you do. You'll be with him soon once I get us out of here."

What kind of maniac kidnapped a child and locked him beneath the ground? Scott wanted to grab his captor and smash his head against the bars. Creeps in their forties didn't frighten him. Especially losers who struck him with a Taser from behind. Let's see how tough the guy was without a weapon. He glanced around the cage, his eyes struggling against the black. There had to be a way out of here. An idea occurred to him.

"Lonnie, we need to make as much noise as possible. We'll drive him crazy and force him to open the cages."

"No," Lonnie said, moaning. "He'll hurt you if you make him angry."

"He can't hurt me. Don't worry. I can take care of myself. I'm not proud to admit it, but I've been in my share of fights. This guy is nothing."

"Don't, Scott."

Ignoring the boy's pleading, Scott followed the bars to the

back of his cell and located the bucket. The stench made his eyes tear up. He walked it to the front of the cell and slammed the bucket against the bars. As he continued to bash the container against the iron, he yelled. Pretty soon, Lonnie joined in. When the racket gave him a headache, Scott grabbed the bars and shook them. His muscles screamed with exertion. Dirt trickled down from the earthen ceiling and crusted his head and shoulders. His hope surged. He'd loosened the bars.

Scott shook the bars harder. More grit cascaded into the cage, though it was impossible to see how much damage he'd done.

"It's working, Lonnie. I'll break us out of here."

His skin prickled with warning. Something was wrong. He had no warning before the light flicked on inside the cells. The creep stood before him with a maniacal grin on his face. Somehow, he'd entered the cells undetected, prowling through the pitch black. How long had he been there?

"I warned you not to test me, Scott."

"Your cage can't hold me, scumbag. When I get out of here, I'll—"

"Yes, yes. You'll beat me up. Is that the master plan, college boy? Are you up to the task?"

"Tough talk. Unlock the cage, and we'll put your threat to the test."

The creep ignored him and wandered to Lonnie's cell. The child slunk away when their abductor pressed his face against the bars.

"I expected more from you, Lonnie. I fear Scott is a negative influence. Shall I correct the situation?"

The creep swung his eyes to Scott with menace. Lonnie leaped out of his crouch and clutched the bars.

"Please, don't hurt him. He's sorry. He won't do it again."

"No, Lonnie," Scott said, anger reddening his face. "You don't have to protect me from *him*. He can't hurt me without his weapons. What did you bring this time, sicko? A gun? A knife? I don't see your Taser."

The kidnapper rolled his eyes.

"I don't require a weapon to control my pet."

"Pet? Is that what you called me? Open the goddamn cage."

Glaring at Lonnie, the creep knelt before the child's cell.

"You can save your friend, Lonnie. The power is yours. Tell me who your father is."

Lonnie glanced between Scott and the creep. His forehead creased with confusion.

"James McKinney?"

"Wrong answer. I'm your father now. You failed the test, and now Scott must pay."

The man rose to his feet and moved with effortless grace toward the neighboring cage. Scott's body tensed with anticipation. This was too good to be true. He'd goaded the psycho into unlocking the door. The man must have a weapon in his back pocket, some means of protection. Scott didn't worry. He'd disarm the man first, then smash his puny frame against the bars, pay him back for the misery he'd caused, and steal the key. Soon, he'd free Lonnie and contact the police.

The creep stood before the door, glaring at Scott through the tops of his eyes. Unhinged. A madman out of a horror movie. Standing naked in the center of the cage, Scott remained calm. He didn't want to rush the man and risk scaring him off. Better to let the prick think Scott was scared.

Scott bit his tongue when the key slipped into the lock. This was another taunt. The creep wouldn't dare unlock the cage and—

He did.

The rusty lock shrieked with bloodlust as the door drifted open. To Scott's shock, the madman peeled off his button-down shirt and tossed it aside. Standing bareback in the cell, the creep twitched his fingers.

Lonnie screamed when the creep rushed Scott, arms flailing maniacally. Scott held his ground, remaining patient. When the creep came within range, Scott punched him square in his face. The man's head whipped back. Blood spilled from his nose.

"You're a dead man," Scott growled.

Scott reached back to throw another punch when the man lunged and wrapped his hands around Scott's throat. The college student coughed and yanked at the psycho's hands. Fingers dug into his windpipe and cut off the oxygen. The man's head fell back and whipped forward, crushing Scott's nose. To his horror, Scott found himself flat on his back with the madman atop him. Doubt crept into him. His heels dug into the soft earth and lost their purchase. Panicked, he bridged and bucked, but he failed to unseat the creep. Behind him, Lonnie cried and screamed, begging the man not to hurt Scott. This couldn't be happening.

Pressing his elbows out, Scott pushed the man's arms away and broke the stranglehold. Gagging, he swung desperately at the creep. The man dodged the blow with ease and spat in Scott's face. A fist struck Scott's temple. The cage spun on an invisible axis as his legs flailed beneath the stronger foe. Still Lonnie cried and pleaded from the next cage. Scott heard the bars shaking, Lonnie's bucket whipping against the cage.

The cell grew dark now. The madman crawled up to Scott's chest and pressed him to the dirt floor. Before Scott threw him off, his kidnapper resumed his stranglehold.

"I warned you, boy."

Scott couldn't breathe. The more he struggled, the deeper he sank into the chilling earth. Atop him, the madman leered down at his beaten foe with an insane smile.

"I'm your father. I'm your God."

Then Scott saw no more.

30

Thomas was waiting inside his office for James McKinney to arrive when Chelsey stopped by the Nightshade County Sheriff's Department and rapped her knuckles on his door.

"These are the people I've interviewed in the Harmony Santos investigation," she said, dropping the file on Thomas's desk.

Thomas paged through the papers.

"A red Camaro convertible. You're right. You don't find too many of those in Poplar Corners. Lawrence Santos saw this car outside his house before his wife disappeared?"

"Down the street, yes. I hoped you'd search the database for anyone driving that car in Poplar Corners."

"I'll put Lambert on the case as soon as we finish with Mr. McKinney." He handed the folder back to Chelsey. "Thank you. I'll keep these confidential."

She held up a hand.

"These are copies. Keep them. And you don't need to thank me. The important thing is we catch Lonnie McKinney's kidnapper."

"Agreed, but I appreciate Wolf Lake Consulting cooperating." Voices from the corridor pulled Thomas's attention. "That must be James McKinney. Do you want to hang out until we finish the interview?"

"Can't. I'm meeting Raven and LeVar at the office in fifteen minutes."

Thomas checked the clock.

"You'd better hurry then. See you at the house for dinner?"

Chelsey hesitated before answering.

"Sure."

He kissed Chelsey on the cheek and thanked her again for sharing her notes. As she exited the building, he worried he was pressing her too hard. She wasn't ready to move in with him. He clutched the case file under his arm and closed the office door behind him.

"You ready?" he asked Lambert as he passed the deputy's desk.

"Let's go."

Lambert fixed his hat and rose to follow Thomas. Across the corridor, Aguilar buried her head in paperwork, her pen flying across the page as she scribbled a signature.

"How about joining us for the McKinney interview, Deputy Aguilar?"

"No thanks," Aguilar said without raising her head. "If I hustle, I'll catch up on this paperwork before my shift ends."

It wasn't like Aguilar to turn him down, let alone skip a crucial interview. Thomas lifted his chin at Lambert.

"Grab Agents Bell and Gardy. I'll meet you inside the interview room." As Lambert strode away, Thomas turned his attention to Aguilar. "You sure everything is okay?"

"Fine."

"It's not my place to ask, but how are the sessions with Dr. Mandal going?"

"Wonderful."

Thomas removed his hat and rubbed his forehead. Why wouldn't Aguilar open up to him?

"My office is always open if you want to talk."

"Maybe tomorrow, Sheriff. There's something we need to discuss."

Thomas scrunched his brow. Whatever Aguilar wanted to talk about, it didn't sound promising.

"All right, then. I'll let you know how the interview goes."

Agents Bell and Gardy were seated beside Deputy Lambert when Thomas entered the interview room. James McKinney, appearing twenty years older than his age, took an open chair across the table. Thomas shut the door and closed the blinds.

"Thank you for coming in this afternoon, Mr. McKinney. I'm sorry I asked you to travel from Poplar Corners."

"I'll do anything if it helps you find Lonnie." Thomas set two water bottles on the table and sat next to Lambert. "Mr. McKinney, I'd like to introduce Agents Scarlett Bell and Neil Gardy with the Federal Bureau of Investigation. And you met Deputy Lambert."

Thomas glanced down the table at Agent Bell.

"Mr. McKinney, do you know Harmony Santos?" Bell asked, opening the folder to her notes.

McKinney thought for a moment.

"Harmony Santos. Isn't that the woman who disappeared a while back?"

"Four years ago, yes."

"I remember her from the news, but I never met her."

"How about Lawrence Santos?"

"Sorry, no. Never met the guy. He's the husband, right?"

"Correct."

"According to the newspapers, the police suspected him for abducting his wife."

"They never proved he took her."

Gardy produced a photograph of Lawrence Santos and slid it across the table.

"Perhaps you've seen Mr. Santos around town," Gardy said.

McKinney studied the photograph.

"He looks familiar. I might have passed him in the grocery store. But we've never met."

Gardy removed a second photograph and passed it to McKinney.

"How about this man? Ever see him around Poplar Corners?"

McKinney took a long time before he answered. Thomas glanced at Lambert in question before McKinney spoke.

"Yeah, I've seen him around. Not sure who he is, though. Does this have something to do with Lonnie's kidnapping?"

McKinney set the photo on the table. Agent Bell tapped her nail on the photograph.

"That's Gerald Burke," she said. "He dated Harmony Santos during college. Where have you seen this man?"

"Around town. He drives an expensive-looking car."

"A red Camaro convertible?" Thomas asked, hoping they'd narrowed the suspect list.

Lonnie's father gave Thomas a confused stare.

"A BMW. What's this about a Camaro?"

Not the car they were looking for. Still, Thomas wondered why Gerald Burke was cruising around Poplar Corners. It was possible they were searching for two kidnappers—the man who nabbed Lonnie McKinney, and Harmony Santos's abductor.

"You ever spot a red Camaro convertible in Poplar Corners?"

"Never. Did Burke kidnap Harmony Santos? Is he the man Lonnie met in the park?"

"There's no evidence Gerald Burke kidnapped anyone. We're considering all possibilities."

Gardy whispered in Bell's ear. Bell nodded and leaned toward McKinney.

"Mr. McKinney, did your son say anything that suggested he'd met the man in the park before?"

"I grilled Lonnie about the stranger. He'd never encountered the man until that day at the park."

"Nobody asked questions about Lonnie at the playground or somewhere in public? Someone who acted a little too friendly?"

"Losing Lonnie was my greatest fear. I would remember if someone asked me about my son."

McKinney halted, and the blood drained from his face.

Agent Gardy tilted his head and said, "You remember someone. Tell us."

Lonnie's father shook his head.

"Mr. McKinney, what is it?"

McKinney reached for a water bottle and took a long drink.

"Last month, Lonnie came into my room crying in the middle of the night. He said the boogeyman was in his closet." Gardy cocked an eyebrow at Thomas. "I blew it off. You know how kids are at that age. The dark scares them, and their imaginations run wild."

"What happened?"

"Nothing that night. I allowed Lonnie to sleep with me. But the next morning, as I vacuumed Lonnie's bedroom, I found dirt on the closet floor. It could have come from Lonnie's sneakers after he played, or . . ."

McKinney's eyes widened in horror.

"My God. What if the man was inside the house?"

31

Thomas waited until Mr. McKinney drove away before he turned to Agents Bell and Gardy.

"What do you make of McKinney's man-in-the-closet story?"

"It's a long shot, but worth checking into," Bell said. "Have forensics examine the kid's closet."

Down the hall, Deputy Aguilar packed her belongings and exited the station without saying goodbye. Thomas followed her from the corner of his eye as he pictured Lonnie McKinney. Was the child locked in some hellish house on the outskirts of Poplar Corners? Thomas hoped the boy was still alive.

"How long did the killer hold the last child he abducted before he dumped the body?"

"Seven days," Gardy said.

"Then we need to find him soon."

Gardy lifted his chin at the rapidly emptying office.

"Appears everyone except the evening shift is headed home. That's probably our cue to grab food before we go over the evidence again."

Thomas glanced at his watch.

"I'm meeting Chelsey for dinner at my house. The two of you are welcome to join us, if you wish to discuss the case."

"Appreciate the invite, but Bell has her eye on a seafood joint on the west side of the lake. Meet you at your place around six?"

"That works for me."

During the drive back to his lakeside A-frame, Thomas couldn't shake the creeping sensation the killer had entered Lonnie's bedroom and hid inside the closet while the boy slept. He recalled his own night terrors—the dirty towels in the corner that appeared as slithering pythons in the dark, a tree's shadow that he swore was a cackling witch or a man with a knife.

The boogeyman.

The Poplar Corners ghost was more than a Peeping Tom. He slipped into homes and stalked people in the dead of night. Did he fantasize about sex and murder while he observed them?

He stopped the F-150 in the driveway and shut off the engine, expecting to find Chelsey's Civic. She hadn't arrived yet. Naomi waved as she wheeled Scout through the yard.

Jack greeted Thomas with endless kisses, tail wagging to beat the band. Thomas removed his hat and set it on the chair before he searched the refrigerator for a cold drink. He checked his messages. Nothing from Chelsey to warn she'd be late.

No sense waiting. He started the water boiling. By the time Chelsey arrived, he'd have dinner ready. The phone buzzed.

"Hello?"

"Good afternoon, Sheriff."

Thomas didn't recognize the singsong voice. A chill ran down his back.

"Who is this?"

"Don't play ignorant, my friend. You know who I am."

Dammit. If the agents were here, they could trace the call.

"Where are Lonnie McKinney and Scott Rehbein?"

"Don't you wish I'd tell?"

"If you did, it might convince me you are who you say you are."

"I'll do you no favors, Sheriff. You spoke unkindly of me. I assure you, I'm not impotent or frightened of the opposite sex. I'm more man than you'll ever dream of being."

Thomas rushed to the window and peered outside as Chelsey's car pulled to the curb. He waved his arms, urging her to hurry. Busy lifting two grocery bags out of the trunk, she didn't see him.

"Why kidnap children? What do you hope to gain?"

"You're wasting time, Sheriff. Where are my manners? Enough about me. Let's talk about you."

"No, let's talk about Lonnie McKinney."

"I'm in control. Growing up must have been difficult, yes? Asperger's syndrome. Ah, yes, I did my homework on you, Sheriff. Bet the other children made life difficult. Back then, kids weren't as accepting of autism as they are today."

"This isn't about me."

"You made it personal when you taunted me on live television. When you were young, you were poor at sports, the gym class klutz because of delayed motor skills development."

Outside, Chelsey stood on tiptoe with both bags clutched under one arm as she closed the trunk.

"Your classmates bullied you, yes? When you called me socially awkward, you were talking about yourself. Don't lie, my friend."

"I had difficulty making friends. So what? Put Lonnie on the phone."

"But not everyone turned their back on you. Not Chelsey." Thomas froze. "Ah, I struck a nerve. Chelsey abandoned you at a vulnerable age and tore your heart out. Poor Sheriff. Yet hope springs eternal, and your paths crossed last year. I don't blame you for carrying a torch. She's quite striking."

"Don't speak her name again."

"Or what?"

Thomas ran to the door and threw it open as Chelsey walked up the ramp. He caught her eye and pointed at the phone. Understanding quickened her pace, and she ran inside and set the bags on the floor. Thomas placed his index finger against his lips. He didn't need to tell Chelsey to phone the agents. She placed the call while Thomas continued.

"Still there, Sheriff?"

"Let me speak to Lonnie. Prove to me he's alive and unharmed."

"Yet you always maintained high integrity, a positive attribute. But you went too far. Because you strove for excellence, everyone around you fell short of expectations. The other children at school, your parents."

"Stop."

Chelsey made a winding motion with her hand. The FBI was tracing the call, and Thomas needed to keep the psycho on the phone.

"You're detail-oriented. Isn't that right, Sheriff? Everything must be just so. If the walk from the curb to the door takes an extra step, you return until you get it right. Everything must be exact. Precise. Am I throwing you off your game?"

"Not at all. Continue, please. This is educational, and I value your opinion."

The caller cackled.

"Don't be sarcastic. You'll upset me again, and you don't wish to anger me."

"What do you want for Lonnie McKinney's safe return? Is it money you're after?"

"Money doesn't motivate me. But respect does. I have one demand."

"Let's hear it."

"Tonight, on the evening news, you will retract your statement and give me the respect I've earned."

"And if I do, you'll release Lonnie and Scott?"

"They belong to me now, Sheriff. You'll not see them again."

"Then why should I agree to your terms?"

The line fell quiet for several seconds. Thomas worried the killer had hung up before he spoke again.

"If you don't do as I ask, I'll tear your *family* apart, my friend. I'll take someone close to you and mail you each body part every Christmas until you're old and shriveled. How would you like that?"

"Release the hostages. Please. Scott has his life ahead of him, and Lonnie is just a child. Listen to reason. You're not a monster."

"I expect your retraction tonight. Meet my demands, or your family pays for your sins."

"Wait. What happened between you and Father Josiah Fowler?"

The call ended. Thomas turned to Chelsey, who still had the FBI on the phone.

"Tell me they caught the bastard."

"Gardy and Bell think he's using a burner. They're working with the cell company to pinpoint his location."

Thomas blew out a breath and leaned against the counter. Chelsey pulled him into her embrace. Her perfume was delicate, fresh, and warming. Normally, everything felt right in the world when Chelsey was in his arms. But his world tore at the seams.

"I overheard the conversation. Will you go on the news and meet his demands?"

"No. I intended to upset him," he said, stroking her hair. "Apparently, the interview worked. But I may have gone too far. I'll never forgive myself if he hurts Lonnie and Scott."

"Don't blame yourself, Thomas."

He held Chelsey at arm's length and met her eyes.

"Until we catch this guy, you can't be alone."

"What's wrong?"

"He's watching you, Chelsey. He warned he'd hurt my family, and I believe he's talking about you."

32

T he sun dipped below the western ridge. Night crept out of the shadows like a vampire that had spent the day hiding from the light. Inky darkness leaked through the valley, coloring the lake black, shrouding the yards and houses, forcing the street lamps to ignite.

Deputy Aguilar turned her RAV4 out of the state park and slalomed between the potholes. After turning onto the lake road, she flipped her high beams on. As she drove, she recited the speech she'd worked up in her head.

"Sheriff, after long consideration, I've decided law enforcement isn't for me. I'm giving you my four-week notice, effective immediately."

She sighed and ran a hand through her hair.

"That sounded cold. I'm not that terrible, am I?"

Lips moving in silence, she rephrased her resignation speech. It still didn't sound right. She respected Thomas, and she loved the people she worked with. They deserved honesty. But she couldn't tell him the ghost of Avery Neal knocked on her door after the witching hour, invaded her dreams, and appeared on lonely roads with a twisted grin on his lips.

Paranoid over hallucinating again, she swung her gaze across the road, expecting to see the dead officer's bloody face staring at her. The windshield misted over, so she turned on the air conditioning to clear the glass. Along the road, a silver-gray morass of fog curled out of the ditch and spilled across the blacktop. She switched her high beams off after the light reflected off the mist. Last month had been one of the region's rainiest, and the drainage creeks still tumbled through the ditches, sparking early evening fogs. Aguilar reached for her radio and pulled her hand back. If she radioed dispatch, she might change her mind about quitting tomorrow.

And changing her mind wasn't an option. She needed to sever ties with the department. Forever. It was the only way to put the Avery Neal nightmare behind her and forget what happened.

The fog thickened and slicked the windshield. She turned on the wipers and eased up on the gas. Both hands gripped the steering wheel as she leaned forward. Visibility continued to drop as the fog blossomed. She tapped the brakes when a shadow moved off the shoulder. One blink, and the figure was gone. Another hallucination, another phantom of Avery Neal emerging from the mist to haunt her. Aguilar grit her teeth and refused to pull over. She wouldn't succumb to illusions. Not tonight.

The SUV rounded a bend. By now the streetlights should have been visible. But the fog swallowed all.

She lowered the window. Outside the car, the lake sloshed against the beach, though it remained invisible. Her speedometer read fifteen, and it seemed like she was flying at warp speed.

A car popped out the fog without warning. Aguilar slammed the brakes and skidded to a stop. The car lay halfway on the shoulder, the other half jutting across the road. Its blinkers flashed blood-red.

Aguilar sat behind the wheel with her heart racing. This wasn't an illusion. She'd come with a hair's width of crashing into the car. Opening the door, she verified her vehicle was on the shoulder and not blocking traffic like the disabled car. A quick glance behind her, and she stepped out.

Night had deepened since she left the park. The fog muted her footsteps as she approached the car.

"Hello? Is anybody injured?"

No reply.

She reached for her flashlight and swept the beam over the rear windshield. Couldn't discern anyone inside. Weird. Did the driver abandon the car and wander down the road? That would be a death wish in fog this thick.

"Can anyone hear me?"

She assessed the vehicle. It seemed in working order. No flat tire, no gas or oil leak. Had she driven faster, she would have wrecked the RAV4 against the car's bumper.

The blinkers kept pulsing like an undying heart. Aguilar rounded the car and knocked on the driver's side window. Nobody sat in the seat, and no keys dangled from the ignition. She flicked the beam across the backseat. Empty.

She glanced back at her SUV. The police band radio sat in the passenger seat. Aguilar didn't have a choice. The abandoned car was a road hazard, and she needed to call it in before someone came around the bend and crashed. She blew out a breath and memorized the license plate. The make and model would be easy to remember—a midnight blue Tesla. She didn't recall seeing any cars like this in Wolf Lake.

Aguilar hustled back to the RAV4 when the gravel crunched on the shoulder.

"Who's there?"

Her first thought was the driver had abandoned the vehicle and wandered down the road for help, possibly losing himself in the fog.

She strained her eyes. The mist concealed the road.

"I'm an off-duty sheriff's deputy. Follow my voice if you're lost. I'll call your vehicle in and get a tow truck to—"

The lightning shock of the Taser struck her chest and flung Aguilar against her SUV. Aguilar's back collided with the grille. Her legs buckled, and she dropped to the blacktop, twitching and squirming as the current scurried through her body like venomous spiders. Her hand reached for the bumper as footsteps approached. A deranged cackle came out of the fog.

"Good evening, Deputy. You're coming with me now."

The fist struck her head and slammed her against the macadam.

Two hands clutched her ankle and dragged her toward the Tesla before she blacked out.

33

F ull dark blanketed the lake shore behind the A-frame's guest house. Inside, Scout Mourning wheeled herself into the front room where Darren, Raven, and LeVar waited at the card table. She'd promised her mother she'd be home before ten, but the voice in her head told her this meeting might run long. Her mind still buzzed from spotting the FBI agents entering Thomas's house. She could hardly believe Agent Scarlett Bell had knocked on her neighbor's door. Though Scout wanted to meet the famous profiler with the BAU, she understood Agent Bell wouldn't visit Thomas's house unless something horrible had happened. Worry sat in the pit of her stomach. Had the killer struck again?

"Now that everyone is here," Raven said, pulling up a map of Poplar Corners on the computer monitor. "Let's begin the meeting."

LeVar rocked back in his chair and asked, "Why did the FBI knock on Thomas's door earlier?"

Scout searched the concerned faces at the table.

"He's pretty good about telling me when something important happens," Darren said, drumming his fingers on the table. "But I haven't spoken to him today. What did you see, LeVar?"

"Not much. Shep was already home when I arrived. While I made dinner, an SUV pulled into the driveway. That's when I noticed the FBI agents."

Darren put an arm around Raven's shoulders.

"You all saw the news, right?" LeVar gave Darren a blank look. "I figured. Nobody watches the local news anymore. Thomas called out Lonnie McKinney's kidnapper. He referred to him as an impotent coward who's afraid of women."

Scout touched her heart.

"That doesn't sound like Thomas."

"He's trying to unsettle the kidnapper and force the man to focus his attention on Thomas. It's a risky maneuver. If it works, the kidnapper will contact Thomas."

"Or attack him."

"That's what I'm afraid of. But if the psycho showed up this afternoon, we would have heard. The other possibility is the unsub will take his frustration out on Lonnie McKinney and Scott Rehbein, and nobody wants that. Let's hope Thomas didn't receive bad news. I'll talk to him in the morning after things die down."

"That makes it even more important we catch this creep and determine if he's the man who kidnapped Lonnie and Scott," said Raven.

Darren lifted his chin at LeVar.

"Tell us what happened the night you visited Poplar Corners."

LeVar told his story to the others. Though Scout remained in the car, she'd witnessed the shadowed figure stalking out of the woods before LeVar's mother drove away. The memory chilled her.

"You think the guy following you was the Poplar Corners ghost?"

LeVar lifted a shoulder.

"I never saw a face. It might have been someone out for a walk."

"In the meadow after dark?" Raven asked. "Doubtful."

"That meadow borders the Santos property. If the ghost stalked Harmony Santos before the abduction, the meadow and woods provided the perfect cover. From my position, I could look into every house in the neighborhood. The meadow stretches around the outskirts of Poplar Corners." He stood from his chair and walked to the monitor. "Check it out. See this cluster of sightings? The McKinney house is right here." LeVar jabbed his finger inside the cluster. "And the woods and meadow run two hundred yards behind the property. That makes it easy for the ghost to sneak into backyards without drawing attention."

"But where did he go afterward? He doesn't live in the woods."

LeVar rubbed his chin.

"That's the part that confuses me. Whoever he is, he's damn proficient. Nobody glimpses the ghost unless he wants them to."

"He wants to frighten people," Scout said, causing the others to nod.

"But by the time a neighbor reports a sighting and the authorities arrive, he disappears."

Scout pushed herself to the computer and typed on the keyboard. She loaded a web page of eyewitness recounts.

"The stories repeat themselves. Someone spots a creepy guy outside their window, then he escapes through the backyard and vanishes."

"Like he's an actual ghost," Raven said.

Darren smirked.

"We can safely rule out that theory."

"He must have escape routes," LeVar said. "Otherwise, someone would have caught him by now."

"We're assuming a lot. This creep might not be the kidnapper. Can we link Harmony Santos to Lonnie McKinney or Scott Rehbein?"

"Raven and I went door-to-door through Poplar Corners yesterday, and Chelsey spoke with Thomas. We can't find a common thread connecting Santos to the McKinney family, and nobody had heard of Scott Rehbein before the news reports."

"It's possible the kidnapper didn't know his victims. All I can say is, I'd love to be there the next time this creep shows his face outside a window."

Scout folded her arms and considered the mystery.

"Following him won't work. The Poplar Corners ghost has eyes in the back of his head. LeVar came too close to him in the meadow, and he disappeared into the trees before we identified him."

"The best stalkers and burglars are keenly aware of their surroundings," Darren said. "We never wanted to admit it when I worked with Syracuse PD. But we caught ninety percent of criminals because they did something stupid. They bragged to their friends about an item they stole. One idiot posted his loot on social media under an assumed name. Like we wouldn't figure it out." Darren shifted his jaw. "But the smart ones? We almost never caught them. They're careful and vigilant."

"So the ghost watches the neighborhood to ensure nobody is following him," Scout said.

"Even if we post lookouts in multiple yards, the odds of us catching him are slim."

"But how often does the ghost look skyward?"

Darren creased his forehead.

"You lost me."

"Instead of following him through the dark, what if we flew a drone over the neighborhood and monitored the footage from a safe location?"

Darren's face lit with understanding.

"That's brilliant. I never would have thought of that. But I don't know jack about flying drones. Do you?"

Scout pressed her lips together.

"Not really. But how difficult could it be?"

Raven searched for drone prices on the internet and clapped her hands together.

"The electronics store in Syracuse stocks several models. Most are a few hundred bucks. It appears the good ones are five-hundred or more. Do we have the funds to afford a drone?"

"I have a hundred in savings," Scout said.

"Forget it," Darren said, pointing at the girl. "You aren't flipping the bill. I'll buy it."

LeVar raised his eyebrows and said, "You don't have to, bro. We'll all chip in."

"I'm not asking two teenagers to empty their bank accounts. This one is on me. But the next time we order pizza—"

"I got you, Skip."

"All right. It's settled. Raven and I will drive to Syracuse tomorrow morning and pick up the drone. But do me a favor and don't crash it through somebody's window. I don't need that much drama in my life. Deal?" They agreed. "Now let's catch this psycho before he hurts someone else."

34

The soil beneath Deputy Aguilar chilled her skin. Darkness swam around her bruised and listless body.

She blinked twice and clutched her head as a migraine crippled her. Where was she? Out in a field? In the middle of a forest with a starless sky overhead?

No. The dark had borders. Unseen walls pressed in on her. She scrambled to her knees and gasped. Not a field, but a cell. Bars ran from an earthen ceiling to the floor and surrounded her on three sides. She must be dreaming. This was impossible.

Aguilar crawled to the bars and wrapped her hands around the cold iron. They felt real enough. No illusion this time. She shook the bars, but they didn't budge.

A thin shaft of gray light bled into the cell through an open door. It was impossible to discern what lay beyond the doorway.

To Aguilar's astonishment, she wasn't alone. Two identical cells stood to her left. In the middle cell, a naked male lay crumpled in the dirt. He didn't appear to be breathing. In the next cell, a child stripped to his underwear and a T-shirt curled in a ball in the far corner of the cage. What was happening?

Aguilar's hands dropped to her body. She was relieved to find no one had stripped her bare. Like the boy, she wore her underwear and the T-shirt she'd hiked in at the state park. A stench hit her nostrils and surged bile into her throat. Human feces and urine. She found the source of the odor in a bucket at the back of the cell. Identical metal buckets stood inside the other cages.

"Where the heck are we?"

The naked male didn't respond. There was just enough light to see his gaping mouth. A trickle of blood ran from his lips to his neck. His eyes were open. Lifeless. Murdered.

The truth slammed Aguilar's chest. The man was Scott Rehbein, the missing college student. Which meant the child had to be Lonnie McKinney.

Panic got her moving. She rattled the bars between her cage and the dead student's. They wouldn't budge.

Movement in the far cell pulled her attention. The boy sat up and rubbed his eyes. Thank goodness he was alive. The child glanced around in confusion.

"Are you Lonnie McKinney?"

The boy jolted and scurried into the dark corner at the back of the cage.

"It's all right. Nobody will hurt you. I'm locked up like you."

A choked sob escaped the boy's throat.

"He killed Scott," the boy said, crying.

"Who did?"

"The man. The bad man who pulled me through the window and locked me in this cage."

Aguilar's eyes flew to the open door. Her vision adjusted until she made out a cylindrical shape beyond the threshold. A water heater. The heater confirmed her vision when a flame flickered beneath the base.

"Lonnie, where are we?"

The boy shook his head.

"Underground. I don't know where."

Aguilar struggled to her feet. Her legs wanted to give out as she dragged her sluggish body toward the front of the cell. The door led to a basement, though the heater concealed the rest of the cellar. Her subterranean cell was attached to a house. This gave her hope. Maybe her abductor had neighbors.

"Have you ever seen him before?"

"Once. In the park. Daddy warned me not to talk to strangers. But I didn't listen. This is all my fault."

Aguilar limped across the cell and knelt beside the bars.

"No, it isn't. You did nothing wrong."

"I left my window unlocked. That's how he climbed into my bedroom. Daddy told me to lock the window, but it was so warm."

"Oh, Lonnie." Aguilar's heart clenched. The boy blamed himself for his predicament. What kind of monster kidnaps children and steals them from a loving home? "I'll get you out of here."

"That's what Scott said. And look what happened."

Lonnie's eyes fell to the mangled college student. Black and purple bruising colored Scott's neck. The killer had strangled him.

Was this her fate?

She ran from one side of the cage to the next, shaking the bars and searching for a weak point. The iron held firm. Whoever this maniac was, he'd built a sturdy cell. Aguilar guessed the bars protruded a foot or more into the floor and ceiling. As she tested the cage again, her skin prickled.

Lonnie's face paled. Aguilar spun around as a shadow moved across the floor.

The man's face lay hidden. Gray light illuminated him from behind. His frame cast a misshapen silhouette across the soil.

"Good. You're awake, Deputy."

"Who the hell are you?"

"Your master," the stranger chuckled. "Welcome to your new home."

Aguilar glanced around the cell.

"Where is *home*?"

"Don't you wish I'd tell you. Somewhere safe, if you are a good little girl and cooperate. Unlike our boy, Scott."

"Murdering college students, kidnapping a child and a sheriff's deputy. You're racking up enough charges to put you away for life."

"As if your foolish sheriff or the FBI could ever catch me."

Aguilar swallowed. He already knew about the FBI agents.

"Oh, you're surprised?" The creep gloated. "I've watched you for weeks, Deputy Aguilar. All of you."

Aguilar strode to the cage and looked up at her captor. She grit her teeth and pounded the bars.

"You're tough when you sneak up on people. What did you hit me with? A Taser? I should have dropped you in the road and dragged you to the sheriff's department."

The man laughed at the ceiling. She made out his face now. He was fair-haired and refined. A wild insanity swam in those intelligent eyes.

"Look at you. So muscular and boastful and sure of yourself. What good did those muscles do you? I bested you, my girl, just as I did poor Scott when he challenged my authority."

"You needed a weapon to take me down."

"The only weapon I require is my mind," he said, tapping his forehead. "I outsmarted you." The stranger tutted. "Poor Deputy Aguilar. Always helping others and trying to do the right thing. Yet it's never enough. You shot a corrupt police officer, and the county forced you into therapy, taking away your womanhood, your purpose in life."

"How did you—"

"I read about you. Your story is as fascinating as it is tragic. But you're a coward, like your sheriff friend."

The creep lunged at the bars. Aguilar slunk away. He grinned in victory.

"You're a failure who's afraid of her own shadow. Submit to my authority and become one of the family, and I swear I'll do you no harm."

"You're insane."

"No, I'm in control." He gestured at the cells. "This is my creation, and you are my pets."

"You can't lock us up forever."

"These iron bars, the key in my pocket, and my superior ingenuity all say I can. Admit it. I won, you lost."

Aguilar padded back to the bars and met his glare. He shot her a condescending smile.

"Tell you what, loser. I'll admit you beat me. Since you have me locked up, you don't need the child. Let Lonnie go."

"You're in no position to make demands."

"It's the right thing to do. Lonnie did nothing to you. Why take your psycho frustrations out on him?"

"Who says I'm frustrated? Perhaps I enjoy the company of a well-behaved pet."

"Stop calling me that."

A snicker.

"I'll call you what you are. Don't test me like Scott did. He challenged me and lost."

"You murdered him in front of a four-year-old child. What kind of animal are you?"

"An animal at the top of the food chain." The creep stuck his face between the bars and leered, running his gaze down her bare flesh. "If I chose, I could slip the key into the lock, open the door, and take you in front of the boy. Show you what it's like to be with a real man. You'd be powerless to stop me."

"I dare you."

"Oh, we'll have fun together, Deputy Aguilar." His tongue slid across his lips. "And when I'm finished with you, you'll know me as your God."

35

Thomas knew something was wrong when Deputy Aguilar didn't show up for her eight o'clock shift. Aguilar never overslept. Since the Avery Neal shooting, even when the deputy was at her most sullen, she remained punctual and dedicated. Aguilar hadn't answered phone calls or replied to texts. At ten, Thomas sent Lambert to her house. He knocked, but no one answered.

His anxiety exploded when a boater discovered a red RAV4 submerged in Wolf Lake. The plates matched Aguilar's vehicle. Divers searched the water for a body and found nothing. The awful truth struck Thomas between the eyes. The killer had taken Aguilar. There were no signs of an accident, no skid marks on the blacktop where her SUV left the road. Somehow, the killer coerced Aguilar out of her vehicle and abducted her.

Now Thomas drove home on the same stretch of road Aguilar disappeared on. He stopped along the shoulder and peered over the cliff, studying the water. A state trooper's vessel bobbed with the current. They were using sonar to search for Aguilar's body.

Thomas had done this to her. The killer promised he'd take

a family member from Thomas if he didn't apologize on televi-sion. After positioning an unmarked deputy's vehicle outside his mother's house, he'd believed his family was safe. What a fool he'd been. His friends and coworkers were family to him, and the killer knew.

Thomas called Agent Bell. She picked up on the first ring.

"No news so far, Sheriff," Bell said.

"What about Aguilar's cell? Can't we trace it?"

"Agent Gardy and I are working with the cell company. Deputy Aguilar's phone hasn't been used since last evening at eight-thirty on the lake road. Either the battery died, or someone removed it."

"I'll wager on the latter."

"Where are you?"

"At the lake. I'm heading home to ensure my neighbors are safe. They're the next targets, Agent Bell."

"We won't allow that to happen." Bell turned away as Gardy spoke in the background. "We're about to talk with the IT coor-dinator at the cell company. Gotta run. I'll keep you posted."

Thomas gunned the engine and raced home. He screeched to a stop outside his driveway and unlocked the door, expecting to find Jack and Chelsey. She'd told him she'd meet Thomas at the A-frame. The house was empty.

"Chelsey? Jack?"

Nothing.

He reached for his radio when the deck door slid open. Thomas brought his gun up and released a breath.

"Whoa, it's only me," Chelsey said, holding her hands in the air.

Thomas sighed and slid the gun into his holster.

"Your car isn't in the driveway."

"I parked at the Mourning's. Naomi needed help to get Scout inside."

He lifted his hands and glanced around.

"Where the heck is Jack?"

"LeVar took him to the state park. What's the latest on Deputy Aguilar?"

Thomas scrubbed a hand down his face. A noise pulled his eyes to the ceiling. Something. The house settling?

"No signal on her cell, and the divers didn't find a body."

"That's a good sign, right?"

"The current isn't strong enough to drag her out. There's no doubt in my mind. *He* took her. And I'm to blame."

"Don't do that to yourself," Chelsey said, wrapping her arms around him. "It's like Agent Bell said. The unsub is escalating. He would have taken someone, regardless—"

"But he kidnapped Aguilar. I made it personal, and now he's going after the people I care about."

"We'll find her. This psycho holds his victims for a week before he kills them, right?"

"That was one kid. Gardy and Bell haven't established a definitive pattern. The unsub changes his routine so we won't catch him."

She rubbed the knot out of his shoulders.

"Stay positive. He bit off more than he can chew with Aguilar."

"Well, he figured out how to catch her and dumped her SUV in the lake with no one noticing." The phone hummed in his pocket. He glanced at the screen. "That's Agent Gardy."

Gardy sounded harried when Thomas answered.

"Are you home?"

"I arrived two minutes ago. Chelsey is here. What's going on?"

"Thomas, we're sending a cruiser to your location. Aguilar's phone started working again. We traced the location."

Thomas widened his eyes as Chelsey stared at him.

"Where's her phone?"

"Inside your house." Heavy silence fell over the room. "Thomas?"

"I'll talk to you in a second, Gardy. There's something I need to deal with."

Gardy was still talking when Thomas set the phone in Chelsey's hand. He lifted his gaze to the ceiling.

"Thomas, what's going on?"

"There's someone in the house," he whispered.

"What?"

He knew every creak, every groan in the A-frame and had memorized where the squeaky boards lay. Thomas held his breath and listened.

The sound came again. A subtle moan as someone moved across the upstairs landing. Chelsey's eyes lit with understanding. She'd heard the noise.

"Thomas?" Gardy's frantic voice came through the phone. "Are you still there?"

Thomas leaned close and whispered in Chelsey's ear.

"Talk to Gardy. Be casual and carry on as if nothing is going on and I'm in the room with you."

Reading his intentions, she shook her head. He slid the gun from his holster and motioned for Chelsey to continue talking. Then he slipped from the kitchen and stood with his back against the wall, eyes angled up the stairs and toward the empty landing. Behind him, Chelsey rattled on with Gardy about something banal. But he read between the lines. The cruiser was two minutes away from his house.

Thomas swung off the wall and aimed his gun up the stairway. He swept it from one end of the landing to the next. The bathroom and bedroom doors stood closed. He always left the doors open, so the air didn't stale. One hand on the banister, Thomas pulled himself onto the first step and stopped. A dull thud came from behind his bedroom door. He looked back at Chelsey, who'd wandered to the border between the kitchen and living room. She had her own gun in her hand, the phone still pressed to her ear as she talked about Deputy Aguilar and how worried they all were. Thomas wondered if Gardy was still on the phone.

He crept up the stairs, his palms slick with sweat, heart like thunder in his ears. A squeaky board lay on the landing between the bathroom and the rail. He gave it a wide berth and arced toward his bedroom. Listened again. He could hear the lake and the wind. Outside, a siren wailed. Thomas cringed. The siren would tip off the intruder.

He stood beside the door, grabbed the knob, and whipped the door open. He swept his gun around the corner. The bedroom was empty. The window stood open, drapes fluttering as wind rushed inside.

His first thought was the killer had set a trap. Was the psycho behind him? Thomas cleared the closet. Nothing. There was nobody in the room, though he noted the bedspread wasn't military-tight as he'd left it. The wrinkled bedspread told him someone had sat on the edge of the bed and awaited his arrival. It might have been Jack, though Thomas doubted it. He didn't see dog hair on the ruffled corner of the bedspread.

He rushed to the window and looked down. It was a long drop from the second-story to the ground. The yard was empty.

Thomas blew out a frustrated breath and turned around, ready to clear the upstairs. He stopped.

Aguilar's phone lay on his nightstand.

36

A fiery slice of sun lay visible over the water when Thomas called the others to the guest house. LeVar gathered with his mother, Raven, Darren, Scout, and Naomi inside the front room. Chelsey stood beside Thomas as the last flare of sunlight flickered and smoldered, as though the lake had doused the flames. Night advanced on the little house behind the A-frame.

They fidgeted in their seats as Thomas stood before them. By now, everyone knew the killer had abducted Deputy Aguilar and broken inside his house.

"I brought everyone together because I won't allow this madman to endanger my friends and family. There's an unmarked cruiser outside my mother's house. She lives in a gated community with twenty-four-hour security detail, so I'm relatively certain she's safe now. But I need your help."

"Anything you need," Darren said, folding his arms. "Deputy Aguilar is our friend too."

"You can help me by leaving town." They all gave him stunned looks. "All of you."

"How can we help if we leave Wolf Lake?"

"Where would we go?" Serena asked.

"You expect us to pick up and leave?" Naomi raised her palms. "For how long?"

"The FBI is here, and we have full support from the New York State Troopers. As much as I value your opinions, I won't be able to concentrate on the case if I'm worried about your safety."

Darren set his hands on his hips.

"I'm a retired police officer. I can defend my home."

Thomas stepped forward and gestured at the others.

"What about everyone else? Naomi and Scout are alone next door. Serena lives by herself on the other side of the lake. And you can't be with Raven every minute of the day."

"I'm a trained private investigator with a gun," Raven said. "I'm not running away. Let me help you catch this guy."

"I grew up around danger," LeVar said, rising to his feet. "I can protect my friends. Say the word, and I'll make sure Naomi and Scout are safe."

"And Serena can live with us," Naomi said, drawing nods from Serena and Scout.

Thomas swung his head back and forth.

"That's not a risk I'm willing to take. You don't appreciate the danger you're in. This psycho kidnapped Deputy Aguilar under our noses and broke inside my house. He waited until LeVar took Jack for a walk. That tells me he's watching us. Maybe even now."

Uneasy murmurs rippled among them.

Raven stood and hooked arms with Darren.

"I'm with Darren and LeVar. If we leave just to get away from this creep, we reduce the chance of catching him. We're making progress on the Poplar Corners investigation. We haven't flown the drone yet."

Thomas folded his arms.

"This isn't up for debate. Look, there's strength in numbers. He won't go after you if you're all together. Take a vacation. Find some sleepy bed-and-breakfast along Lake Ontario and buy a few rooms. If you stay, you're all sitting ducks."

Darren ground his teeth.

"We're close to catching him, Thomas. Just a little more time. That's all I'm asking for."

"Darren, I trust you to defend yourself. But we're too spread out, too thin. He'll go after the person who's alone."

The state park ranger paced to the window and stared out at the lake. Darkness spilled down from the ridge, cloaking the land. Were it not for the first stars, the night would have rendered the lake invisible.

"There might be another option."

Thomas leaned against the wall.

"I'm listening."

"The state park. Until school releases for summer, cabin rentals run at low capacity. What if everyone moved into the cabins?"

Thomas opened his mouth to protest and stopped. That wasn't a horrible idea.

"Tell me more."

"Well, we only rented one cabin this week, and it's on the far side of the clearing. If everyone took cabins near mine, we could watch each other's backs and still work on the case."

Scout, who hadn't spoken to this point, bobbed her head.

"That's perfect. We'd all be together, which means we could investigate full time."

Naomi and Serena shared an agreeable glance.

"Think about it, Thomas," Darren said, pointing up the hill toward the park. "I've had security cameras in place since the burglaries. No chance the killer sneaks up on us without me catching him."

"And we'd be just up the hill," said Raven. "LeVar and I can work with Chelsey on the Harmony Santos case and help the others catch the Poplar Corners ghost."

Thomas chewed his lip. He'd feel more comfortable if they left town. But if everyone stayed together at the campgrounds, he could monitor them.

"All right, I'll agree to that."

LeVar gave Scout a high-five.

"Can we move in tonight?" Scout asked.

As Scout packed, voices carried from the kitchen, where Naomi conferred with Serena and LeVar. The teenager laid a suitcase open on the bed and wheeled herself to the dresser. Guessing they'd live at the cabins for three days or longer, she spooned clothes into her arms and hauled them back to the suitcase. Her mother had already agreed to keep Scout out of school through the week, provided Scout emailed her assignments to her teachers and studied every day. Final exams weren't until the end of June, so this was the perfect time to miss a few school days.

A nervous butterfly fluttered inside her chest. The break-in at the A-frame highlighted the danger they were in. But if the team stayed together, they'd keep each other safe.

And they'd catch the creep. She was sure of it. With no school to worry about, Scout could concentrate on the investigation and work day and night to catch the so-called ghost.

Her mother knocked before entering.

"Are you packed?"

Scout zipped the suitcase.

"I am now."

"What about your toothbrush?"

"Oops, I forgot."

Naomi raised an eyebrow.

"You're rushing, Scout. I realize you're excited, but slow down. We can't drive back and forth to the house if you forget something."

"You're right. It's just that this is the first time I've worked full-time on a case. It's like being a real investigator."

Naomi planted a kiss on Scout's head.

"I know it's your dream and you'll make it happen." Her mother fought not to stare at Scout's legs, but Scout noticed. "You will. Someday. I believe in you."

LeVar and Serena stood beside their bags in the entryway when Scout trailed her mother into the living room. Naomi set Scout's suitcase down and caught her breath. Smirking, LeVar lifted his chin at Scout.

"Bring enough clothes? You spending a few weeks in the Bahamas?"

"I always come prepared," Scout said.

"Well, I'll need a forklift to hoist the suitcase into my car. If I ruin my back, you and I will have words."

They packed LeVar's Chrysler Limited beneath a minefield of stars, the crickets singing around them. As LeVar helped Naomi and Serena with their bags, he kept glancing across the road toward the thicket, as though he sensed eyes on them. Then he scooped Scout into his arms and placed her on the backseat beside Naomi. Serena slid beside LeVar in front.

LeVar locked the doors and fired the engine. Through the rear windshield, Scout watched the darkness until the Chrysler began the steep climb into the state park.

37

Bright light shone from the ranger's home and two neighboring cabins when LeVar's car pulled into the welcome center at Wolf Lake State Park. Darren worried until he saw all four remaining members of the investigation team pile out of the Chrysler. Thomas was right. They needed to stick together. That was the only way to keep everyone safe.

An elderly couple rented a cabin at the far end of the lot. Their lights were off, the seniors turning in after sunset. Otherwise, the grounds were vacant.

LeVar pushed Scout's wheelchair. Darren and Raven helped Serena and Naomi with their bags. Scout and Naomi took the cabin beside Darren's home. The cabin featured a handicap-accessible shower. LeVar and Serena would share the next cabin over. After they dropped off their belongings, they gathered inside the ranger's home. The clock read nine-thirty, and Naomi and Serena already had heavy eyelids. Raven set pizza and chips on the table. Darren walked the cabin perimeter with a holstered weapon, checking every shadow until he was satisfied nobody was creeping around the grounds.

When he returned to the cabin, the others sat around the table. He gestured at four monitors on the counter.

"After the break-ins, I installed security cameras around the cabins. They'll come in handy over the next few nights, or however long it takes before we catch this killer. Nobody sneaks into camp without me knowing."

LeVar's old running mate from the Harmon Kings, Rev, had spied on LeVar's guest house from the state park while he robbed cabins. The robberies prompted Darren to set up a security system. Now the monitors displayed color views of the grounds, the gain finely tuned to peer inside shadows.

"We should post guards," LeVar said, glaring at the monitors. "I volunteer to keep watch tonight."

"We'll work in shifts," Darren said. "LeVar, you monitor the grounds from eleven until three. I'll relieve you from three to seven. By then, the sun will be up."

"Bet. I got this covered."

"We can help too," Serena said.

"No sense in all of us losing sleep," Darren said. "LeVar and I can handle the job and grab enough sleep to be useful during the day."

"I'll allow it," Raven said, shooting Darren a meaningful glare. "Provided you sleep through the morning. I'll work at the welcome center until you're awake."

Darren nodded, understanding he couldn't run the park and keep his friends safe at the same time.

"So we're in agreement. Scout." The girl looked up. "Sift through the sightings data and give me your best guess where the ghost is hanging out in Poplar Corners. Tomorrow night, when the sun sets, we strike."

"Are we flying the drone?"

"You bet. Which also means you need to figure out how to fly that sucker so we don't crash it into a tree."

"I'll help," Naomi said. "We'll test the drone over the state park and ensure the video signal is strong."

"Excellent idea," Darren said. "Find how far we can fly the drone before it exceeds its range." Darren fell silent until he won their attention. "Remember, this isn't a vacation. We're safe here as long as we're vigilant and look out for each other. Our cabins sit side-by-side. I won't allow anything to happen to you." Darren wasn't much for speeches. He cleared his throat. "Now, dig in and help yourself to pizza and chips. We might be here for several nights, so let's make the most of it."

As the team dished pizza onto paper plates, Darren's eyes slid to the window. The night thickened, brushing up against the pane like an immortal foe.

He hoped the others understood the danger they were in.

38

Father Josiah Fowler emptied the last of the bourbon into his glass and guzzled it. He set the drink on his desk with a hollow plunk. The church was empty at this time of night, his staff at home in bed or inside the neighboring rectory. He didn't trust the church after dark. It made strange noises when he was alone. Distant creaks that echoed through the corridors, occasional groans that sounded too much like footsteps moving among the pews.

His head swam when he stood up from his chair. The priest clutched the desk until he found his footing. With a moan, he locked his office and passed through the gloomy corridor. He peeked his head inside the church school classroom, as if searching for phantoms, before climbing the stairs toward the vestibule. Each footfall echoed back to him.

Inside the vestibule, he stared inside the church. Two statues of angels holding water bowls welcomed guests. In the semi-dark, their eyes appeared haunted and accusatory.

Fowler wiped the inebriation off his face, locked the doors so the angels couldn't follow him home, and descended the steps outside the church. The stars were sharp tonight. Boundless.

His legs wobbled as he gripped the rail. Had he murdered that woman, Lana Gray? He remembered climbing into the car, his head spinning with drink. He'd known driving was a terrible idea, that he should have called a cab or slept the bourbon off in his car before he twisted the ignition. Then the yellow dividing line seemed to warp and undulate as he weaved from one shoulder to the next.

That was the last he remembered of the drive.

The next morning, there were questions from the sheriff and his deputies. Sheriff Gray's wife was dead, the grille of the car crushed against a tree. A witness claimed Fowler had crossed the centerline moments before Lana Gray rounded the bend. But no one proved the priest caused the crash. It might have been ice or the frigid night. Perhaps she fell asleep at the wheel. Maybe...

A scuffling sound pulled his eyes around the church. Last month, a raccoon had gotten into the garbage can and spilled trash across the grass. But this noise sounded too heavy to be a raccoon.

He stopped and stared. It was too dark to see past the bushes.

"If you're looking for something to steal, you're out of luck. Try a bank."

Fowler chuckled at his own joke. But uneasiness tinged his drunken laughter. He recalled that old saying, *whistling past the graveyard*.

His eyes fell. It was hardly pious to assume the worst. What if the person needed help?

"Hello there. Are you injured? Call out to me, and I'll help you."

A loud thud made him jump. His hands clenched. Something sinister walked among the darkness.

Picking up his pace, he crossed the lawn and started up the

rectory sidewalk. The lights were off inside. Everyone had turned in for the night except Fowler. Bordering the walkway, four lamps cast dimly lit pools across the concrete. The priest yearned for the light, yet it seemed so far away.

Footsteps swished through the grass as a shadow blackened the outer wall of the rectory. Fowler held his breath and hurried forward, his heart a metronome in his throat, sweat breaking out along his back.

He cried out when the silhouette lurched out of hiding and blocked his path. For a moment, his frantic mind conjured images of vampires, demons, and the devil.

"Good evening, Father."

Though shadows concealed the man's face, Fowler recognized the voice. The man from the confession booth. The animal who'd left the woman's hand inside the box. Fowler suddenly wished he'd broken his oath and cooperated with Sheriff Shepherd.

"Go away. You've caused enough terror, haven't you?"

"I promised we'd meet again, and I never break a promise."

"The child. Did you—"

"I showed the boy mercy. Unlike you."

"Who are you?"

The man stepped into the lamplight. Silvery illumination highlighted his fair hair and wild eyes. Fowler knew this man. He'd been but a boy when Fowler last encountered him. An innocent, doe-eyed child. It had been a huge mistake, a moment of weakness. If the priest could turn back time . . .

"Do you remember me, shaman?"

"I'm so sorry."

The knife thrust into Fowler's belly and twisted. Hot, crippling pain tore through Fowler as his legs gave out. The priest toppled forward, and the ghost cradled him in his arms, almost lovingly, before setting him on the sidewalk. Fowler glared wide-eyed at the murderer as blood bubbled out of his stomach. He opened his mouth, but no words came out. The ghost dropped to his knees.

"I'll see you in hell, pretend priest."

Justice Thorin plunged the blade into Fowler's chest.

39

Aguilar's internal clock warned her the kidnapper hadn't visited the cells in twelve hours. Which was unusual. Her abductor crept into the underground lair every six to eight hours, sometimes through the cellar door, other times through a trapdoor that led to the outside world. Aguilar had glimpsed blue sky the last time the creep opened the trapdoor and climbed inside. Where was he? Had he abandoned Aguilar and Lonnie to starve and die?

She paced the cage in absolute darkness, the soil rough against her bare feet. Her skin rippled with goosebumps. It was as if the underground enclosure trapped the departed winter, storing it until the leaves changed. She longed for sunlight and people and rush-hour traffic jams. Yet sometimes she was thankful for the dark. That way Lonnie didn't see her stripped to her underwear and T-shirt, her dignity stolen. She'd become a caged animal who only existed to amuse her captor.

After every step, she tested the bars, searching for a weak spot. Along the front of the cage, she rattled the iron enclosure and discerned more wiggle than she'd found with the other bars. Her foot stepped into a clump of soil and rock. She'd noticed the pile when the kidnapper shone light into her prison, but hadn't thought about it until now. Someone had found the weak point and shook the bars until soil cascaded from the dirt ceiling. Now that she thought about it, a similar clump lay in Scott Rehbein's cage. Had the college student discovered a loose bar before the psycho murdered him?

Hope raced through Aguilar's body. She clutched the bars and yanked back, her heels digging into the ground for leverage as her back strained. After she failed to dislodge the bars, she shifted her weight forward and shoved against the cage, arms outstretched and locked at the elbows. No hope. The bars refused to budge.

A slice of milky light spilled beneath the basement door. Not from the sun. The creep must have turned on the cellar light. Illumination arrowed across the floor and caught Lonnie's cage. The boy curled on the cold ground, stripped as she was, his body facing away. Was he breathing?

"Lonnie? Can you hear me?"

The last time their captor descended into the cells, he brought sandwiches. Something store-bought this time. After he removed the food from the plastic wrappers, Aguilar read *Doug's Deli* on the label. The name didn't ring a bell or help her determine their location. Lonnie, bone thin with his ribcage jutting against his flesh, had eaten his sandwich, while Aguilar refused the meal. Now Lonnie was unresponsive and unmoving. Aguilar worried about poison.

If it was the last act of her life, she'd free Lonnie and return the child to his father. On her knees, Aguilar assessed the opening at the bottom of the cage, where she slid food trays and the bucket to the kidnapper. Despite her diminutive size, she couldn't squeeze through the opening. Too small, even for Lonnie. But the opening might allow her to snatch her captor by the leg or injure him. She needed a weapon.

Amid the suffocating darkness, Lonnie moaned. It was a painful sound, the whimper of a dying animal. She swung her eyes to the child, thankful he was alive, yet terrified he wouldn't live much longer.

"What's wrong, Lonnie? Tell me where you hurt."

The child squirmed and kicked out as though battling monsters in a dream. Then he rolled to his side and faced Aguilar. The shaft of basement light caught the child's face, and Aguilar gasped. He was dying.

"Lonnie, look at me. I need you to keep your eyes open and stay awake."

"It hurts."

"What hurts?"

"My tummy."

Aguilar scurried to the bars and averted his gaze from the dead student splayed in the center cell.

"When did the pain start?"

"I don't know," Lonnie said, clenching his eyes as tears leaked down his cheeks.

"Try to remember. Was it after you ate?"

He bobbed his head. The son-of-a-bitch poisoned the boy. Now she couldn't trust the food he brought them. They'd starve if the poison didn't kill them first.

"If you're sick and have to throw up, it's okay. That will get the bad stuff out of your stomach."

Whatever life trauma drove the creep to hurt people, it wasn't a valid excuse. There was no greater crime than harming a child. Lonnie rubbed his eyes.

"Did he poison Scott?"

The boy shook his head.

"Scott talked back to him, so he . . ."

The words trailed off. Aguilar swallowed.

"He unlocked Scott's cage?"

"Yeah, because Scott wanted to fight him. Scott thought he could win, but the man hurt him. He hurt Scott until he stopped breathing."

So it was possible to goad the psycho. Lonnie must have noticed the idea floating behind Aguilar's eyes. The boy struggled to his knees and grabbed the bars, staring at her with pleading eyes.

"He'll kill you too. He's too strong. Nobody can win against him."

"Lonnie, I'm a deputy with the Nightshade County Sheriff's Department."

Hearing her own words shot a wave of confident energy through Aguilar's body. The night the creep fooled Aguilar and shot her with the Taser, she'd planned to quit. It occurred to her that the Avery Neal dream hadn't afflicted her since the kidnapping. Perhaps real nightmares superseded the pretend ones. Escaping this hellhole with Lonnie gave Aguilar a sense of purpose, reminded her of why she'd become a sheriff's deputy. Until the world was safe from sickos like their abductor, she wouldn't rest.

"I'm not afraid of him. He can't hurt me."

"Yes, he can. He hurt Scott, and Scott's a boy."

Aguilar lifted her head and found Lonnie's silhouette in the dark. She wore a wry smile.

"Women are as strong as men, Lonnie. Don't worry about me. The next time he visits, I'll make him angry. I haven't decided what I'll do yet, but I need to force him to enter my cell."

"He put his hands around Scott's neck and squeezed. Scott wasn't strong enough. I don't want him to hurt you. You can't beat him."

Aguilar's gaze fell to the broken college student. She wouldn't die in front of Lonnie. And she refused to let the creep best her.

"Please, don't make him angry," the boy wept.

"Stay strong for me." She straightened her back and repeated her words. "I'm a deputy with the Nightshade County Sheriff's Department. And I won't stop fighting until you're home with your daddy."

40

Chelsey lowered the visor to block out the morning sun. She parked a block from Gerald Burke's residence and observed people moving about the neighborhood. A man wearing headphones and running sneakers power-walked along the curb. Two women in yoga pants and sweatshirts chatted as they walked their dogs.

An idea fluttered through her head. There were two kidnappers loose in Nightshade County—the psycho who murdered people in the Great Lakes region and New England, and the person who captured Harmony Santos. She'd read Agent Bell's profile of the killer—a malignant narcissist who considered the world beneath him. Gerald Burke fit the bill. Harmony's old boyfriend claimed she'd *settled* when she married Lawrence Santos. It was obvious Burke never got over Harmony. But would he kidnap his old girlfriend and commit murder?

And there was still the matter of the wedding photographs. Every time she examined the pictures, she sensed eyes on Harmony. Chelsey searched for Gerald Burke in the photos. But she never found Harmony's old boyfriend glaring at her as Lawrence claimed. What was she missing?

Chelsey stepped from the car and locked the doors with the key fob. When the women in yoga pants approached, they allowed the dogs to sniff Chelsey and say hello. Chelsey knelt and patted their heads.

"Beautiful dogs. What are their names?"

"This is Dunes," the woman on the left said, stroking the dog's fur. The dog was an unidentifiable mix—black lab, but smaller.

"And Cujo," her friend said, holding the brown-coated beagle at the end of the leash.

The name made Chelsey chuckle. She recalled the infamous monster dog from the Stephen King novel.

"I take it you live in the neighborhood."

"We're neighbors," Cujo's mother said, pointing toward a Tudor and Cape Cod across the street from Gerald Burke's house. "Are you buying the Baumann House? It's a tremendous deal, if you like a large yard."

The friend shook her head.

"I wouldn't. Clint barely keeps up with our lawn. I can't imagine how he'd maintain a half-acre. But people keep coming by to check out the Baumann place."

Chelsey removed a card from her wallet.

"Actually, I'm a private investigator." The neighbors shared a wary glance. "Don't worry. None of your neighbors are in trouble. I'm searching for someone. A woman. Perhaps she came around four years ago."

The neighbors dug in their heels as the dogs tried to drag them down the street. Chelsey swiped through the images on her phone and located a picture of Harmony Santos.

"Here she is," Chelsey said, holding the phone up.

Dunes's mother scrunched her face in concentration before she shook her head.

"Sorry, she doesn't look familiar. Are you sure you have the correct neighborhood? We know everybody on the block."

Cujo's mother bent over to study the picture. She tapped a fingernail against Chelsey's phone.

"I've seen her."

Chelsey stiffened.

"Where?"

"It was a long time ago. Probably four years, like you said. She visited my neighbor across the street. Mr. Burke."

The woman's mouth twisted on Burke's name.

"So you know Gerald Burke?"

"Can't say we're cordial, but he comes and goes. He's not the most neighborly person on the block."

"You can say that again," her friend said in agreement.

Chelsey found another picture of Harmony Santos, this one from her wedding day.

"Do you recall seeing her on any other occasion?"

"No, just once. Not that I'm a busy-body. I assumed she was dating Mr. Burke, but I never saw her after that."

Chelsey questioned the women for another minute before leaving them with business cards and a request to call if they remembered anything else about Harmony Santos. She continued down the road, her body buzzing with excitement. Harmony Santos had visited Gerald Burke around the time of her wedding. Had she cheated on Lawrence?

Chelsey waited until she reached Gerald Burke's house before looking behind her. The women disappeared around the corner with their dogs. Next door, a lawn contractor drove a mower, the roar of the engine loud enough to cloak Chelsey's footsteps. With nobody paying attention, Chelsey slipped around Burke's house and followed the path toward his back-yard. The driveway was empty. Burke was at work and wasn't due home until this afternoon.

A hedgerow blocked the neighbor's view. Hunched over, Chelsey sneaked along the house and peeked through windows. The dining room held a cabinet stocked with fine china. She moved to the next window and stopped. A first-story bedroom. Chelsey stood on tiptoe and peered inside, squinting until her eyes picked out the bed and dresser. The window was open to the screen, the translucent curtains open halfway. An antique dresser lay against the far wall. The king-size bed took up half the room.

It was the bedside table that drew Chelsey's attention. She recognized Harmony Santos in the framed photograph. The woman appeared several years younger than she'd been in the wedding photos. The picture must have been taken during college when Burke dated Harmony. So Burke still carried a torch for his old girlfriend. Keeping a photograph for that long pointed toward obsession. Chelsey wondered if Burke kidnapped Harmony because she refused to leave Lawrence.

"What the hell are you doing?"

Chelsey yelped and spun around. Gerald Burke glared down at her, his hands curled into fists.

"Oh, Mr. Burke. I knocked, but you didn't answer."

"So you sneaked around my house and stared into my window?"

"No, I was just—"

Burke took a dangerous step toward Chelsey. She felt the furious heat rippling off his body.

"Did you find what you were looking for, Ms. Byrd?"

"Tell me about the photograph."

"What photograph?"

"Of Harmony Santos. You keep it next to your bed."

The corner of his mouth twitched.

"That's none of your business."

"You claimed you had nothing to do with Harmony's disappearance, and you broke up during college. Yet you kept her photo. That's a little strange, don't you think?"

Another step closer.

"Harmony and I were meant to be together. She never should have married that loser. Harmony was never happier than when we dated."

"Did you kidnap Harmony Santos when she refused to leave Lawrence?"

"You're sick. Get off my property before I call the police."

"I have witnesses from your neighborhood who saw Harmony at your house four years ago. Did you have an affair with Harmony?"

"You've got it all wrong. I never hurt Harmony. She needed protection."

"From who? Lawrence?"

Burke placed his hands atop his head and walked in a circle, his eyes angled toward the sky.

"I don't know who the guy was."

"That's convenient. Why wouldn't Harmony seek protection from her fiancé?"

"Probably because I could protect her better than the wimp who gave her a ring."

Chelsey wasn't sure she believed Burke.

"Tell me everything."

Gerald Burke folded his arms and leaned against the wall, eyes squeezed shut.

"Harmony returned to college after her wedding. She was working toward her masters, taking classes part time."

"Lawrence Santos didn't mention this."

"Because she didn't tell him." When Chelsey lifted an eyebrow, Burke sighed. "Harmony worried Lawrence couldn't support them and she'd end up the breadwinner. I guess she didn't want to embarrass Lawrence. She only took one class that spring. Harmony intended to go full time the following fall."

"What college?"

"Kane Grove University."

"You said Harmony needed protection. From who?"

Burke lowered his voice.

"She wasn't sure."

"Come on, Mr. Burke. Give me more than that."

"A guy started following Harmony. She never got a good look at his face, but Harmony was pretty sure he had blonde hair. He kept appearing. Sometimes in the quad, other times in the parking lot. At first, she blew it off as coincidence. Then she saw him outside the grocery store in Poplar Corners. What are the odds some guy from Kane Grove University would pop up in that cow town? That's when she came to me."

"What did you do?"

"The next day, I followed Harmony to school and ensured nobody bothered her. After that, she never saw the guy again." Burke puffed out his chest. "I scared him off."

If Burke was telling the truth, Harmony had a stalker.

41

Two hours had passed since sunset. Darren wondered if they were wasting time.

"You got anything, LeVar?"

After a second of silence, LeVar replied over the radio.

"That's a negative. Nothing out here but mosquitoes the size of bats."

"All right. Let's give it another fifteen minutes before we call it a night."

Darren placed the radio on his hip and scanned the woods through his binoculars. He sat in his Silverado in the public park, where Lonnie McKinney had encountered the stranger. The door was open, the field lit by fireflies as night sounds encompassed the dark. The playground equipment slumbered at the far end of the field, shadowed and silent. Twice he stopped the binoculars when the trees rustled. Both times, an animal scampered into the woods.

He set the binoculars on the seat and turned the laptop to face him. The screen showed an animated image of Poplar Corners from a few hundred feet above ground level. Video displayed a bird's-eye view of the town as the drone drifted over forest and backyards. The pictures fascinated Darren, though they hadn't spotted the so-called ghost yet. He worried the stories of a Peeping Tom staring through windows were legends or gross over-exaggerations. But years as a police officer taught Darren to remain patient. The chaos usually started after officers let their guards down.

The clock read eleven. He yawned and picked up the radio.

"How are you holding up, Scout?"

Scout Mourning sat inside LeVar's Chrysler Limited on the opposite side of the meadow with her mother and Serena Hopkins. They'd parked on the access road behind the neighborhood where Lawrence Santos lived.

"Trying to keep the drone in the air."

"You're doing a terrific job. The pictures are amazing."

"Hold on. I'm taking the drone over the neighborhood again."

The radio went silent as Scout concentrated on flying the drone. He watched the woods until footsteps approached the truck. A flashlight swept across his eyes as Raven climbed into the cab.

"See anything out there?"

"Nope. It appears the ghost took the night off."

Darren didn't like Raven hunting through the park on her own. He only agreed after she promised to keep her radio on at all times and never leave the park grounds. The problem was, once she wandered several steps from the truck, she disappeared into the night. Darren let out a relieved breath now that she'd returned.

"Scout's flying the drone over the neighborhood," he said, rotating the laptop so Raven could watch. "I told her to stick to the area between the meadow and the backyards. If our Peeping Tom shows his face, that's where we'll catch him."

"Is LeVar still in the meadow?"

"Yeah, and complaining about the bugs."

"Can't take a city kid to the country."

They resumed their watch. Nothing moved in the park as the clock ticked toward midnight. If the ghost didn't appear soon, Darren would call off the search. He didn't feel right about keeping everyone up late.

"Darren, there's someone in the field."

Darren sat up and turned up the radio.

"Come again, LeVar."

"Someone's out here. Between the Santos house and the meadow."

"Scout, are you copying this?"

"I'm redirecting the drone now," Scout said.

"Keep the drone above the trees. Don't spook our target."

Darren and Raven stared at the screen as though watching a tense scene from a suspense movie. The drone swept over the meadow and shot toward the Santos home. Grass and field flew by as the drone whistled over Poplar Corners, invisible except for an occasional flash of red light. Houses passed in a blur before the drone slowed. Now it hovered over Lawrence Santos's backyard.

"She's damn good at flying that thing," Raven said.

"You can say that again."

Darren bent forward and squinted his eyes. An aluminum shed stood along the fence line between the Santos property and the meadow. He was about to ask LeVar if he was sure someone was sneaking around the property when a silhouette slipped through the yard. Raven enlarged the picture.

"What was that?"

"It moved too fast. I can't tell."

A second later, the shape reversed course and bounded toward the fence, leaping it with ease. Darren groaned.

"Congratulations, LeVar. You caught a deer."

No reply.

"LeVar, do you copy?"

~

SCOUT'S TONGUE protruded between her lips as she worked the controls. She directed the drone over the trees, cursing when power lines appeared in her picture. Pulling up, she sent the drone skyward and swept it across the meadow. The radio squawked in Scout's lap.

The windows were up, and Serena's perfume cloaked the interior of LeVar's car. Scout's mother fought to keep her eyes open as the hour grew late.

"Why isn't LeVar answering?" Serena Hopkins asked from the front seat.

Scout glanced over her shoulder and checked the window. The meadow encroached on the car, the night somehow untrustworthy. June bugs crawled across the windshield. Scout turned her attention to the drone and bit back a curse. The momentary distraction nearly sent the drone into a tree. It was difficult to concentrate while the radio buzzed with activity.

Naomi opened the door and stepped onto the access road. She clutched her elbows with her hands and stared into the meadow. No sign of LeVar.

"Maybe his battery died," Scout said as she began to worry. LeVar should have returned by now.

She turned the drone for another sweep of the neighborhood when a shape moved along the tree line.

"I've got movement a hundred yards behind us," Scout said.

Naomi climbed into the car, shut the door, and engaged the locks. Serena stared at Scout.

"Is it LeVar?"

"I can't tell. Whoever it is, he's moving toward us."

Darren's voice came over the radio. He'd left the park with Raven and expected to arrive in five minutes.

Scout glared at the unknown figure on the laptop screen. The drone was too high to identify the person. She took it lower, risking a crash. The shadow vanished inside the thicket, then reappeared fifty feet ahead.

"Scout," Naomi said, staring at the monitor. The teenager was too focused to answer. "Scout!"

"Not now, Mom. I'm dodging trees."

"He's coming toward the car."

Serena and Naomi locked eyes. The keys dangled from the ignition. Serena appeared torn. If she drove them to safety, she'd abandon her son. And LeVar wasn't answering his radio.

"Give me a second," Scout said, wiggling the controller as if she played a video game. "I'm taking the drone lower."

The drone descended and hovered over the man.

Naomi covered her mouth with her hand.

"That's not LeVar. Serena, we need to go."

Serena's eyes were full moons.

The drone was close enough for Scout to see the Chrysler, the gray soil of the access road, and the unknown man striding toward the car. Closer with each step. Close enough that she should be able to see him through the windows. But all she saw was the black of midnight.

"Serena, start the car!"

Naomi's voice shocked Serena out of her daze. The woman twisted the key as the grass rustled behind the car. Scout swung her head around and screamed at the ghostly face emerging from the darkness. She was vaguely aware of the video image twirling end over end as the drone spun out of control. The Chrysler shifted into drive as a second figure shot out of the woods and collided with the stranger.

"Don't leave! That's LeVar!"

Serena slammed the brakes. The Chrysler rocked as Naomi turned around. They couldn't see anything, only the meadow rustling as the two figures fought. Naomi leapt from the car with Serena behind her.

A shout. LeVar staggered onto the access road with one hand clutching his head. Blood trickled between his fingers. The teenage boy fell into his mother's arms as Naomi stood between them and the meadow.

"Scout, where is he?" Naomi shouted over her shoulder.

Scout redirected the drone before it struck the ground. The grass whirred past the screen for a split second before the drone took to the air again. She navigated the drone back to the access road, where it buzzed over their heads and rocketed toward the meadow. There was no sign of the man who attacked LeVar. Just endless wilderness bordering the neighborhood.

The door opened. Serena and Naomi helped LeVar into the car. He fell into the passenger seat with a nasty gash over his eye.

"What happened?"

LeVar grinned at Scout.

"The scumbag jumped me from behind. Knocked me out for a minute or two. But I got me some payback." LeVar winced as Serena worried over his injury. "He ran toward the woods. Don't let him get away."

"I'm trying!"

Scout couldn't find the Poplar Corners ghost. He blended into the terrain and vanished from the camera. By the time he emerged from hiding, it might be too late for the drone to catch him. Scout sent the drone toward the forest, skimming the trees. Then over the meadow, the drone flying a few dozen feet above the ground, no longer hidden from sight. She cursed, unable to find LeVar's attacker.

A shape lurched out of the forest and angled across the meadow. The ghost made a beeline toward the park.

"I see him," Scout said, chewing her lip as sweat poured off her forehead.

Naomi, Serena, and the bruised LeVar crowded into the backseat for a better view of the laptop screen. Scout wanted to tell them to back off, but if she took her eyes off the screen for a second, she'd lose the ghost again.

The man vanished inside a thicket. Seconds later, he reappeared along the meadow. Now he was only a minute from the park grounds.

She pushed the drone faster. It gained on the ghost with every stride he took.

As the drone whirred over the rural outskirts of Poplar Corners, the man vanished.

"That's impossible," Scout said, poking a finger at the screen. "He was right there."

As she searched for the ghost, the drone circled around. It dove toward the thicket and buzzed over open land.

The ghost had vanished.

42

Ainsley Witherspoon was a grizzled man who walked hunched over. Thomas worried the man might tumble down the embankment as he led the sheriff and Deputy Lambert toward the Nightshade River. Every other word out of Witherspoon's mouth was a curse, and he sounded as if he gargled broken glass.

It was after midnight. The river stretched the moon's reflection into a twisted, unrecognizable deformity. Thomas aimed the flashlight at the water.

"Where did you see the body, Mr. Witherspoon?"

Witherspoon hacked into his hand and stumbled over a clump of grass. Lambert caught the man before he went head over heels into the rushing current.

"Was fishing off the shore when a guy floated past. Christ, I never seen nothing like it." With Lambert's aid, Witherspoon waddled down to the bank, where he caught his breath and pointed toward a clump of leaves and debris. A tree had toppled into the river, forming a dam. "He's right there."

Thomas followed Witherspoon's finger. The light picked out

the dam. And something else. A leg clothed in black pants bobbed out of the water like a madman's buoy.

"Goddamn kids come down here to drink. One falls in every few years. You can't fix stupid."

Witherspoon spat.

"I don't think that's a kid," Lambert said, stepping closer to the bank.

A shiver rolled through Thomas. With Lonnie McKinney, Scott Rehbein, and Deputy Aguilar missing, the last thing he wanted to find was a dead body.

Lambert glanced over his shoulder.

"I'll run back to the cruiser for ropes and my hip waders."

"Unnecessary," Thomas said, peeling off his jacket.

"Sheriff, you can't gauge how fast the water is moving at night."

"I'll make it. Take Mr. Witherspoon back to his vehicle and get the FBI agents down here."

Before Lambert could protest, Thomas dropped into the river. The water rushed thigh-deep around him, tugging, twisting, trying to knock him off balance. He took measured steps through the water, staying as close to the bank as the debris allowed until he approached the dam.

The river ramped over the tree in a continuous gushing roar. He could see more of the figure now. It wasn't a kid, like Witherspoon assumed. This was a full-grown adult, judging by the size of the black shoe jutting out of the water. Thomas's face slicked with mist as he reached the body. Lambert's flashlight fell over the dam, and Thomas held up a thumb to confirm he'd reached the corpse without incident.

As he fought to dislodge the dead man from the debris, sirens and whirling lights appeared up the hill. The state police had arrived, along with Claire Brookins and the county medical examiner, Virgil Harbough. Trooper Fitzgerald dropped into the water beside Thomas.

"He's stuck beneath a branch!" Thomas shouted over the rushing water.

Fitzgerald nodded and helped Thomas free the body from the debris. The corpse turned over and floated atop the current. Dead eyes stared up at Thomas.

"That's Father Fowler," Thomas said, too stunned to react.

"The priest from St. Mary's?"

With Trooper Fitzgerald's help, he dragged the corpse ashore and knelt along the bank, exhausted and dripping wet.

"We've got another one for you, Virgil," Thomas said as the medical examiner eased down the slope beside Claire.

Virgil took one look at the dead man's face and blanched.

"Is that—"

"It's Fowler. And I don't think he drowned."

"This is bad business, Sheriff. Someone brutalizes a man of God and throws him in the river. What next?"

Virgil shook his head and examined Fowler's body.

With the flashlights aimed at the priest, the beams picked out Fowler's blood-soaked shirt and battered face. Virgil assessed the wounds as Claire snapped pictures. Behind them, Agents Bell and Gardy arrived in their SUV. Bell was the first down the slope.

"What do we have, Sheriff?"

"Father Josiah Fowler. His visitor returned to St. Mary's for one last confession."

Bell knelt beside Thomas and ran her gaze over the bruises.

"Multiple stab wounds plus blows to the priest's face. This was an act of rage. Are you certain there have been no scandals inside the church?"

"None that I could dig up."

"That doesn't mean they don't exist."

Gardy stood back to give Virgil and Claire room. He folded his arms.

"Fowler refused to discuss the confession, but the killer murdered him anyway." Gardy glanced at Bell. "Forget about escalation. The unsub is going over the edge. Multiple abductions, and now a brutal attack on a man from his past."

Thomas stood.

"What does that mean for Deputy Aguilar?"

"It means we need to find this guy. Quick."

"Lambert," Thomas said, calling his deputy over.

"Yeah, Sheriff?"

"Send the forensics team back to St. Mary's, and canvas the hell out of that neighborhood. Someone had to see something. The unsub stabbed and beat Fowler to death."

Lambert hustled back to his cruiser. When Thomas turned, he found Agent Bell glaring at him with those interrogating blue eyes.

"Fowler's past is the key to finding our unsub, Sheriff."

"You still believe the molestation theory."

"It fits. Our killer attended St. Mary's church as a child. If I'm correct, the abuse occurred twenty to thirty years ago."

"That's not a lot to go on."

"In order for the abuse to occur, Father Fowler must have had time alone with the boy. An altar boy, perhaps. A kid who attended church school."

"I doubt the church keeps records of who attended Sunday classes."

"Be creative," Gardy said. "Communion and confirmation photos, class pictures. People keep those pictures for lifetimes."

Bell bobbed her head in agreement.

"It will take time to track down old photos," Thomas said. "I'll get started."

"Find them quickly," said Bell. "Now that the unsub murdered Fowler, there's no telling who he'll attack next."

43

The basement door stood open.

Aguilar was thankful. The stench inside the cells —a stew of musty earth, blood, rotting flesh, and excrement—brought tears to her eyes. With the door open, she could breathe again.

And she could see. The gray light allowed her to mark the loose bars with a tiny rock she'd scraped out of the soil. Two bars on the left side of her enclosure wiggled when she shook them. She was strong, but she couldn't bend iron. She needed to find how far the bars sank into the earth. The bars probably ended in the pits of hell, Aguilar thought. She knelt beside the cage and cleared the soil away.

"Lonnie, find me a rock. Something large and sharp enough to dig with."

The boy didn't move. He slumped in the corner, his head hanging between his knees.

"Lonnie."

The child's head snapped up. He looked around the enclosure, confused where he was until the awful reality returned to him.

"Like a shovel?"

"Yes, a rock I can use as a shovel."

He sagged his shoulders and wandered to the rear of the cage. The boy had spent most of yesterday vomiting into a bucket. Thankfully, their kidnapper removed the waste during his last visit. Lonnie's color still worried Aguilar. His energy levels seemed a tad higher. But it was obvious the kidnapper had poisoned the boy.

Aguilar's eyes flicked to the door. The creep last visited the cells several hours ago. No telling when he'd return. As Aguilar jiggled the loose bars, Lonnie sifted through the dirt.

"Something like this?"

Aguilar turned. A palm-sized rock stuck out of the wall at the rear of Lonnie's cell.

"That's perfect. Can you pull it out of the wall and toss it to me?"

Lonnie clawed at the dirt until the rock loosened. Holding the stone in the palm of his hands, he walked it to the side of the cage.

"Ready?"

"Ready. Toss it here."

Lonnie heaved the rock. It clanked off the bar inside the dead college student's cell and fell to the ground.

"Sorry."

"No worries. I can reach it."

Aguilar lay on her side and stretched her arm inside the neighboring cell. The rock taunted her, a fraction of an inch beyond her fingertips. As she wiggled her body closer to the bars, she looked straight into Scott's dead, milky eyes. A beetle skittered across Scott's lips. She blinked and glanced away. Straining, she pressed her body against the bars. The iron chilled her flesh as the rough edges bit into her skin. She let out a gasp when her hand closed over the rock.

The size was perfect, and the sharp edge made the rock an efficient tool for digging. It would also serve as a weapon. The creep hadn't thought of everything, not that it was possible to remove every rock from the underground enclosures.

Aguilar dug into the soil and pushed the dirt into a pile. After the hole was two inches deep, she grasped the loose bars and gave them another tug. No change. Working harder, she scraped at the soil until the sweat poured off her body and matted her hair against her face. Salty perspiration stung her eyes.

She was getting somewhere. The hole was six inches deep, the mound piling higher. She tested the bars. A little more wiggle. Keep digging. Don't stop.

The groan of the cellar steps warned her to stop digging and toss the rock toward the back of the cage. She leveled the soil over the hole. Smoothed it over. Aguilar held her breath as a shadow cut across the threshold.

The creep leaned in the doorway. He appeared different now. Not smug and amused by his captives. Fury swam in his blood-shot eyes.

"What are you doing?"

Aguilar lifted her chin.

"Nothing."

"Don't lie to me. I punish liars."

She lifted her palms and gave him an exasperated look.

"Lonnie is sick because of the food you gave him. I'm making sure he's all right."

"You're up to something, deputy. I see the deception in your eyes." He walked to her cage and curled his hands around the bars. There was a bruise over his left eye. "I didn't poison the child. I'm his father, and it's my obligation to keep him safe."

"By locking him up and leaving the lights off?"

"Would you prefer I kept the lights on while I was away? So you can go back to doing whatever it was you were doing before I arrived?" He jiggled the bars. Aguilar cringed, hoping he wouldn't test the bar she'd loosened. "You're wasting your time. These bars run deep into the earth. No matter how hard you tug, you won't dislodge them. Accept your new home. You'll be here for a long time."

"If you care so much about Lonnie, unlock his cell and drive him to the hospital. He needs a doctor."

The kidnapper swung his gaze to the boy's cage.

"Is that true, Lonnie? Do you wish to leave as Scott did?"

Lonnie wrapped his arms around his chest and shook his head.

"No, sir."

"No, Father, Lonnie. Say it."

"No, Father."

The creep grinned and turned to Aguilar.

"See? That wasn't so hard, was it? The boy obeys, as will you." He leered at her. His tongue touched his lips. "Perhaps you need convincing."

"What happened to your face?"

He touched his forehead. Aguilar spotted another bruise on his arm and a welt on his temple. Good. Maybe he attacked someone, and the victim fought him off.

"It's not your concern."

The creep paced along the cage. His eyes fixed on the smoothed over soil beneath the weakened bars. When Aguilar was sure the man had figured out her escape plan, he swiveled on his heels and placed his hands behind his back.

"I will bring the child medicine for his stomach. And fresh water. Happy?"

"And if he's still sick?"

"He'll be fine, deputy. You worry too much."

He departed through the open door and closed it behind him. Absolute darkness filled the cell.

But the dark wouldn't prevent Aguilar from finding the stone and digging her way out of the cage.

44

At two in the morning, the moon vanished behind the hill and plunged the state park into a deeper darkness. Darren's body hummed with adrenaline. He paced the grounds, his gun and radio at his hip. Darren didn't expect the man who attacked LeVar, potentially the psycho the FBI pursued, to follow them to the state park. The Poplar Corners ghost fled after LeVar fought back. Knowing how tough the former gang member was, Darren suspected LeVar injured his foe. The ghost was probably holed up and nursing his wounds.

LeVar hadn't required stitches. A bandage over his brow stopped the bleeding. He'd wear a goose egg on his forehead for a few days, but the teenager showed no signs of a concussion.

What if LeVar had arrived too late? The ghost tried to attack Scout, Naomi, and Serena. A chill rippled through Darren's body when he pictured Raven alone in the park with that maniac creeping through the night. Too close for comfort.

Darren rounded the cabin where Scout and Naomi slept. The lights were off, one window open a crack to invite cool air inside. His sneakers swished through the grass as he confirmed they'd locked the door. Serena and LeVar's cabin stood silent against the night, though Darren suspected LeVar was awake.

At the edge of the campgrounds, Darren leaned against a tree and blended with the night. Now and then, branches snapped and dry leaves rustled inside the forest.

His phone lit up. He'd kept the ringer on silent so he wouldn't disturb the others. Reading Thomas's name on the screen, Darren answered.

"Everyone safe up there?"

Darren glanced at the cabins.

"Safe and secure."

"Keep your eyes peeled. Our killer was active tonight."

"Now what?"

"We fished Josiah Fowler out of the Nightshade River."

"Father Fowler?"

"He's dead, Darren. The killer stabbed him in the chest and stomach and beat the hell out of Fowler's face. Whoever this guy is, he's out of control."

A twig snapped behind Darren. He reached for his gun before a raccoon scampered across the trail.

"Thomas, someone attacked LeVar in Poplar Corners tonight."

"Is he okay? What happened?"

"A few bumps and bruises, but he's fine. I'm convinced it was the Poplar Corners ghost."

"Can LeVar identify him?"

"It was too dark, and the guy jumped LeVar from behind. But Scout flew the drone over the meadow and caught the ghost moving through the forest."

Thomas drew in a breath.

"That's the break we need. I want that footage, Darren. Can you send it to me?"

"I downloaded the video files after we returned. I'll send

them to your email. There's something strange about the footage, though."

"What's that?"

"The drone tracked him through the meadow and into a thicket. A second later, the guy disappeared. I thought the video glitched, or we lost several seconds of footage. But we captured a continuous stream until the drone landed."

"Maybe he ran out of the trees and ducked inside a garage. You're certain he emerged from the thicket?"

"Positive."

Darren recognized Agent Gardy's voice in the background.

"All right, Darren. Send me the files, and I'll have the Harmon lab enhance the video."

"I'll send them now. Call me if anything changes."

Darren crossed the clearing and unlocked his cabin. In the bed, Raven curled under the covers, her even breathing like gentle waves. He kept one eye on the window as he set the laptop on the kitchen table. After he emailed the footage to Thomas, he filled his mug with coffee, checked his weapon, and stepped into the night.

Nobody was getting past Darren. He'd die before someone harmed his friends.

45

Mrs. Langstaff nervously adjusted her shawl. Thomas worried about the elderly woman. She leaned on a cane as she brushed a tissue across her eyes inside the St. Mary's church vestibule. Mrs. Langstaff had been with the church for as long as Thomas could remember. Until recently, she'd seemed ageless. Now every movement made her wince, and her face appeared skeletal in the half light.

"Are you certain it was Father Fowler? He was inside his office when I left at eight o'clock. What was he doing at the river?"

Thomas caught the woman when she stumbled.

"Why don't we sit down, Mrs. Langstaff?"

She sniffled and glanced around, as if confused where she was. Thomas led her to a padded bench beside the entry doors. Her cane clicked against the floor and rang hollow against the vaulted ceilings.

"Did Father Fowler expect a visitor last evening?"

"No, nobody visits that late."

"Did you notice anyone outside when you left? A vehicle beside the curb, perhaps?"

"Nobody."

Thomas sighed. He'd expected as much. As he questioned Langstaff, Thomas glanced through the open doors. Deputy Lambert conferred with Agents Bell and Gardy outside the rectory. Lambert had cordoned off the walkway with police tape after discovering blood on the concrete.

"I remember you from when I was a boy. How long have you been with St. Mary's, Mrs. Langstaff?"

"For three of your lifetimes, Sheriff."

"So you were here when Father Fowler first arrived."

"Oh, yes. I've seen my share of priests come and go. There was Father Magdalen when I was young. That was a long, long time ago. But Father Fowler was special." She cried into her tissue. "I can't believe he's gone. Who would do such a thing?"

Thomas waited until Langstaff composed herself. A question poised on the tip of his tongue. Did anyone suspect Fowler of sexual abuse? Langstaff's love for Fowler convinced Thomas she'd never accept such a rumor.

"It's possible Father Fowler knew the man who attacked him. We think the murderer attended St. Mary's when he was young."

Langstaff placed a hand over her mouth.

"No, that can't be."

"I'm interested in communion classes from two and three decades ago. Does the church keep photographs that far back?"

"Yes, they're kept inside the rectory."

"Would you show me?"

The elderly woman gave Thomas a worried look before she nodded. He helped her down the steps and walked beside her to the rectory. Her hands trembled, making it difficult to fit the key into the lock. Inside the rectory, Langstaff hobbled to a bookcase and removed a white photo album adorned with a gold cross. Someone had placed the communion photos in chronological order with the dates written on the back.

Thomas flipped through the photos as Langstaff fretted, worried he'd crumple the well-kept pictures. He paged back two decades and removed ten years of photographs. The name of each child was handwritten on the back, the names painstakingly arranged in order. In each picture, the children in front sat cross-legged with their hands pressed together in prayer. The taller children stood in back.

"May I borrow the photographs?"

"It would be better if I made copies."

"Please. I promise I'll keep them safe and return them in a few days. I wouldn't ask unless it was important."

She gave him a reluctant nod, and he tucked the folder of communion photos beneath his arm.

Agent Gardy waited outside the rectory when Thomas emerged from inside.

"As Agent Bell requested," Thomas said, handing the folder to Gardy.

The FBI agent sifted through the images.

"These are perfect. Bell is sure our killer is in one of these pictures."

"There must be twenty kids in each. Over a decade, that's two-hundred names."

"Remove the females," Gardy said. "That gets us down to a hundred."

"Still too many," Thomas said. "I've got three kidnapping victims to locate, and I'm running out of time."

Thomas peered over his shoulder. Old Mrs. Langstaff leaned in the rectory doorway, watching them. The woman's faith was strong. She loved her church, and she only saw good in the parishioners. Thomas thought of his mother, a St. Mary's devotee who'd supported the church, even after the Thea Barlow murders.

It seemed unthinkable that this house of worship produced two serial killers.

46

Through a window cut into the front door, Chelsey watched the blonde-haired FBI agent stride across the parking lot toward Wolf Lake Consulting. She'd held reservations about meeting with the BAU profiler. Scarlett Bell was a household name, a star among people fascinated with darkness and death. But everything Thomas had said about Bell made Chelsey think she'd like the agent. Bell was a rebel, unafraid of angering the higher-ups. And she uncovered truths hidden from the naked eye.

It had been an uneventful morning after last night's murder. The forensics team had picked blonde hair off Father Fowler's shirt, despite the priest bobbing in the water for an hour or more. Yet no one had noticed a vehicle along the river or a man dumping a body into the rapids. Hadn't Harmony Santos told Gerald Burke her stalker had blonde hair?

"Thank you for agreeing to meet with me," Chelsey said, offering her hand. "We met at the sheriff's station. I'm Chelsey Byrd."

"The private investigator, yes. I read the interview notes you shared with Sheriff Shepherd. Excellent work."

Chelsey led Bell down the hallway and into the office.

"Always happy to help, especially when innocent lives are at risk. Did you ever find records for a red Camaro convertible in Poplar Corners?"

"No, but I'm intrigued by the vehicle."

"How so?"

"It fits the killer's profile. Not saying someone who drives a high-end muscle car is a narcissist. But I'd expect a malignant narcissist to flaunt his power with the clothes he wears, the vehicle he drives, the way he carries himself."

Chelsey's partners, Raven and LeVar, were at their desks, splitting attention between the Harmony Santos case and the attack in Poplar Corners. Both believed the cases were related—the Peeping Tom had kidnapped Harmony Santos four years ago. Chelsey made introductions before leading Agent Bell to her desk. Bell pulled up a chair and scanned the wedding photos laid upon Chelsey's desk.

"So you wanted my opinion?"

"It's crazy," Chelsey said, biting a nail as she flipped through the pictures. "Ever since Lawrence Santos dropped off the wedding photos, I've had a creeping sensation that Harmony's kidnapper is in the pictures. But nobody sticks out. What's really weird is I'm most uncomfortable when I look at pictures of Harmony."

Agent Bell's face remained unreadable as Chelsey slid the pictures across the desk.

"And you want a second set of eyes."

"If you'll be so kind."

Bell anchored her hair behind her ear and spread the pictures out. She focused on the men in the photos, shaking her head as she eliminated potential suspects.

"I don't see anyone sneaking peeks at the bride, if that's what you're suggesting."

"Not exactly," Chelsey said, releasing a breath. "The more I study the pictures, the more they creep me out. It's like the killer is staring me in the face, and I can't see him. This must all be in my head."

Bell's eyes slipped from one photo to the next, her nails tapping against the desk. Chelsey worried she was wasting the agent's time. In a moment, Bell would stand and shake her head, confirming Chelsey's imagination had run amok.

Yet she didn't.

Agent Bell stacked several photos together and pushed them aside. Five pictures remained on the desk. They were all closeups of Harmony Santos. The truth hit Chelsey when Bell's gaze swung to her.

"Strange the groom never appears in these pictures," Bell said. Her eyes sharpened. "It's a wedding reception, right? These photographs are all of Harmony Santos. Notice how the lens zooms in, cutting out distractions. Lovingly. Almost obsessively, don't you agree?"

Chelsey palmed her forehead. How had she missed it?

"The photographer."

Before Chelsey confirmed Agent Bell's suspicion, she swiped through her contact list and phoned Lawrence Santos. The phone rang several times. She got his voicemail.

"Hi, Mr. Santos. This is Chelsey Byrd at Wolf Lake Consulting. I had a question about the wedding photos. If you could call me back as soon as possible, I'd appreciate it."

Chelsey didn't wait long. As Bell rearranged Harmony's photographs, Lawrence Santos returned her call.

"Ms. Byrd, I received your message. Sorry, I just stepped out of the shower."

"No worries, Mr. Santos." She blew out a breath. "So I'm going through the wedding photos again."

The tension rose in the husband's voice.

"Did you find Harmony's kidnapper?"

"Not yet. Who was the photographer?"

A few seconds of silence passed.

"That was four years ago. Harmony hired the guy. Hold on. Maybe I have his card."

Chelsey trembled with anxious energy as a desk drawer opened and closed over the phone. Papers rustled before Santos returned.

"I got it. Phil Streeter. He has a studio in Kane Grove. What's this about?"

"Just double-checking a lead. Thank you, Mr. Santos. I'll get back to you soon."

"Phil Streeter," Bell repeated, rolling her chair to Chelsey's side of the desk as Chelsey typed on her keyboard.

The website loaded.

"I found him. Phil Streeter, wedding and portrait photographer. Artistic, documentary, and modern photography."

"Is his picture on the website?"

"I'm looking." Chelsey ran her eyes over the screen until she found Streeter's bio. "Here it is."

She clicked his profile. A dark-haired man in his forties smiled amiably.

"He's not blonde."

"But he took those closeups of Harmony."

Bell clicked her tongue.

"Most wedding photographers have a partner."

"Good point."

Chelsey dialed Streeter's number and held up a finger as the phone rang.

"Streeter Photography," the man answered.

"Good morning, sir. Are you Phil Streeter?"

"Yes, I am. Are you interested in hiring my studio?"

"Actually, I'm a private investigator in Wolf Lake."

Streeter gave a lighthearted chuckle.

"So you're a female James Rockford. Am I in trouble?"

"I'm investigating a woman's disappearance from four years ago. Harmony Santos. My records show you photographed her wedding. Do you remember the Santos wedding?"

"I remember all my clients. But that wedding sticks out."

"Why?"

"The news. I couldn't believe it when I saw that poor woman's picture on television."

"You were around Lawrence and Harmony all afternoon. Do you recall anyone causing trouble, someone paying close attention to Harmony?"

"If I had, I would have told the authorities. Nothing like that happened. The Santos wedding was wonderful. The family enjoyed the reception, and they treated me like an old friend. I pray nothing bad happened to Mrs. Santos."

"Do you have a partner, Mr. Streeter?"

"Not at the moment. It's difficult holding on to talented photographers. After I teach them the trade, they all want to open their own studios."

"Did you employ a second photographer for the Santos wedding?"

"Absolutely not. I'm the sole photographer for weddings."

Chelsey pressed her lips together. She'd run into another dead end.

"So you didn't have a partner four years ago."

"I did, but he's not with the studio any longer. Thank goodness."

"Who was your partner, if you don't mind me asking?"

"Heck, no. I don't mind. A pretentious fellow by the name of Justice Thorin. He's a bigwig with a local university."

"Kane Grove?"

"Yes, how did you know?"

Chelsey snapped her fingers and gave Agent Bell a thumbs-up.

"So Justice Thorin worked for you?"

"Mostly post-production. I'll give the devil his due. He's a master with Lightroom and Photoshop. I photograph clients, but Thorin made the pictures shine. I never understood how he did it. A splash of color enhancement here, a contrast adjustment there. The man has an eye for image editing."

"Why did you let him go?"

Streeter groaned.

"Justice Thorin is a conceited prick. And a perfectionist. In his opinion, the photographs were never good enough. He upset a client on the phone, so I told him he needed to go. A shame. He really is talented."

After thanking Streeter for his help, Chelsey turned to Agent Bell.

"Thorin did post-production for the Santos wedding."

"Imagine the hours Thorin spent alone and hunched over a computer, staring at Harmony."

"So those closeups of Harmony, the ones that never included Lawrence Santos . . ."

Agent Bell nodded.

"Thorin cropped everyone out of the picture except the woman he obsessed over."

"And then he took her."

47

"It feels right," Thomas said, thinking aloud. "And he lives in Poplar Corners."

Agent Neil Gardy sat across from the sheriff's desk, one ankle propped on his knee, his fist pressed against his mouth. Chelsey and Agent Bell had called about Justice Thorin, Phil Streeter's former assistant.

"The same town Harmony Santos disappeared from," Gardy said. "And he's a professor at Kane Grove, where a stranger with blonde hair stalked Santos."

"Justice Thorin's staff photo shows he has blonde hair. What are the odds we'll match his hair to those found on the victim?"

"Pretty good. But we'll need a stronger case before a judge gives us a warrant. Didn't you say there were no red Camaro convertibles registered in Poplar Corners?"

"Right." Thomas typed at his keyboard and checked Justice Thorin's vehicle registration. "My records say he drives a blue Tesla." He called up Thorin's history and clapped his hands together. "But he owned a Camaro four years ago."

"So he gets rid of the Camaro and buys another high-end vehicle to impress people."

"Agent Bell described him as a narcissist. This must be our guy, Gardy."

"The coincidences are starting to add up. We need to tie him to the other murders. He's a distinguished professor with awards listed on his bio. Ten bucks says he travels a lot."

"Ten whole dollars? Don't break your bank account, Gardy. I'll call the university."

Gardy stepped out of the room to place a call while Thomas waited for someone in the fine arts department at Kane Grove University to answer. After a long wait, a woman picked up. She sounded rushed and out of breath.

"Kane Grove University, fine arts department. This is Professor Felicia Armstrong. How may I help you?"

"Yes, this is Thomas Shepherd with the Nightshade County Sheriff's Department. I'm looking for a professor named Justice Thorin."

A pause.

"Professor Thorin didn't come in today."

"Is today his day off?"

"No. He missed three classes, and he's supposed to administer final exams in two days. I just covered his image editing class. Did something happen to Professor Thorin?"

"I need to speak with him." Thomas glanced at the notes on his desk. Agent Gardy had listed the abductions and murders in the Great Lakes, Mid-Atlantic, and New England he'd tied to the unsub over the last eight years. "Tell me something. Does Professor Thorin teach at other universities, perhaps as an adjunct professor?"

Armstrong scoffed.

"Doesn't he wish?"

"I don't follow."

"Professor Thorin . . . never mind."

"Please, tell me what you were going to say."

"I don't like to speak ill of others. But why not? He screwed me today by sticking me with his classes. Professor Thorin has a bit of an ego. He only teaches at Kane Grove, but he's a frequent speaker at universities around the northeast. He volunteers to speak. It's not like every institution in the northeast clamors for him. He'd spend every day on the road if Kane Grove let him."

"I noticed he won his share of awards."

"The man has talent. I'll give him that. Professor Thorin isn't considered a big deal nationally. But if you speak at universities ten, fifteen times per year, people believe you are."

Agent Gardy returned to the room. Thomas held up a hand.

"Mrs. Armstrong, I'm putting you on speaker. I'm here with Agent Neil Gardy with the Federal Bureau of Investigation."

"Did you say the FBI? What's going on?"

Without answering Armstrong's question, Gardy read her a list of dates from the last eight years which matched disappearances and murders tied to the unsub.

"Can you tell me if Professor Thorin traveled on these days?"

"I'll try. We have a Google-based staff calendar that goes back several years. What's the first date again?"

Gardy read it back to her.

Armstrong muttered to herself.

"Sorry. Our internet is slow today. Hold on." After a moment, Armstrong said, "Yes, Professor Thorin spoke at Bates University that Friday."

Gardy nodded at Thomas. They had a match.

"Let's try another day. How about four years ago on May the fourth?"

Armstrong confirmed the date as she typed.

"Wow. Professor Thorin spoke at Western University that evening. How did you know he traveled on that date? Is he in some kind of trouble?"

Gardy and Thomas shared a glance. They had their man.

Gardy read Armstrong the rest of the dates. Every murder lined up with Thorin's travels.

"Professor Armstrong," Thomas said. "If Thorin returns to the university today, or you hear from him, call me immediately."

Armstrong's voice quivered. She sensed something was horribly wrong.

"I will. Sheriff, should I phone campus security? Am I in danger?"

"You're not in danger. But you need to stay away from Thorin if he returns to the school. We'll call campus security."

After Armstrong hung up, Thomas opened his desk drawer and removed a folder. Intensity blazed in his eyes as he divided the stack of communion photographs and handed half to Gardy. They scanned the names written on the backs of the pictures. Thomas couldn't find Thorin. With a frustrated huff, he started over, certain he'd missed the unsub. It was Gardy who found him first.

"Bingo. Justice Thorin from twenty-eight years ago."

Gardy flipped the picture over and jabbed his finger at a boy in the back row. Thomas held his breath. He expected to find a monster, a psycho with crazed eyes, or a devil with horns protruding from his head. Instead, he stared at a blue-eyed child, who seemed the epitome of the good old American boy. Except for the wary fear tingling through his eyes. While the others smiled at the camera, Thorin stared out of the corner of his eye.

At Father Fowler.

48

The creep left the cellar door open again. Just a crack. Enough to spill dim light into the cells.

Aguilar's muscles screamed. Her body dripped with sweat, the dirt and grime coating her flesh like a second skin. Beside her, the mound of excavated dirt grew taller. Every time she needed a break, she smoothed the soil into the corner of her cage. The slope became obvious despite her efforts to level the soil. And there was no hiding the gaping maw in the ground beneath the two loose bars. She'd clawed away three feet of earth. How deep did the damn bars go? With her arms exhausted, she shoved her shoulder against the cage. The bars shifted three inches.

She was almost out.

Lonnie shivered on his side. His skin had paled since the last time their kidnapper visited, the child's face cadaverous and sallow.

"Wake up, Lonnie. Sit up and look at me."

The boy didn't reply. Terror skittered on spider legs across Aguilar's skin. Was the boy dead?

Neither Lonnie nor Aguilar had eaten in the last twenty-four hours. Maybe longer, as the concept of time didn't apply underground. She needed food. Energy. Something to replenish her lost strength.

Breathless, Aguilar grasped the bars and hung against the cage.

"We're almost out. Hang on a little longer. Please."

The boy moaned and shielded his eyes from the light shaft. At least he was alive.

Though conserving strength was a priority, it was crucial to give the boy hope. Aguilar rattled the bars, pulling clumps of soil out of the ceiling. His eyes widened.

"See what I mean? Another ten minutes, and I'll break us out of here."

Lonnie shook his head.

"He'll kill you."

"He'll kill me if I don't get us out of here. Stay awake. The second I break through the cage . . ."

Then what? It occurred to her she had no way of breaking Lonnie out. Without the key, it would take Aguilar hours to dig under Lonnie's cell.

There was no choice. She'd wait for the creep to return and attack him, then steal the keys and unlock Lonnie's cell.

The boy slumped against the cage. His eyelids fluttered.

"Please, Lonnie. Stay awake."

He gave her a fatigued, bone-weary smile that tore her heart in half. The kidnapper visited every several hours. He was due to return. When he did, he'd spot the hole the second he entered the enclosure.

An idea came to her. The psycho had left water bottles in each cage. She hadn't touched her bottle, suspicious of its contents. Lonnie's bottle lay in the corner. Aguilar needed the creep to believe Lonnie was moments from dying. The boy already appeared on death's edge. It wouldn't take much convincing.

"When he returns, you need to distract him."

The boy gave her a blank look.

"I mean fool him. Drink from the water bottle, but don't swallow. Hold it in your mouth. Do you understand?"

Lonnie nodded.

"When he's outside the cage, spit the water and pretend you're throwing up. Can you do that?"

"I think so."

She searched the cage for some way to hide the hole she'd excavated. No choice. She'd feign sleep and lie across the hole when the creep returned. Which could be any second now.

Aguilar grabbed the rock and scraped another inch out of the ground. She'd lost two fingernails. Blood dripped down her blistered, callused hands. Ignoring the pain, she tore through the earth and tossed the soil into Scott's enclosure. Bits of dirt and sediment covered his face.

Her arms trembled. She was in no condition to break through the cage, let alone fight for their lives. In the gym, she pushed herself past preconceived limits. If she'd squatted two-hundred pounds during her last workout, she added another five pounds this time, or push through an extra set. In doing so, she overcame the impossible and broke personal records. But today was different. She'd never encountered exhaustion this crippling. And she'd never tested her limits after a day of fasting.

Aguilar tossed another inch of earth into the neighboring cage. She should have spread the dirt across her cell, so it wasn't obvious. Too late for that now. Another scrape of rock against soil. Blood slicked her hands. Her heart wanted to leap through her throat.

When her endurance betrayed her, she slumped against the cell and wept, certain she'd never break through the cage.

The bars shifted. She caught her breath and opened her eyes.

The two loose bars hung ajar. If she had time to recover her strength, Aguilar felt sure she could shoulder her way through the opening. But she was too tired.

The way out lay before her. Mocking. An ironic grin dimpled her cheeks. She wasn't sure if she should laugh or cry.

One glance at Lonnie got her moving again. The boy hung against the cage, face squashed between the bars, gaze fixed on her. There was hope in his eyes.

Aguilar dragged herself to her feet and shoved against the cage. Straining. Sweat pouring down her brow and stinging her eyes. The bars shifted outward. Not far enough for her to squeeze through.

She rested for a moment and tried again. Failed. She wasn't strong enough.

Her eyes flicked to Lonnie a second before a stair creaked inside the cellar. He was coming.

"Hurry!"

Aguilar nodded at the boy and pushed harder. The bars refused to bend.

The kidnapper's shadow preceded him, the black outline of his head drawn against the soil outside the basement door.

"Remember what to do," Aguilar said, staring at the boy.

Lonnie dropped to the ground and twisted the cap off the water bottle. Aguilar fell over the hole and lay flat on her back, her eyes open to slits as the creep entered the enclosure.

The kidnapper glanced from Aguilar to the boy. The sanctimonious smile vanished when his eyes landed on the child. Lonnie retched and spilled the water out of his mouth. Perfect timing.

Alarmed, the creep ran to Lonnie's cell. When he looked back at Aguilar, she closed her eyes and pretended she was unconscious. Aguilar's body felt like rubber. Her heart pumped at a disturbing rate as she struggled to control her breathing. Just a little longer. Another few seconds to summon what remained of her energy.

"Lonnie, where do you hurt?"

The boy pointed at his belly. Jamming his hand into his pocket, the creep glanced at Aguilar with indecision. He'd refused to take Lonnie to a doctor. Was he worried the boy would die on his own? The creep would lose power over life and death if fate stole Lonnie first. Or did he care for the boy?

"I have medicine upstairs. Wait here while I—"

Lonnie moaned and spit out more water. He'd held some back, Aguilar thought with wonder. Smart boy.

The creep turned his back on Aguilar and knelt before Lonnie's cage.

Then he removed the key from his pocket.

The moment the kidnapper worked the key into the lock, Aguilar opened her eyes. She sat up, moving with cat-light silence as the man swore beneath his breath. The lock rattled. He swore again as the mechanism jammed.

A black, furious shadow grew against the kidnapper's back as Aguilar rose to her feet. It seemed to Aguilar he should have sensed her behind him, as one might sense the tracks rattling between his feet before the train arrives. Her back crackled and popped as she straightened. He didn't notice.

She grasped the bars and gritted her teeth. Placed one leg in front of her and leaned forward, her muscular body at a thirty-degree angle to the enclosure.

The creep jiggled the key. The lock refused to open as Lonnie pretended to vomit again. In frustration, the psycho shoved the keys into his pocket and turned. His eyes widened in shock.

Aguilar bellowed and threw her body against the cell. The bars burst forth, and she tumbled out of the enclosure with a mask of rage drawn against her face.

The kidnapper threw up his hands as Aguilar barreled into him.

49

"Justice Thorin. Six Aurora Road in Poplar Corners, NY," Thomas repeated over the radio.

His foot pushed down on the gas pedal, and the cruiser shot down the interstate with Agent Gardy beside him. Bell watched Thomas through the mirror, again reminding him of his psychologist, Dr. Mandal.

Lambert's voice came over the radio.

"Read you loud and clear, Lambert," Thomas said.

"Sheriff, the results came back from forensics."

"That was fast. What did we learn?"

"Get this. Forensics matched the hair fibers on Fowler to hairs from the confession booth."

"We figured that. So it's the same guy."

"There's more. They also pulled a hair out of the wooden box the unsub left inside the booth."

"And?"

"It doesn't match the others. But Lawrence Santos gave Harmony's hairbrush to the department after she went missing. It's a positive match. The unidentified hair from the box belongs to Harmony Santos."

Thomas's stomach turned over. The evidence suggested the severed hand belonged to Harmony Santos. Had the unsub held Harmony captive for four years?

"Where are you now, Lambert?"

"Leaving the station. New York State troopers are en route to Poplar Corners. I'm ten minutes behind you."

"Meet us on the access road. That's the best way to approach Thorin's house without him seeing us."

As they raced toward the town, Gardy studied a digital map of the terrain.

"Six Aurora Road is near that meadow. The one the Peeping Tom disappeared in." He turned the laptop so Bell could see. "How did he get from the thicket to his house without the camera catching him?"

Bell scrunched her brow.

"Hand me the laptop. Sheriff, is the drone footage on this computer?"

Thomas met her gaze in the mirror.

"It is. Check the video directory. Why?"

"We're missing something important. Hold on."

One more exit until they reached Poplar Corners. Thomas clutched the steering wheel and pushed the cruiser faster. Gardy stared into the fading daylight. They both knew how the day would end. Thomas only hoped Thorin had spared his victims.

They were halfway to their destination when Bell inhaled.

"Remember when your friends said the ghost disappeared in the meadow?"

"Yeah. Did the video glitch?"

"He didn't disappear. He descended."

"What?"

"I'm watching the video frame by frame. He appears to drop into a hole. Then there's a flash of light, as if the moon reflected off a metal object."

"Like the hinge on a trapdoor?"

"That's what I'm thinking."

Bell handed the laptop back to her partner. Gardy replayed the video in slow motion.

"I'll be damned. There's a hidden entrance to an underground enclosure."

Thomas took the exit and said, "That explains how he disappears before anyone can catch him."

Gardy nodded.

"And it gives us another entrance into his house. It's possible he keeps his captives underground."

Thomas glanced at Bell. If anyone understood the psycho's motivations, it was the BAU profiler.

"Why does he keep them underground?"

"Besides the obvious reason—no one will hear the screams —concealing them underground dehumanizes his captives and feeds his God complex. He's master of his domain, and he can work in total secrecy. Imagine the time and effort it took to build a subterranean enclosure. This is his masterpiece and his refuge. I expect we'll find cages, some method of containing his victims. I also believe the enclosure is attached to the house with an entrance through the basement. This allows the unsub to visit his captives anytime he desires. And the enclosure gives him an escape route into his home, in case someone catches him peeking through windows."

A cold shiver rolled through Thomas.

"Did he hold Harmony Santos for four years?"

"Underground? Doubtful. My guess is he brought her inside the house, fed her, cleaned her up. Perhaps he chained her so she couldn't escape. I can't imagine a civilian surviving four years underground. If I had to guess, Thorin only spares captives who meet his desires and submit to his will. The others, he murders."

Trooper Fitzgerald awaited Thomas and the agents on the access road. It was a quarter-mile walk through the meadow to reach Justice Thorin's property. Two more state trooper cruisers pulled along the roadside as Thomas climbed out of his vehicle. After conferring with Gardy over the digital map, the other troopers drove across Poplar Corners to cut Thorin off if he attempted to escape.

Deputy Lambert arrived and hurried to the group. Determination narrowed his eyes. Though Aguilar and Lambert ribbed each other, they'd become close friends over the years. Lambert would walk through fire to save Aguilar, and she would do the same for him.

"You believe he's hiding Deputy Aguilar underground?" Fitzgerald asked, adjusting his hat.

Clouds smothered the moon and stars, throwing the meadow into deep darkness.

"Along with Lonnie McKinney and Scott Rehbein," Bell said. "It's your call, Sheriff. How do you wish to do this?"

Thomas studied the map and pointed at the property.

"Deputy Lambert and I will enter the enclosure through the trapdoor. Lambert, grab the bolt cutters out of my trunk. I assume Thorin keeps a padlock on the door."

Lambert nodded and ran to the cruiser.

"The rest of you, split up. Agents Gardy and Bell, take the front door. Fitzgerald, go in through the back. We'll coordinate by radio and enter at the same time. No mistakes. Strike him fast. Don't give him time to react."

Lambert returned with the bolt cutters. Thomas held their eyes.

"Ready?"

They were.

Gardy and Bell drove the sheriff's cruiser to Thorin's house while Thomas and Lambert entered the meadow. The weeds grew past their chests. When the wind blew, the grass and weeds danced like decrepit scarecrows. Except for the occasional light in the distance, Thomas saw nothing except the overgrowth in front of them. The meadow seemed to isolate and trap him.

"Thorin keeps them alive for seven days, right?" Lambert asked, pushing a milkweed stalk aside.

"If Agent Bell's theory holds up, Thorin held Harmony Santos captive for four years. Don't worry. Aguilar is alive."

"What about the child?"

"Stay positive. We have to believe the captives are alive and unharmed."

"If he hurt Aguilar, I swear I'll . . ."

Lambert bit off the rest of his statement. The deputy grit his teeth, eyes intense.

"I feel the same way. Maintain your composure, deputy. We only have one shot to get this right."

50

Aguilar tasted blood on her lips. Not all of it was hers.

The creep staggered, his nose broken and askew. But he wouldn't stop. No matter how many times Aguilar bashed him with punches and kicks, the kidnapper kept coming. It was as if demons drove the man.

He lashed out with a wild swing. Aguilar ducked and slammed a fist into his ribcage. The creep buckled and stumbled against the wall while dirt rained down on their heads. For a moment, Aguilar pictured the enclosure caving in on them, burying them for eternity.

The psycho still had the keys in his pocket. Without them, Aguilar had no hope of breaking Lonnie out of the cell. She lunged and drove her shoulder into his stomach, lifting the man off his feet. His back struck the wall. He cried out and swung with his elbow. The point clipped Aguilar's temple and dizzied her. The cells rotated. Before she shook off the vertigo, he screamed and barreled into her.

Aguilar landed on her back with the creep on top. His hands wrapped around her throat and squeezed. Behind them, Lonnie cried inside the cell and begged the man not to hurt Aguilar. This couldn't happen. She refused to fail the boy.

But the man was stronger than she'd expected. As he straddled her stomach, she pried at his hands, unable to move him. Insanity and victory colored his bloodshot eyes. His face was a gory, disfigured mask. But he was relentless, too powerful for Aguilar.

She bridged and fought to unseat him. He removed one hand from her throat. As she gasped for air, he struck her jaw. Blood spilled from her mouth.

The hand returned to her neck. He strangled Aguilar, squeezing with inhuman strength. The gray light dimmed. Lonnie's voice drifted away as her legs writhed across the soil.

"You dare to challenge me?" the monster yelled. He turned his head toward the child. "This is what happens when someone disobeys. Watch me kill her, Lonnie."

Aguilar drove her elbows against his locked arms and broke the stranglehold. She sucked air into her lungs, desperate to breathe, desperate to survive. The creep yanked her head up by the hair and rained blows down on her face. The fists flew at Aguilar in a blur.

She'd almost lost consciousness when he stood over her—one hand still clutching her by the hair—and dragged her to Lonnie's cage. Her splayed legs scrambled for purchase. Then she was on her hands and knees in front of the child, her head yanked back at an inhuman angle. His eyes locked on hers.

"Tell the boy, deputy. Tell him who your God and master is."

"Go to hell."

"We're already there."

He bashed his fist against her face. Blood drooled from her mouth and puddled in the dirt.

"Say it. I am your God and master. Do it, or I'll open the cage and kill the child while you watch."

"Okay, okay. Don't hurt Lonnie."

He released her hair and grinned. She barely recognized him beneath the blood.

"I'm waiting, deputy."

Her chest heaved. She couldn't suck enough air into her lungs as the earthen walls seemed to close around her. She couldn't die here. Let him murder her in the fresh air beneath the stars or sun. Anywhere but here.

"Let her go, please," Lonnie sobbed.

The man gripped Aguilar's hair and pulled her head back again. A warning danced in his eyes. If she didn't surrender to his wishes, he'd murder Aguilar and Lonnie.

She screamed and grabbed his forearms, ripping his hands from her hair. In one motion, she flipped him over her shoulders. His body struck Lonnie's cell and rattled the bars.

Aguilar fell back on her hands and fought to regain her strength as the creep squirmed on the ground, holding the small of his back.

"You bitch!"

Aguilar's eyes widened as he crawled to his hands and knees. Nothing stopped him. As she struggled to her feet, he rose to meet her.

His murderous screech deafened Aguilar. He dove forward, arms outstretched, hands seeking her neck. She twisted away and slammed a fist against his cheek. His legs wobbled. He supported himself against the dirt wall and spun around.

"You'll have to do better than that."

He came at her again. His body collided with Aguilar and drove her toward the open cellar door. She crashed through the opening and struck the water heater. Before she recovered, he tossed her across the concrete floor. The basement whipped past in a blur as the black wall of darkness beyond the window told Aguilar it was night. She reached out, searching for a weapon.

He yanked Aguilar's hair and threw the deputy across the floor again. Her body crumpled against a support beam.

The creep stalked forward, taking his time. He'd kill her slowly. Beat her until the life left her body.

When he was within arm's reach, she kicked out and drove her heel into his belly. He doubled over and held his stomach.

Aguilar sprang to her feet. The kidnapper sneered and grabbed an old, dirty vase off the floor. He whipped it at her head. She ducked, and the glass exploded against the wall.

He approached with arrogance. When the creep grabbed her neck, Aguilar thrust her elbows between his and knocked his arms away. Her punch rocked his head back. Another blow flattened his ruined nose. The confidence left his eyes.

The psycho stepped backward before Aguilar threw her body into his and smashed him against the floor. He scrambled to his knees. Instead of attacking, he fled toward the cells. But Aguilar was right behind and caught him inside the dark enclosure. With a howl, she tossed him against the cage. He crumbled to the ground, his back wrenched.

Before he could defend himself, she kicked his head and whipped his neck sideways. He lay on the ground, clawing at the dirt, struggling to rise. His arms quivered and gave way, and he fell flat against the ground.

Aguilar mounted his back and bashed his face against the earth. The fight left his body. He dropped flat and lay there, unmoving. She wasn't sure if he was unconscious or dead.

She stole the key from his pocket. One eye on the fallen psycho, she staggered to Lonnie's cell and slipped the key into the lock. As their captor had discovered, the lock was jammed.

"I wanna go home," Lonnie cried.

The boy curled in a fetal position. He was in obvious pain, his pallor worsening with each breath. Aguilar cursed. There had to be a way to free Lonnie from the cell.

A metallic, snapping sound brought her head around. To her shock, the trapdoor opened. Night air descended into the underground cells before the first set of legs climbed down the rusty ladder. She knew immediately it was Thomas. At the same time, two muffled thuds echoed from somewhere in the house. Someone had breeched the doors.

The sheriff dropped to the ground and glanced around in horror. His eyes stopped on Aguilar, who collapsed to her knees and cried. She didn't believe she'd ever see another human face again. Lambert dropped into the enclosure next. He took one look at Aguilar and helped her to her feet, supporting the injured deputy with her arm slung over his shoulder.

Thomas checked the psycho.

"He's breathing," the sheriff said.

"Get Lonnie out of the cage," Aguilar pleaded as she leaned on Lambert. "The cell. It won't open."

She handed Thomas the key. As the sheriff worked the key into the lock, Lambert set Aguilar on the ground.

"Hold on. I'll use the bolt cutters," Lambert said.

Aguilar slumped against the cold bars and closed her eyes. Lambert grunted. The iron snapped. He used the bolt cutter on three bars before he tore the cage open and climbed inside. With Thomas's help, he carried the boy out of the cell.

Aguilar forced her eyes open and pushed up to her knees. The child was unresponsive. No, they couldn't be too late.

Thomas called for an ambulance as Lambert carried the boy through the cellar. Two figures appeared—Agents Gardy and Bell from the FBI. Trooper Fitzgerald joined the agents.

"Let's get you out of here," Thomas said as he helped Aguilar to her feet.

She staggered past Agent Bell. Fitzgerald took one of Aguilar's arms, Thomas the other. Together, they helped her limp through the cellar. Her bare feet stepped on broken glass.

She winced before Thomas and Fitzgerald lifted Aguilar and carried her over the shards. They were almost to the stairs when an inhuman scream came out of the cells. Fitzgerald set Aguilar down and reached for his gun.

The psycho rushed Agent Bell, who fell back and landed on the cellar floor. Gardy yelled and grabbed his arm. The psycho wielded a bloody shard of glass as he lunged at Agent Bell. He'd already sliced the shard across Gardy's arm. Aguilar called out in warning before Bell's legs shot up and snaked around the psycho's head. She twisted her body in one quick, decisive motion.

The kidnapper's neck snapped. His body slackened and collapsed.

Gardy held his bleeding arm with one hand. The other aimed the gun at Bell's attacker.

Thomas trained his gun on the psycho and asked, "Is he dead?"

Agent Bell rose and stared down at her foe.

"It's over."

51

The night was a confusion of swirling emergency lights and raised voices. Seated beside Thomas, Deputy Aguilar huddled beneath a blanket while the paramedics carried the psycho to the ambulance. A bloody sheet covered his body. His name was Justice Thorin, and he taught fine arts at Kane Grove University. What drove a distinguished professor to kidnap innocent people and murder them?

The emergency workers had already removed Scott Rehbein's body from his underground cell. Lonnie McKinney left in an ambulance ten minutes ago. Thomas spied the question on Aguilar's face.

"The paramedics stabilized Lonnie McKinney. His father is on the way to the hospital. You saved that boy, Aguilar."

She lowered her head and wept. The nightmare was over, but she wondered how long the events would haunt her. For the rest of her life, she assumed.

She stared in wonder at the English Tudor house. In her mind, she'd pictured a ramshackle home, something out of *The Texas Chainsaw Massacre*. Instead, Justice Thorin lived in a stately home with five acres of land that stretched back to the meadow. He kept the lawn mowed, and landscaped the front yard with rose bushes and tulips. The vast lot lent Thorin privacy. The closest neighbor was almost a block away.

She couldn't bring herself to look at the trapdoor. Aguilar never wanted to see the cells again.

A van pulled to the curb.

"It's the media," Thomas said with a groan. "Let's get you out of here before someone points a camera at us."

Aguilar accepted his hand. She limped with him behind the house while Deputy Lambert and four troopers held the news crew back. Thomas set Aguilar on a hanging swing in the backyard. It seemed incongruous that a psychotic murderer would enjoy the tranquility of a cold drink on a swing. But wolves wore sheep's clothing, and the devil hid behind details. She knew Thomas wanted to ask her what happened in that dark hellhole. He swallowed his questions, and she silently thanked him for giving her time to process the madness. As she rested her head on his shoulder, Agent Bell approached with an armful of clothes.

"I believe these are yours," Bell said, handing Aguilar the clothes she'd worn while she hiked through the state park. "We found them in Thorin's closet."

The peaceful hike seemed as if it had occurred months ago. She was afraid to ask what day it was.

"Thank you," Aguilar said, though she felt squeamish knowing the psycho had touched her clothes.

Bell lifted her chin at Thomas.

"We should give Aguilar some privacy while she changes."

The sheriff blinked.

"Right. I'll be out front, helping with the media if you need me."

Aguilar handed the blanket to Bell. The BAU profiler raised the blanket while Aguilar slipped into her shorts and T-shirt.

After the deputy pulled on her socks and hiking sneakers, she thanked Bell.

"Anytime. Besides, I wanted a few minutes alone with you."

The agent's inquisitive eyes fixed on her. Aguilar clutched her elbows with her hands.

"All right."

"I watched you while I gave the profile."

Aguilar glanced away.

"Okay."

"You planned to quit law enforcement."

Aguilar's mouth went dry.

"How did you know that?"

Bell's eyes softened.

"Because we're more alike than you believe, deputy. Guess how many times I've wanted to quit my job."

"But you're considered the BAU's top profiler."

Bell shook her head.

"What I do comes at a price. Every time I enter the mind of a killer, a part of me dies. Justice Thorin isn't the first person I've killed. When the tabloids write about the murderers I take down, they treat the body count like the final score of a baseball game." Bell held Aguilar's eyes. "But I remember every life I ended. No matter what they did or how many people they hurt, their deaths haunt me. I don't want to play God."

Aguilar rubbed the tears out of her eyes.

"When does the hurt go away?"

"It never goes away. Not completely. But it gets better when we stop blaming ourselves. Real monsters walk among us, deputy. They hide behind friendly smiles, and we never learn of their atrocities until it's too late. Consider the lives you saved by shooting Avery Neal." Aguilar held her breath. "I know about the shooting. You did what you needed to do. How many people would Neal have murdered had you not acted? He would have killed the entire Massey family and any officer who suspected him. The psycho murdered his own partner. You saved Deputy Lambert and Trooper Fitzgerald. Remember your heroism the next time the ghosts come calling. You saved countless lives by ending one. And Neal forced your hand."

Aguilar couldn't respond. Her shoulder shook as fresh tears welled from her eyes. Agent Bell rubbed her shoulder and stood.

"I should speak to the media before I talk myself out of it. There's someone who wants to see you."

Aguilar wiped her eyes and drew in a calming breath. To her surprise, Trooper Fitzgerald stood over her with his hat in his hands. Over the trooper's shoulder, Aguilar watched Agent Gardy descend through the trapdoor. Fitzgerald cleared his throat.

"How are you holding up?"

Aguilar shrugged.

"I'm alive. That has to count for something."

"You're a hero, deputy. I'm not just talking about how you saved Lonnie McKinney. You saved my life, as well."

"You would have done the same for me."

Fitzgerald nervously tapped his hat against his legs.

"I'd like to think so."

"But what?"

Fitzgerald sighed and lifted his gaze to the night sky.

"The nightmares haven't stopped since the shooting." Aguilar swung her head to Fitzgerald. The trooper nodded. "It's not just you. I haven't slept right since. But Avery Neal's ghost doesn't haunt me. My failure keeps me up at night."

"What are you talking about?"

Fitzgerald pressed his lips together.

"I froze. When Neal started shooting, my brain locked. Were it not for you, I'd be dead."

"You fired back. I saw you."

He issued a mirthless laugh.

"Yeah, after you shot Neal and saved my ass. You also saved Deputy Lambert. He didn't freeze like me, but his shots flew wide."

Aguilar grinned.

"Lambert never could hit the broad side of a barn." She set her elbows on her knees and dropped her head. "But he's a terrific deputy and an even better person. Maybe we're all too hard on ourselves."

"I guess we're both due some soul searching."

Fitzgerald turned away, and she grabbed his hand.

"Hey, you did your job. Don't fool yourself into believing you didn't. You covered Lambert and me. The only reason I shot with accuracy is because you fought by my side."

The trooper's eyes misted.

"Thanks, Aguilar. I love this job. Every day I wake up and hope there's someone out there I can help. Thanks for reminding me."

As Fitzgerald walked away, Aguilar pondered what he'd said. It was as if he'd mirrored her thoughts and expressed her fears. A sense of calm fell over Aguilar.

Thomas returned. She didn't argue when he demanded that she go to the hospital. The doctors would treat her injuries and replenish her fluids. But the healing had already begun deep inside Aguilar, in the places their instruments couldn't reach.

She was going to be okay.

52

Puffy clouds checkered the sky above Wolf Lake, reflecting off the water like insoluble shreds of cotton.

Thomas carried the baby back ribs from the A-frame to the grill. His friends mingled, some nursing beers, others content with the pristine view and friendly conversation. Darren worked the grill while Naomi finished cooking a pot of baked beans inside.

As Thomas approached the grill, the sweet scent of wood smoke caught his nose.

"Oh, dude," Darren said, taking the plate from Thomas's hand. "Those look amazing."

"Imagine how they'll taste."

Darren laid the ribs on the grill one at a time. Barbecue sauce sizzled against the grates.

"Another case solved, and we're still alive to talk about it."

"I understand why you left the force, Darren. I'm unsure how much longer I can handle murders and kidnappings."

The park ranger glanced at Thomas through the tops of his eyes.

"This was a tough one. But they aren't all this bad."

"That's what I keep telling myself." Thomas lowered his voice. "Justice Thorin buried his victims beneath the cages. Over a dozen bodies. Agent Bell predicted everything, as if she'd stepped inside Justice Thorin's brain. Our old friend, Dr. Astrid Stone, led the excavation."

"The forensic anthropologist who uncovered the skeleton below Lucifer Falls?"

"Right. An hour into her dig, she pulled a decaying arm out of the ground. It still had gray skin on it, so the kill must have been recent. The arm was missing a hand."

"Harmony Santos."

"Yep. Thorin kept her alive for four years. Can you believe it?"

"It's horrible. So Aguilar . . ."

"Yeah," Thomas said. "We found five bodies beneath her cell. When she dug down to loosen the bars, she missed a skull by inches."

"How is she processing the situation?"

"Like any of us would. It will take time. Right now, she's happy to be alive."

"And Lonnie McKinney is alive because of Aguilar. That's the part that makes all the horrors manageable. How's the boy doing?"

"The kid must have someone watching over him. He spent one night in the hospital and went home the next morning. Talk about a survivor. The father says Lonnie will need counseling. But the boy survived food poisoning and multiple nights in a cold, dark cell."

Thomas fished a strawberry and watermelon kombucha out of the cooler and twisted the cap off. He took a sip and puckered his lips. Aguilar had convinced Thomas to drink kombucha, but the initial sip always smacked him with a sour punch. He raised the bottle and clinked it against Darren's beer.

As Thomas took another sip, he spotted Aguilar and Lambert in the yard.

"Speaking of Aguilar, I need to speak with my lead deputy. You can handle the ribs by yourself?"

"Shep, the only danger is whether I'll eat the ribs before they make it to the picnic table."

"I trust you. Besides, my security cameras will catch you in the act."

Darren laughed and flipped the ribs.

Sheriff Gray slapped Thomas on the back as he passed. They shared a greeting, and the former sheriff gave Thomas's kombucha a cockeyed glance. Last evening, Thomas and Gray had spoken for two hours about Father Fowler. Though they'd never prove the priest drove Lana off the road, Gray finally had closure.

Lambert and Aguilar were speaking with Serena and Raven when Thomas walked over.

"Thanks for coming," said Thomas.

"Wouldn't miss it for the world," Lambert said. "Baby back ribs? I'm feasting tonight."

"Contain yourself," said Aguilar, nudging Lambert with her elbow. "I looked forward to this all day. Can't tell you how much I need this."

Thomas touched her arm.

"You're welcome here anytime. I've told you this before, but anytime you need quiet, drive over and sit by the lake."

"I may take you up on that offer." Aguilar glanced at Lambert. "Sheriff Gray wants company."

"Is that your way of getting rid of me?"

"I need to speak with Thomas for a minute."

Lambert shrugged and walked off. Thomas wiped the hair off his brow.

"What's going on?"

"Walk with me to the water. There's something I need to say."

They strolled together through the thick grass. A boat motored across the lake, pushing waves against the shoreline. Aguilar turned to Thomas, but kept her eyes on the water.

"The night Thorin kidnapped me, I was rehearsing a speech."

"A speech?"

"Thomas, I planned to resign the next day."

Thomas swallowed. He sensed Aguilar was struggling with the Avery Neal shooting. But he never believed she'd leave the job she loved.

"And now?"

Aguilar set a hand on her hip and stared out at the lake.

"I finally understand everything Dr. Mandal taught me. It still hurts, but I realize Neal brought everything upon himself."

"You did your duty, Aguilar. Lambert and Fitzgerald owe you their lives."

"Choosing between Neal and two fellow officers was an easy decision. But I'll never come to grips with taking someone's life."

Thomas shifted his jaw.

"Good. That's what keeps us human." She glanced at him. "You think I don't lose sleep over the Jeremy Hyde and Thea Barlow cases, that I don't wake up in the middle of the night and picture Skye Feron locked inside a psycho's house for six years? We're the gatekeepers, Aguilar, the guards standing between society and the monsters who prey upon the weak. As Agent Bell says, it comes at a price."

Aguilar fell silent as the water sloshed over the shore. Seagulls squawked overhead.

"If you need to walk away, I understand. Nobody will think less of you."

She shook her head, and Thomas was surprised and relieved to see confidence gleaming in her eyes.

"I'm not going anywhere, Thomas. Besides, how are you gonna run Nightshade County without me?"

"I can't."

"Exactamundo, Potsie." Aguilar turned toward the others as Scout wheeled herself down the path. LeVar walked beside the teenager. "So the amateur investigators helped with the rescue?"

"They did. Scout caught Thorin on camera with a drone. I never would have thought of that. A brilliant idea, really."

"It's a shame Scout never met the FBI agents before they flew home. Scout meeting Agent Bell would be like any of us hanging out with our favorite celebrities."

Thomas hid his smile and gestured at the party.

"Let's make our way to the grill before Darren steals the ribs."

Serena hugged Thomas next to the picnic table and planted a kiss on his cheek. His face reddened.

"What masterpiece did you concoct this time, Serena?"

"Naomi and I baked a sweet potato pie that will knock your socks off. The secret ingredient is—"

Thomas held up a hand.

"Don't tell me. Let me guess after the first bite."

"You'll love it. But you only get one guess."

Chelsey stepped off the deck, with Tigger and Jack trotting beside her. She carried a grocery bag of snacks under one arm. She kissed Thomas as Jack ran circles around them. Tigger seemed embarrassed by Jack's excitability.

"Did you know there's an SUV parked behind LeVar's car?"

Thomas cleared his throat.

"Must be a neighbor. How was work?"

"I shouldn't complain because we need the business. But the infidelity cases are growing tiresome."

"Too many Casanovas running around the village. The lake is rather romantic, don't you agree?"

She bit back a smile without answering. He took the grocery bag as she bent to pet Jack. They wandered back to the party, taking their time and enjoying each other's company. Thomas set the snacks on the picnic table and called to Darren.

"How much longer on the ribs, ranger?"

"Another ninety minutes. You can't rush perfection."

"You better not be stealing samples."

"Ticket me, Sheriff."

A gust of wind kicked up and scattered paper plates across the lawn. As Scout chased the plates in her wheelchair, Thomas jogged over to collect the items. He stacked the plates and placed them under a soda bottle.

"I watched the drone footage, Scout. Where did you learn to fly a drone so well?"

"YouTube videos. But you only saw the good parts, not the footage where I almost smashed the drone into a tree."

"Well, you had a helluva week. Were it not for your footage, we wouldn't have found the underground enclosure. And you prevented an armed robbery. Not a bad week, if I may say so."

She wore an embarrassed smirk.

"Mom says I should become a profiler someday. But I'm not sure. How am I supposed to climb ladders, take down robbers, and chase serial killers?"

"I'm certain there are consultant positions that don't require you to fight anybody." Thomas glanced at the A-frame from the corner of his eye. "But I'm not a profiling expert, and there's only so much advice I can lend."

Scout dropped her eyes.

"I wish I'd met Scarlett Bell before she left. There were so many questions I wanted to ask. I suppose I can write to her again."

"Or you can ask her now."

Scout lifted her head when Gardy and Bell emerged from the A-frame. Gardy wore another gaudy Hawaiian shirt and mismatched shorts. Scout swallowed.

"Is that—"

"They fly back tomorrow afternoon. Agent Bell refused to leave until she met the one and only Scout Mourning."

A tear trickled out of Scout's eye as Gardy and Bell made a beeline toward the teenager. Dressed in casual attire—jean shorts and a tie-dye sleeveless tee—Scarlett Bell didn't look like the FBI's lead profiler. Already, she fit in with their Wolf Lake family.

"So you must be Scout," Bell said, bending to shake Scout's hand.

Scout stammered.

"I, uh . . ."

"Do you know how long I've wanted to meet you?"

"Me?"

"Hell, yes. After the work you did tracking down Justice Thorin, we're practically partners now."

Gardy blanched.

"What about me?"

Bell tilted her head at Gardy.

"You see the way he dresses? I can't take him anywhere." Bell inhaled and closed her eyes. "Dinner smells unbelievable. How long before we eat?"

"The grill master says ninety minutes," Thomas said.

"Perfect. That gives us time to catch up with Ms. Mourning. Is there a quiet place we can talk?"

LeVar called to them from the picnic table.

"The guest house is all yours."

"Well, then. Let's talk careers in criminal profiling."

Agent Gardy pushed Scout's wheelchair down the concrete

path as Bell walked beside them. Scout turned her head back to Thomas and mouthed, "Thank you," before they disappeared inside LeVar's home.

Thomas swallowed the lump in his throat. He found Chelsey staring at him.

"That was a beautiful thing you did."

Thomas scratched behind his head.

"It was the least I could do."

"You made her year, Thomas." Chelsey kissed his lips. "Every day, you remind me why I love you so much."

He placed his hands on her hips.

"You're no slouch, yourself."

She set her hands on his shoulders and stared into his eyes.

"The answer is yes."

"Yes? What are we discussing?"

"I see what Raven and Darren have, and I can't wait any longer. Thomas Shepherd, I want to wake up beside you and share every moment. If you'll have me, I'd like to move in."

"You're serious? How soon?"

"Let's spend the night together and work up a plan for moving my things to the lake. I'll call the realty agency in the morning."

Thomas's smile stretched ear to ear.

"I can't believe this is happening."

Chelsey stared down at her legs, where Jack and Tigger frolicked on the lawn. Then she held his gaze.

"I love you, Thomas Shepherd."

Thank you for reading The Shadow Cell.
Ready for more of the Wolf Lake thriller series?
Read book seven now!

GET A FREE BOOK!

I'm a pretty nice guy once you look past the grisly images in my head. Most of all, I love connecting with awesome readers like you.

Join my VIP Reader Group and get a FREE serial killer thriller for your Kindle.

Get My Free Book

www.danpadavona.com/thriller-readers-vip-group/

SHOW YOUR SUPPORT FOR INDIE THRILLER AUTHORS

Did you enjoy this book? If so, please let other thriller fans know by leaving a short review. Positive reviews help spread the word about independent authors and their novels. Thank you.

ACKNOWLEDGMENTS

No writer journeys alone. Special thanks are in order to my editor, Kimberly Broderick, for providing invaluable feedback, catching errors, and making my story shine. I also wish to thank my brilliant cover designer, Caroline Teagle Johnson. Your artwork never ceases to amaze me. I owe so much of my success to your hard work. Shout outs to my advance readers: Donna Puschek, Mary Arnold, Mary-Ellen Schwandt Leidy, and Teresa Padavona, for catching those final pesky typos and plot holes. Most of all, thank you to my readers for your loyalty and support. You changed my life, and I am forever grateful.

ABOUT THE AUTHOR

Dan Padavona is the author of the The Darkwater Cove series, The Scarlett Bell thriller series, *Her Shallow Grave*, The Dark Vanishings series, *Camp Slasher, Quilt, Crawlspace, The Face of Midnight, Storberry, Shadow Witch*, and the horror anthology, *The Island*. He lives in upstate New York with his beautiful wife, Terri, and their children, Joe, and Julia. Dan is a meteorologist with NOAA's National Weather Service. Besides writing, he enjoys visiting amusement parks, beach vacations, Renaissance fairs, gardening, playing with the family dogs, and eating too much ice cream.

Visit Dan at: www.danpadavona.com

Made in the USA
Middletown, DE
04 January 2023

20990819R00170